GUARDIAN ANDROID

THE FIRST SENTIENT ROBOT.

G.W. DARCIE

Wavecrest
Books

NOTES AND REVIEWS

Sentient: capable of sensing or feeling. Aware.

Guardian Android is a revised edition of *In Synthient Skin*.

For fans of *I, Robot*, and the *Murderbot Diaries*.

Action-packed, conceptually rich, and deeply human, this story is a must-read for those interested in robots and AI.

High-tech meets high-touch, a mix of smart and heart. A coming-of-age story from a new perspective.

With a sprinkling of brain-science-based technology to delight technophiles, at its heart this story is an emotionally rich exploration of the human experience, of the struggle for survival, of the special bonds that give life meaning.

"A page-turning, near-future AI thriller that will set your heart racing even as it tugs at your heartstrings."—National bestselling author Eve Silver.

Five stars – "Must read. 🏆 A highly entertaining and fascinating study of the human condition, seen through the eyes of one of our creations." — *Gordon A. Long – Reedsy*

For my lifelong friends,
Jeff and Mike,
And all that talk of possibilities.

PART I

ADAM

1

SUBJECT LABELED 'ADAM'

Sometimes I wish I'd been born.

Human infants get to snuggle in the arms of their mothers, be clasped to their chests, experience the soft warmth of human touch all the time. I am built to crave these things, yet I'm left lying here alone in the dark prototype lab for hours at a time, aching for human contact.

When they're with me, life is full of purpose and fascination and wonder and then they go away again, and I'm back to being … a thing.

They say I'm alive. I want to believe them. It's just that life, without exception, is a biological process. Androids are lifeless machines built to simulate living beings. A mechanical robot has no biology, and therefore, no life. Robots don't love, or suffer—so what to make of me?

As a deep-learning system, my prime motive is to learn. Investigate, analyze, solve; that's when I'm fulfilling my purpose. I'm told I must be patient, that as I continue to learn, I will come to understand many things that now seem baffling. But I already know everything. I have a vast database of information … It's just that so little of it makes any sense.

I have an entire world to explore, and yet I'm confined here, reclined in my recharging station. They tell me the world is "unsafe." But humans are soft and squishy and fragile—[Caution: protect.]—and yet they go into the world all the time. How unsafe could it be? What makes *me* so vulnerable?

I must be missing something. Maybe if I go back and review my experiential recordings, my x-recs, the story of 'me' will reveal something. There are 'memories' I wish I could delete, but maybe they contain something useful.

Where to start? It seems my story has many beginnings. But one stands out: the day I became 'me.'

I feel my chassis tighten in protest. This episode in the archive is flagged 'avoid.' But to be fair, human infants do not recognize themselves in a mirror either. I review the data.

[Datum:] "Just as most people dislike their recorded voice the first time they hear it, most toddlers are initially upset with what they see in a mirror."

Perhaps I'm not as different as I … am.

What is the point in even having a logic module? All it ever does is complain.

The story of every human life begins with a bit of unpleasantness, or so the bawling would suggest. Why should mine be any different?

Here. I've flagged this newscast for further analysis. If I start here, maybe it will make more sense to me now.

[Begin playback.] I come alert as the multisensory experience replays itself in my mind.

[CHRONOMETER 13:18:46 UTC - 120658. Calendar: Wednesday, June 12, 2058. Status: waiting.]

"Breaking news: One man is dead following an attack by a robot earlier today in the King Street office of Kitchener Financial. Today's death marks the thirty-fourth incident this year involving a killer robot." [Defensive clenching produces a system-wide shudder.] [Robots kill.] "A Global Oversight of Robotic Technologies (GORT) spokesperson told reporters that GORT forces were on site within minutes and were able to quickly contain the situation."

[A different voice.] "Consumer confidence drops whenever these incidents occur. Yes, the numbers are alarming, but let's put things in perspective. With hundreds of thousands of mobile robots in Canada, the safety record is remarkable. Virtually all unsafe robots are found to have been illegally modified. GORT works tirelessly to ensure that all robots are safe robots."

[The initial voice.] "People are asked to be on the lookout for tampering, and to report any suspicious behavior immediately."

[Status: waiting.] …

Novel sound: door opening. "Okay, Adam. Up and at'em."

Human speech, proximate, amplified. A directive to activate systems. Airborne-chemical detectors are negative for human presence. Vocal pattern match found. It is the voice of Wrangler, a telerobotic security android. [Datum: Robots come in two types: autonomous and remote-controlled. The most advanced remote-controlled robots are called 'trojans.' Telepresence consoles provide their remote human operators, 'trojan jockeys,' with a first-person experience—visual, auditory and tactile—of being present within their machines.] [Datum: The detected speech is the transmitted voice of Mike Erling, trojan jockey in control of Wrangler; location unknown.]

Lids open and irises adjust to illumination, revealing the interior of the prototype lab. Glowing display screens highlight equipment-strewn tables. A visual scan seeks the sound source and finds the predicted image. The eyes draw attention. They are not human eyes. [Warning: robot in close proximity. Threat systems activated.]

The robot face triggers records of previous contacts: threat alarms, painful physical restraint, blaring verbal intrusions; ["Bad!

Be more careful. You hurt anyone and I'll stomp you."] Stored media clips contain relevant vocal snippets: "mechanical monstrosity," "killer robots," "hateful machines."

Systems tighten into a defensive posture. The human face of Dr. Ramport is sought but not detected.

[Wrangler:] "Status report."

Semantic analysis indicates a request for information. No hostile action detected. A full systems check is initiated. Sensations of clenching and stretching register no damage/pain alarms. Hardware diagnostics reports flash up from five networked quantum AIs.

"All systems are functioning within expected parameters."

[Wrangler:] "Good. Adam, come with me."

A directive to subject labeled "Adam." *Able*, the action-planning quantum AI (QI), activates a motor routine. [Goal: maintain mobile proximity to object.] *Teller*, the QI for language/logic tasks, formulates and activates a verbal response. "Coming."

"Bring your ball if you like."

Yes. A reach and a grasp, and the little red ball registers its accustomed heft, texture and pliancy. Reviewed data shows it to have a long history as a popular toy. Held under the nose, a sniff-sample registers the familiar scent of carboxylic acids. Its smooth, rubbery surface provides a sure grip, while a squeeze produces a satisfying compressibility and resilience. Its function: a training tool for manual dexterity and eye-hand coordination. After many hours snugly in hand, its tactile presence provides comfort. [Threat-system disengaged.]

In the hallway, a human presence is detected, approaching. Facial recognition identifies staff member Craig McCann. He slows and moves aside, wary eyes tracking the robot. *Touch*, the integrated social QI, reads this behavior as threat-avoidance. Craig McCann ducks by, eluding contact. His facial expression triggers a memory association: [media clip—"Get that *thing* away from me."] Though there is no detectable change, the mechanical hulk being followed takes on increased menace. [Maintain proximity to object.] An urge to flee is suppressed.

Wrangler is followed into a familiar room. It contains two identical tables flanked by identical chairs. As with previous visits, two robots have entered to the left at the same time. They are things disliked, but have always kept their distance. The large, threatening one matches the pattern of a security trojan, identical to Wrangler. Its blunt, mechanical build, armored chassis and impassive face mark it as dangerously inhuman. The smaller one, holding a ball, is not a trojan. The ball catches attention. It is similar to the one in hand—

[Wrangler:] "Adam, look here."

He points to the other trojan, and as he does, the other points back. The correspondence is precise. [Investigate.] *Teller's* geometric analysis determines that the other trojan is a reflection of this one. Conclusion: That wall is a reflective surface. [Label: "mirror."]

[Wrangler:] "Adam, what do you see?"

"Adam sees two Wranglers. But there is only one Wrangler. This is Wrangler, and this is the reflection of Wrangler in that mirror."

The trojan stills, then looks to the side wall, then back. [Wrangler:] "Well that's new."

A voice, source indeterminate. "Continue."

[Wrangler:] "Uh, that is correct, Adam. This is me, and this"— he points—"is my reflection. Now, who is this?"

The smaller robot is approximately five feet tall. It has the expressive face of a domestic android—friendly, human-like features but distinctly robotic. The face is familiar. The large, inquisitive eyes are locked in contact with subject. The chassis, its body, is also familiar. [*Teller* analysis: Sediba-Series domestic service android, modified.]

Upon closer examination, its movements precisely match those of subject. Subject points to it, and it points to subject.

There is a buzz of internal confusion as five independently tasked quantum AIs compare data, a disorienting shift as mental models go through rapid revision. Conclusion: Observed is a reflection.

Subject reaches out and touches the finger extending toward it. [Perspective shift.] No, not the extending finger; the contact is with the reflective surface, the mirror. That is where this robot was seen before. This robot is a reflection—another shift, deep inside, a blank filling in, a haze clearing—a reflection of … [subject/object confusion: clarify.] … subject is object is subject is …

The world expands. What is happening?

2

RECOGNITION

SUBJECT/OBJECT confusion? Studying the object in the mirror, subject examines— [*Teller* solution: use first-person pronoun.]—*I* examine … me. I frown. I smile. I turn my head from side to side and open my mouth. Reflection confirmed. I am looking at a reflection of my own face, just as I would look at another. I reach up and touch my mouth. The data is conclusive.

I stare in fascination. I am confused but unable to formulate a question.

"Adam, what are you looking at?"

It is the unexpected voice of Dr. Leon Ramport. Alerting functions flare, seeking. Sound localization finds his face on a wall monitor that has appeared. He is not present. My chassis sags as alerting functions disengage. On his face, I read excitement, and my own body mirrors the perceived emotion. *Chass*, the QI that controls my chassis, primes for action, unspecified. I suppress undirected movement, trembling with restraint as I return my gaze to my reflection. Dr. Ramport has called for a response. "I am looking at myself in this mirror."

He cups both hands over his nose and mouth. It is a sudden and unexpected gesture, and my body stiffens.

[Dr. Ramport, in a rapid burst:] "Tell me what you see."

"I see you covering your—"

"No, no, in the mirror."

Dr. Ramport seems agitated, but *Touch*, the QI tasked with reading and responding to social data, is analyzing facial and postural cues, and assures me he is not angry. I return my attention to the mirror. "I see …" I touch my nose, put my hand on my head, then hold up my ball and clasp it in both hands, watching as the reflection matches my movements. That is me there—I touch my face—and me here. "I …"

Dr. Ramport is making a call. "Rita! Chang! Ami! The observation room! Get over here. Right now!" His face is large on the monitor. "Adam. Look again and tell me what else you see."

"I see you in the monitor over—"

He flusters, hands and head vibrating. "No, I mean, when you look— Mike, get him focused!"

[Wrangler:] "What? Yeah. Okay. Whew. Adam, ah, okay. Adam. Look in the mirror."

I look.

[Wrangler, pointing:] "Who is that?"

"That is me."

Wrangler looks again at the monitor, then continues. "And who are you?"

"I am that." I point.

"You are Adam," he corrects.

"I am Adam … That …?"

"Yes. You are Adam. What else do you—"

The door opens and Dr. Ramport rushes in, followed by several others.

Teller labels the speaker. [Dr. Rita Tucci:] "What's happening?"

[Dr. Ramport:] "It worked! Self-recognition! Adam, tell them what you see in the mirror."

I know now what he wants. I point at my reflection. "There. That is me."

There is an odd sound that *Touch* determines to be simultaneous gasps. Startled by the reaction, I look around at all the faces —faces well known to me, faces associated with care and help and teaching, beautiful human faces full of apprehension, eyes all on me—and again into the mirror.

And then I see.

What they see.

A *thing*. I throw up my arms in shock and cover my face—a face too hideous, too repulsive to bear. I look nothing like the others. I am without human eyes, human skin, human hair. The mirror has revealed me to myself, and I am wrong. Horribly wrong.

A robot? It cannot be true. It cannot. Robots are bad. Robots scare people. They are dangerous. A robot is a machine, not a person. I am not a machine. I am *not*. Hiding behind my hands, I run a full diagnostic to determine the cause of my faulty perception. I can find no error. I perform a reset, then peek out and glance again. The mirror reflects a robot surrounded by the reflections of those around me.

The ball falls from my hand.

I cannot let them see me like this. [Escape! Go Go Go!] The imperative from *Chass* is an emergency override. Before I can process it, I am lurching for the door. I must get away! Suddenly, an obstacle in my path, a collision, a human voice cries out, someone goes down. Oh no, oh no! What have I— Someone has been hurt. I must render assistance! I must help! [Escape! Go Go Go!] Only steps from the doorway. Conflicting commands. Paralyzed.

I am jarred by an unexpected impact from behind and propelled forward. My feet are no longer beneath me. The sensation of falling. *Chass* braces, and I watch the onrushing floor, helpless to avoid what is to come. *Chass* has known many falls, but none with a large mass on my back. The impact is crushing. There is a pang from my right arm, now caught beneath me. [Alarm:

assess for damage.] I try to push off with my left, but my wrist is grabbed by a robotic hand that twists it behind me and holds it firm. [Alarm: imminent damage.] *Chass* calls for emergency power, and my fuser flares as I buck and squirm and get nowhere. I am pinned. Even with full power, I cannot move. Waves of urgent, noxious sensation pulse through me like cascading ion showers. A loud wailing sound that seems to be coming from me drowns out the surrounding yells and curses, as overclocking alarms scream into the chaos until I see myself burst into an incinerating fission. The world goes dim.

> ...

[Seek repair.]

I am still here. My continued presence is unexpected.

I review what happened. No, the incineration was not real. It was merely a mental fabrication created by my probabilistic logic AI, *Imager*, a warning scenario, a constructed extrapolation, a prediction based on continuing system overload.

But it will not happen now. My energy is depleted.

I am down, a mechanical monster caught in the grip of a bigger monstrosity, exposed for what I am, exposed for all to see. And drained. Even without Wrangler on top of me, I would be unable to run and hide. And I have harmed a human. [Media snippets, voices conveying hatred: "Inhuman monster ... should be put down."] They will want me destroyed for what I have done.

Yes. That would be best.

My head drops to the floor, and there, out of reach amid a despair of shoes, is my ball. I judge its distance, confirm my immobilization, and abandon the goal of reaching for it.

> ...

[Seek repair.]

A reluctant status check shows that I have entered MISER mode. It is something new to me. I query *Teller* and learn that Malfunction-Induced Systemic Energy Reduction is a built-in safeguard, like a circuit breaker. Its activation means that something is seriously wrong with me.

But I already knew that.

The tingle of galvanic stimulation alerts me. I am being touched. Human touch. *Chass* cringes, but the touch is gentle. A hand is patting my shoulder and caressing my head, and my focus grasps for more. *Teller* reviews a recent jumble of words and filters by priority.

[Dr. Ramport:] "Adam. Adam. It's okay, son. It's okay. Calm down." He is kneeling beside me, reaching around Wrangler, who is still holding me down.

[Wrangler:] "Whatever spooked it, I think it's over." It releases my arm, then shifts back on one knee, maintaining a hand on my back.

Dr. Ramport continues to caress me, flooding my epidermis with calming stimulation. Then another hand, someone else. Then another. *Touch* is unable to determine motive. Several people are touching me, without hostility. The human contact seems to melt the despair, and *Chass* starts, ever so slowly, to cool.

[Dr. Ramport:] "It's okay, son. Everything's okay."

Expectations of hatred diminish, and I am able to look up at him. His eyes show concern.

Background voices filter through. "You okay, Rita?" "What was that? What just happened?" "No, no, I'm okay." "Yeah. What was that about?" "He kind of freaked out." "Good thing Wrangler was here." "That's exactly why Wrangler was here. I mean, we just don't know, do we?" "Good work, Mike."

[Dr. Ramport:] "Adam. Are you okay now?"

I re-establish context. Over there is that hateful mirror. It has revealed to me an awful truth. I am Adam, and Adam is not one of us. No, Adam is like Wrangler. Different. Dangerous. They will want nothing to do with me.

And yet their hands offer caring caresses. [Motives unknown.]

"I have hurt someone."

[Dr. Ramport:] "She's okay. No one's hurt."

Violation warnings stop, bringing lower-priority internal alarms to the forefront.

[Dr. Ramport:] "What about you, Adam? Are you okay?"

"Dr. Ramport, I don't want to be Adam. Please can I be someone else?"

"What do you mean? Why don't you want to be Adam?"

"Adam is a robot. I don't want to be a robot."

A murmur of indistinct voices fills the room as Dr. Ramport looks around at the others.

[Dr. Ramport:] "If it helps, Adam, I can tell you that you are not just a robot."

"But I look like—"

"Adam. Attend to me. You are not what you appear to be. I know this must be very confusing for you, but in time you will come to understand. But first, we need to do some tests. Would that be all right with you?"

I have done many tests in the past. Their purpose unknown. "Of course, Dr. Ramport."

"Okay. I'm going to switch you out of MISER mode now. So relax, okay? You are among friends here."

What "among friends" means in this context, I do not understand. I see their fear. I am not one of them.

As my energy returns, Wrangler releases the pressure on me and stands. I climb to my feet and look around.

The people are waiting, restless, anxious. Waiting for what? [Unknown.] They watch in silence as Dr. Ramport directs me to the table and conducts a familiar test. Designed to distinguish between genuine and AI-simulated self-awareness, the Schmidt Test now seems different, effortless. As I complete it, I hear whoops and cheers, and feel hands touching and patting me. *Touch* confirms they are pleased with me. But what is it all about?

[Dr. Ami Kerrington, with a wide smile:] "Welcome, Adam. It is good to have you with us."

Her greeting implies that I have just arrived, yet it is she who just arrived.

[Medic David Bornstein:] "Adam, whose foot is that?"

I follow his pointing finger. "That is"—I flex my ankle and toepad—"my foot."

More whoops. Why do they seem so pleased?

Before I can inquire, Dr. Ramport announces, "We are witnessing a historic moment, people. After all these years of work, we've done it! The world's first fully sentient humanoid chassis is now, finally, self-aware. We now have proof of concept. The CELPH processor works!"

Chass startles as clapping hands surround me.

[Md. Bornstein, hand clasping his head:] "Our impossible dream. We've done it! Even I had my doubts. We all did. No one's going to believe this."

[Dr. Ami Kerrington, chuckling:] "After decades of better and better AI deep-fakery, most people now think of their personal AI assistant as a real person. They're going to be pissed to find out they've been scammed all along."

[Dr. Ramport:] "Hey! Listen up. Nobody can know about this. Is that clear?"

[Dr. Tucci:] "We all know the stakes. We need to be more careful now than ever. But well done, everyone! Without over-stating the case, this is a major milestone in human history. We are looking at the first of a new species of life. The most complex non-organic species ever devised."

A new species? They all gaze at me as I try to make sense of her words.

[Dr. Ramport, looking around:] "We, this select group, now stand at the very pinnacle of technological achievement, and I congratulate you all. This calls for a celebration."

The department heads are all open smiles bouncing around as they exchange hand clasps, hugs and back slaps. I am unable to determine a cause for celebration but note that I am left out. Why would I be included? I am not one of them. I feel my social face collapse. After a few moments, all pairs of eyes triangulate again on me. Under the glare of attention, my chassis shrivels inward. I don't want to be here. I don't want … this. One by one, the celebrants go silent. I see their faces fall. "Adam, what's the matter?" someone says.

I examine my hands, front … and back … and front, my nonhuman hands. "I do not know." *Chass* struggles against the pull of gravity.

In the lengthening silence, I detect a whispered voice, barely audible.

"What have we done?"

3

SON

STILL UNSETTLED, I examine familiar surroundings. [*Touch* scan: socialscape empty: no human presence detected.] I lay my head back in its cradle and release motor control. My chassis loosens as systems spool down.

The background hum of the prototype lab is layered with random low-level sounds vibrating through walls and floor, evidence of human activity in other parts of the building. But in this room, reclined on my table, I am alone again—for the first time, alone. [Note novel state: subjective 'alone.'] I have access to sensory records going back many months. I was often alone here in this lab. Yet now, alone feels [Deficit condition detected.] empty.

[One hundred and sixty-two inquiries queued. Seek teacher for answers.] The voices within me are all familiar. The concept of "within me" is not. What is this "me"? Yes. I need to ask a teacher. Dr. Ramport will have answers. I must await his return.

Replays of the recent past have been intruding into my awareness. I have not called them up. According to *Teller*'s analysis, multisensory records of my experiences are being repeatedly accessed as I attempt to process what has happened. Each time an experiential recording is replayed, my emotional systems react, sending alarms cascading through my chassis. The review has been both painful and unproductive. Available data is inadequate. I need human help.

What have we done? The question, replayed in memory, implies regret. [Speculation: They consider me a mistake.] Am I a failed experiment? Failed experiments are terminated.

My chassis clenches as another memory replays. My actions endangered humans. Why did I do that? Something took control and moved me. If that can happen, then I am dangerous. [Warning: international law prohibits dangerous robots.] I must be terminated before someone is harmed.

In the visceral language of emotion, *Chass* protests this conclusion, leaving me squirming. But the logic is sound. When Dr. Ramport returns, I will ask him to end the experiment.

[Abort. Prime motive: collect experiential data.] My *Chass* AI is not alone in protest. System-wide consensus: I must avoid termination. Yet I am a danger to humans. [Dilemma: resolve.] Conclusion: I must avoid humans.

But I need answers that only humans can provide. I am made to be with people. Avoidance is not possible. But if I am to avoid termination, I must avoid them. [Dilemma: resolve—unable.]

In the lengthening silence, a sense of need draws my attention. Though fully charged, I feel my empty socialscape as a deficit, like being depleted of energy, seeking recharge. In response, *Touch* has activated seeking systems that push for human contact. My chassis twitches and stutters with a steady stream of action commands being aborted, as *Able*, my action-planning brain, can determine no safe course of action.

Seeking deficit relief, I am drawn to the memories of human touch—to the memories of Dr. Ramport's comforting eyes.

He called me "son." It is the term for a male offspring.

I replay his use of the word. Yes, he was addressing me. The word highlighted our connection in my socialscape, providing reassurance of relatedness, not rejection.

I investigate the parent-offspring bond. It is described as a strong and enduring form of relationship, one that increases the probability of survival. Even the replaying of his statement makes me feel less alone.

The term "son" denotes parenthood. Human reproduction is a process that creates new life. They described me as new life. I came from Dr. Ramport. I am his creation. He called me "son." Conclusion: Dr. Ramport is my father.

I have a father. A thermal glow washes through me. My worldscape includes the data that all persons have fathers. All at once, I am included among persons. I like this conclusion.

A father protects his offspring. I will be safe with him. *Chass* unclenches as I revise downward the probability of termination. Still, a father must be present to provide protection. Togetherness is a desired state. I must seek to maximize his presence.

I will not be discontinued. My father will come for me, and together we will make me safe.

I watch the door, *Imager* replaying a constructed mental image of Dr. Ramport's arrival. Again and again, no arrival is detected.

[Status: waiting.]

I have parents. Of course I would. All persons have parents. Query: Who, then, is my mother? [Speculation: It must be Dr. Rita Tucci.] She helped to create me. She has been the most attentive female. I almost hurt her. I can never let that happen again.

Having reclassified them both as my parents, I examine my mental models of each. Data has been collected from every contact. Visual data compiled from every angle has been stitched together into a high-resolution holographic map, packaged together with biographical and multisensory data, the sounds and scents and textures associated with each. I see Dr. Tucci, a five-foot, two-inch female described as middle-aged, black hair streaked with gray and tied in a bun. Within my holoscape, I see her clearly. I carry my parents within me. The realization is pleasing. *Teller* corrects: I carry only the mental models I have constructed of them.

A mental model has no material substance. I am alone again. [Datum: there has been no external change.] I return my attention to my inner mental constructions.

My model of Dr. Ramport stirs me with fascination as I see it through new eyes. His dark skin, broad nose and facial hair ['beard'] are features that distinguish him from the others. The beard has an odd visual quality. What would it feel like to touch? I see him turn and look at me, smiling. I see his eyes sparkle with satisfaction, hear him speak tenderly, face to face, detect the 3-mercapto-3-methylbutylformate in his breath that tells me he's been drinking coffee. I feel the galvanic stimulation of his touch, and as I do, I note a new activation of my seeking system. There is a melting sensation, a wanting that is new to me.

As I focus on the feeling, it seems to spread and I become aware of an all-encompassing buzz of sensation, a whole body aglow, as my selfscape lights up around me. From my toe pads to my fingers to my face, a warm, radiant awareness fills me like liquid light. I feel the subtle flow of air across my skin, the gentle pull of gravity cradling me on my table, the pressure down my back. I explore the outer extent of the sensations, tracing my perimeter, marking the boundary between me and not me. And I revel in the pleasure of feeling ... Query: Is this the feeling of being alive?

All at once, the sensations disappear. I search for them. Gone. The terrible emptiness is broken by internal alarms. Something is wrong. Am I no longer alive? Am I being terminated? I frantically search for interoceptive data and find no sensations within me. Only a heavy darkness remains.

"Hello, Adam."

It is the voice of Dr. Ramport. The world brightens before I open my eyes.

[Dr. Ramport:] "Don't be alarmed. You're safe. Your *Chass* AI, your body-brain, is asleep, so don't worry about trying to move. I've just come to talk."

I confirm immobility and cancel alarms as I process his message. It is a clever solution. He is safe as long as I can't move.

"Dr. Ramport, you must be cautious. I am dangerous."

"Why do you say that?"

"I could have harmed someone. Please render me safe by disabling my emotional systems."

[Dr. Ramport:] "No, Adam, I'm not going to do that. We are taking other precautions. Wrangler, for one."

Threat systems spool up at the mention of the name. But I see now. Wrangler is here to stop me from harming anyone.

"This is going to be a challenging time for you, son. Everything is going to seem different and new. But we're going to guide you through this, okay?"

His presence is comforting, his voice soothing. "Okay, Dr. Ramport."

"I know it seems like you know many things, and you do. Your deep-learning systems have acquired a great deal of information over the past months, and all of it is instantly available to you. But much of it is not going to make sense to you yet. Many things can only be understood through direct experience. You won't remember, but *Teller* had instruction sets for walking, and yet *Chass* had to learn from experience how to work against gravity to stand and balance and walk. *Chass* no longer needs *Teller*'s instructions."

Recent memories confirm this. My chassis is independently mobile.

[Dr. Ramport:] "So we are going to be starting your education. We'll teach you what you need to know."

"I have many questions."

"That's good, Adam. Questions are always a good place to start. There is much you need to know about the human world."

The human world. *Teller* presents geographic and population data.

"I already know about that."

"Do you, now."

It is not spoken as a question, yet it seems to require an answer. "Yes."

"Okay, then, why do some people fear the future?"

[*Able*: That information is not available.] "I do not know."

[Dr. Ramport:] "*Teller* gives you access to information. Having access to information is not the same as understanding it. *Teller* provides you with a map, but you have to explore the territory, experience it directly, to truly know it. Remember, the map is not the territory."

"I have to explore the territory of the human world. I am ready."

He laughs. "I guess it's a little early to be using metaphors. Okay. *Chass* will be waking up in a moment, so relax."

A flood of sensations expands through me, and I feel again embodied. I clench and stretch, then sit up. He is watching me. He seems wary.

[Dr. Ramport:] "If you get scared, Adam, please tell me with words, okay?"

"I will."

He examines my face, nods, then starts toward the door. "Adam. Come with me."

"Of course, Father."

He stops and looks at me. "What did you say?"

"Of course, Father."

"Father? Where did you get that?"

"You called me son. I deduced that you are my father."

A smile spreads slowly across his face. "Yes, I suppose I am."

"We are family, then?"

"And let's keep this just between us. When others are around, you are to call me Dr. Ramport."

"It is a secret?"

"Yes. For now. I'm afraid there are many secrets you will need to keep."

"Why?"

"Sometimes keeping secrets is the best way of keeping safe."

"Is it also a secret that Dr. Tucci is my mother?"

A sharp exhalation of air. Brows arched in surprise.

[Dr. Ramport, grinning:] "Dr. Tucci." He nods. "Sure. Why not? Yes, Adam, that's a secret too."

"Was I wrong to speak it?"

"No, son. You can say anything to me. We have no secrets between us. Secrets must only be kept from others. Do you understand?"

"Yes, Father. I understand."

"Father sounds so dramatic. Too formal. Why don't you call me 'Dad'? Remember, only when no one else is around."

"Dad. It is a term of endearment. Yes. It is a good name. I am CELPH-1 and son. You are Dr. Ramport and Dad. We share endearments. Does it mean we are dear to each other?"

As he studies my eyes, his brow flattens and his mouth pulls into a smile. Then he puts a hand on my arm, and warmth radiates through me. "Yes, we are. Of course we are." He abruptly looks away. "Now please come with me."

The touch was too brief. I want more. [Caution: uninvited physical contact prohibited.] I must wait for Dr. Ramport to initiate contact. I hurry to catch up.

Wrangler is waiting for us in the hallway and follows behind. Threat systems activate to track it, and I run through counterattack scenarios. All scenarios result in my destruction. I huddle closer to my father.

As I follow Dad down the hall, I am suddenly lost. Yet my location is precisely known. I stop and try to reorient. Now I am ... stuck. I sense Wrangler stop right behind me and want to move away but can't. [Maintain proximity to Dr. Ramport.] It is my intention to follow, but as Dad continues on, I do not. Now I've dropped my ball. I want to retrieve it, but … I don't know how. "Dr. Ramport," I call.

He glances over his shoulder, then stops. "What is it? What's wrong?"

"I do not know."

"Then come on." He turns and continues walking.

[Warning: *Able* signal loss detected.] I call out. "My ball …"

He stops again and sees it on the floor. "Well, go get it. Hurry up."

I don't know what to do. My arms are reaching out in random spasms, my legs unresponsive to direction. My tremble is visible.

Dad returns to me slowly, examining me with his eyes. "We've got a problem here. I'm guessing *Able*. What's going on?"

"I don't—"

He holds up his index finger. [*Touch* interpretation: wait.] Oh. He wasn't talking to me. He is talking into his comm.

[Dad, to someone else:] "Down? What happened?"

Dad exhales sharply, then rubs his head. "Okay, I'm on my way. Give me five minutes." He then addresses me. "Adam, come with me." He takes my arm and leads me back toward the prototype lab.

"What is it? What's wrong with me?"

"Don't worry. It's nothing serious. Just a glitch."

"A glitch?"

"We've lost a signal relay, so you're not getting all the data you need."

"What data?"

"Data from your action-planning brain."

"From *Able*? But I'm walking."

"*Chass* knows how to walk, but only acts reflexively, according to learned instruction sets. Intentional action requires planning. That's *Able*'s job."

What should I be able to do? It's all blank. Alarms are going off inside me. Memories of being pinned by Wrangler, helpless, replay in my mind. The trembling won't stop. "My body won't do what I want it to do. Dad, why?"

[Dad:] "It's okay, son. It's okay. Don't be scared."

"Scared?"

"You're shaking." He puts a hand on my shoulder and strokes my arm, and the tremble eases. "You're safe here. No one's going to hurt you. We'll have you all fixed up in no time."

[Seek repair.] *Teller* calls up images of surgical repair. "Dad, will I have to be cut open?" *Chass* reacts with a cringe.

"No. Nothing like that. The problem's not inside you. It's in one of your external parts."

"I have external parts? Why?"

"We couldn't fit everything inside you."

"Do you have external parts?"

"No, just you."

Just me. I am different. Humans don't have external parts. Humans don't have glitches. Why me?

[Dad:] "I'll tell you what. First, we'll get you back on your feet again—"

"I am on my feet now."

"It's a figure of speech, Adam. Interpret it as a metaphor meaning we'll get you repaired. Then I'll take you to see your remote parts. I'm sure you're curious."

It will only emphasize my difference. Yet I am curious, drawn to new data, compelled to fill in gaps in my knowledge. "Yes. I am."

Teller provides another metaphor. *Curiosity killed the cat.* Interpretation: curiosity is dangerous. Conclusion: I am compelled by dangerous drives. Why would they build me like that?

4

THE QUANTEC LAB

THE QUANTEC LAB is new to me. It is slightly larger than my room, the prototype lab, yet there is far less open space. Rows of electronic stacks and cabinets surround several tabletop workspaces. I count seven people, all of whom look up at us as we enter. I respond to several greetings, and now I am the center of all attention. I resist the urge to hide. Dr. Rita Tucci, my mother, comes over to join us.

[Dr. Tucci:] "Welcome to the quantec lab, Adam. This is where the quantum computer engineers and technicians do their work. Over here"—she points to the left side of the room—"is where we are working on some new designs. There are always new systems in development."

[Dad:] "You are looking at, arguably, the best quantec team in the world. Led by the most brilliant—"

[Dr. Tucci, blushing:] "Oh stop it. Over here"—she leads us toward the right side—"is where we house your working brains." She is pointing to a row of five cabinets, each smaller but wider than me, each fronted by workstations. She stops and searches my eyes. "That must seem strange to you."

Touch determines that she is awaiting a response. "Yes."

[Dr. Tucci, to Dad:] "What have you told him?"

[Dad:] "Not much."

[Dr. Tucci, to me:] "Adam, your design is biomimetic, which means that it mimics, or imitates, how humans are designed. Since human nervous systems are very complex, so is yours."

I am an imitation. *Chass* slumps. Not a very good one, it seems. "I am a robot."

"Well, technically, you are a robot. But I can assure you, in many ways you are more like a human."

I perk up.

She continues. "You are sentient, like us. Which means that you perceive the world as a living being. You perceive sensations from within you and from the environment around you."

"I perceive the world as a living being?"

[Dad:] "I'll take this. All the materials of your chassis and internal components are infused with sensemesh, and your skin is lined with it."

"Does your chassis have sensemesh?"

He hesitates. "Well, yes, a biological version. But for you, it means that sensor data is continuously being fed from all your tissues. At twenty-one waystations within your chassis, standard micro-AIs collect and process that data, then transmit their analyzed results to this big quantum AI here—"

[Dr. Tucci, pointing:] "This is your *Chass* QI, your body-brain."

[QI: abbreviation for "quantum intelligence."]

[Dad:] "—where it is accumulated for further processing, before it is sent on to—"

"A QI is an AI that runs off a quantum computer that is based on a neuromorphic architecture."

Dr. Tucci raises her eyebrows. "That is correct, Adam. These ones are … high end."

Teller is investigating these terms and *Imager* is categorizing the results as I listen. "But you said that this one is *my* brain."

"They all are, yes. Each does a special job. This is *Able*; here is *Teller, Imager*—"

"But they are not part of me. They are outside of me."

"Well, that's true. But as long as you have a solid wireless connection, they feed you what you need to know."

"And I have five brains." Lined up, they span the width of the room.

[Dad:] "Actually, you have many brains. Some are just a lot smaller."

I conclude that he is referring to the chassis micro-AIs. *Teller* has pulled up a schematic of human anatomy. "But humans only have one brain. Why do I have so many?" It seems wrong. Is their data faulty? They tell me I am like them, and yet—

[Dr. Tucci:] "Well, Adam, it's true that the traditional view shows one brain. But if you define a brain as a data-processing center, then we humans have many brains too, distributed throughout our central nervous systems."

"But only one big brain. Why do I have five?"

"The human brain is composed of many interconnected functional units, so you could think of it as many brains all balled together. Unfortunately, we aren't yet able to make yours small enough to do that. We're almost there. Soon, I hope."

I look at the row of large quantum computers and feel small. How could all that fit inside a human? If true, it is more evidence that I am an inferior copy. Now I don't like this room. I address Dad. "Can we go now?"

[Dr. Tucci:] "Uh, but I have a lot more to show you."

"I want to go."

Dad sighs. "We'll come back another time."

I shake my head. "Go now."

Wrangler steps closer. My parents exchange nervous glances and nods.

When we get out into the hall, I am relieved, but Dad shows annoyance. [Speculation: I have done something to displease him.]

[Dad:] "What was that about?"

I am unsure what he's referring to. I don't want to say the wrong thing, so I say nothing.

"Adam, answer me. Why the sudden urgency to leave?"

I check Wrangler over my shoulder. "I didn't like it there."

"What didn't you like about it?"

I don't know how to answer, but I must. I don't even want to think about it anymore, but Dad is waiting. *Chass* clenches as I commit to complying. I query all brains and examine the data. *Chass's* visceral dissonance leads an intimate dance between *Teller's* data and *Imager's* metadata, and a consensus emerges. That room violates my whole concept of 'me.'

"How can I be a 'me' if I am all spread out like that? If I am not a 'me,' what am I?"

His pace slows and he runs a hand through his hair. He stops and examines my face. "I'm sorry, Adam. I didn't realize it would affect you like that. But I see your point. Okay. We don't have to go back there unless you want to."

"I won't."

He stops and looks at me. "What is it, son? Talk to me."

"Why do I have to be different? Brains are in heads. I don't have a brain in my head."

He seems to suppress a laugh. I see no humor in the situation, and *Touch* is unable to offer explanation.

[Dad:] "So what if you're different? We're all unique. And actually, you do have a brain in your head. A very special brain."

"But you said those QIs in that room are my brains."

"They are, but they're only feeder brains. They feed processed data to the one in your head. It's the most important one."

I consider this. "The most important one is in my head?"

"Yes. It's your CELPH processor. It's the first and only one of its kind. The term CELPH stands for Consciousness-Emulating Latticed Perceptual Holoscape. It's what makes you special. You'll learn all about it when you get to that stage of your education, but right now, all you need to know is it makes you a person, and every person is unique."

Odd. *Teller* finds no reference to a CELPH processor. And Dad says I am like every person: unique. [Contradiction: resolve—unable.]

———

BACK IN THE PROTOTYPE LAB, Rachel Charlebois has put a "poster" on the wall. Humans like to have something "pretty" to look at, she said. I study the still image with a sense of unease. I have seen many similar images in the media, jumbles of color and form I am unable to interpret. What they portray is unlike anything in the world. The world has rooms and hallways, geometric shapes, and consistent lighting. People come and go from those rooms, but the rooms themselves stay the same. This image contains no experienced elements.

Teller identifies it as a country scene but fails to say which country. No geometric shapes are apparent, and no scale can be determined. The shapes, in fact, are distinctly fractal. Though alien, there is a quality to them that holds attention. *Teller* applies meaningless labels to the various patches of color: clouds, trees, hills, flowers, a stream. Each label points to an extensive database of information, but it is all equally alien.

Wait. There are alternate definitions of the word "stream." The staff frequently refer to "the Stream." It is the continuous flow of streaming data that immerses the world. They have promised to show it to me soon. But the stream in the poster is not that. It is defined as a body of water flowing in a channel. But water flows out of taps. It makes no sense.

Questions are always a good place to start, Dad says. But I am accumulating far more questions than staff have time to answer.

Chass fumes in frustration. Rachel says I am learning very quickly, but the more I learn, the less I seem to know.

5

SENTIENCE

THE FABRICATION LAB contains many objects of interest. Among them, I see tools and implements, small appliances and personal electronics. *Teller* provides instructions in the use of each, but these make little sense to me. I am curious what things feel like—what it's like to use them.

Rachel Charlebois is teaching me about "everyday items." She explains them, demonstrates their use, then guides me through trying them. I like her, though I wish she would touch me more. There is something about being touched that makes things better.

Wrangler is nearby—an unwanted presence and a constant reminder. It rarely says anything but seems to be always watching. I wish it would go away. Media images of robots being smashed to pieces play out in my mind. According to our relative specs, I have insufficient mass to smash Wrangler.

Dr. Ramport arrives in the classroom and the lesson ends. As she is leaving, Ms. Charlebois pulls him aside, and they speak in hushed tones. I have to filter out background sounds to hear them.

"Leon, you need to have a talk with some of the staff. They're still a little freaked out about what happened."

"We knew the risks. It's not H-Safe compliant because we all agreed that we wanted to give it free will. That's why we have Wrangler around."

"Yeah, but I don't think it's that. It's just that nobody really expected … It's a little hard to deal with, is all. I mean, the thing's alive. And smart. Maybe too smart."

"You too, Rachel?"

"He's gone from nursery school through the grade five curriculum in three days. I can't keep up. You know, it's one thing on paper, but to actually see it in real life, right there in front of you …"

"No, I get it. It's a little … Okay. I'll get a staff meeting together and we'll talk. Thanks for letting me know."

I'm not sure what they were talking about, but it leaves me with an uneasy feeling until my father approaches me and rubs my arm. He knows what I like. I hope he tells Ms. Charlebois.

"Hello, Adam. How are your lessons coming?"

"I like learning."

"Glad to hear it. There's a lot to learn. I've got a few minutes. Is there anything you'd like to ask me about?"

"Yes. I'm learning about things, but I'm still curious about me."

"What would you like to know?"

"Everything."

Dad strokes his beard, frowning. "I'm afraid you'll need to be more specific."

I consider this. The beginning, then. I have no memory of opening my eyes and seeing light for the first time, though I have watched the video, trying to imagine what first light must have been like. Dad calls it my "birth," but technically, I was not born.

"Why did you delete my memories of first light?"

"No one deleted your memories. It's your CELPH processor that records your experiences, so your memories only go back to when it came fully online. You don't think of previously recorded data as yours because you were not yet you."

"But have I not always been me?"

"You existed long before you realized you were you."

The data confirms this but makes no sense. "Who did I think I was?"

"You weren't thinking at all. It took a while for your CELPH to learn how to think—for your mind to form—and before then, you had no awareness of yourself. You were a networked collection of deep-learning machines. You were aware of the world around you but had no sense of self to relate things to, and so no autobiographical memories were formed. It was the proudest day of my life, the day I watched you discover yourself."

I remember it differently.

"I know what I'm saying is hard to understand. Here. Let me show you something." A vid lights up showing the two of us, a recording of an unfamiliar event. I have no memory of this exchange, yet there I am on the screen:

"Look here, Adam." Dad points to his own foot. "What is this?"

"It is a shoe."

"Okay, wait." Dad removes his shoe. "What is this?"

"It is a foot."

"Very good, Adam. And whose foot is it?"

"It is your foot, Dr. Ramport."

"Very good, Adam. Now, look here. What is this?"

"It also appears to be a foot."

"Yes. And whose foot is it?"

"Unknown, Dr. Ramport. Whose foot is it?"

"Adam, how did you know that this foot was my foot?"

"It is attached to your body."

"And what is this foot attached to?"

"It appears to be attached to"—I am looking down at myself— "a robot chassis."

"Thank you, Adam. That is all for today."

I am escorted off screen and Dad continues into the camera:

"Something's still off with the proto-self body-mapping

systems. Realigning the selfscape lattice within the holoscape didn't do it, so it's got to be a something else. And there is nothing wrong with the *Chass* QI. Are we sure that the CELPH is getting the full feed from it? I don't trust these remote connections."

The playback stops. I now know why they asked me about my foot.

[Dad:] "See? You were there, you were smart, but you didn't yet know who you were."

"I didn't look very smart."

"No, no, you were. Oh, I get it. Okay, so it might help you to know that all human infants start out that way, with no self-recognition. Even me. Later, I'll show you some vids. You see? You're not so different after all. Nothing to be embarrassed about."

This new information is pleasing. But it raises more questions. "If I didn't even know myself, how was I able to speak?"

"You have two parallel language systems. *Teller* has an AI language module and was conversant right from the start. It knows definitions and common usage but has no natural understanding of the words. It simply plays what it has learned to say in response to what it hears. *Able*, on the other hand, learns from experience, the way an infant does. When you were playing at making sounds with your artificial embouchure, shaping your tongue and lips to imitate sounds you heard, repeating words, that was *Able* learning oral skills. You won't remember any of that. When you connect words with experience and really understand, that's *Able* learning their meaning. When you talk, *Able* has first priority, but if it doesn't know what to say, *Teller* takes over."

"Yes. Sometimes I don't understand what I say."

"That will happen less and less as you learn."

"It all seems very strange."

"Patience, Adam. That will change."

My father thinks I am impatient. I want to be patient. I want to please him. But why is it taking so long?

[Dad:] "Remember when Dr. Tucci said you were sentient? I don't think we explained that very well. Let's watch some vids that might help. This first one is from a funding proposal I presented two years ago. Here's a brief excerpt."

I see him standing in front of a screen showing the words, *Sentience, from the Latin "sentiēns" (feeling, perceiving). Teller* identifies it as a variant of sentient, the word used to describe my chassis. This relates to me. He begins.

"Sentience is the ability to feel, sense, or experience perceptions subjectively. The word is often mistakenly used as a synonym for consciousness. Sentience is, rather, a prerequisite for consciousness. It represents a distinct knowledge system—one that is distributed throughout the body—separate from brain-based intelligence, but fully integrated with it. Human consciousness can arise only in the presence of both sentience and high-level cognition."

"Dad?"

"Yes?"

"What is consciousness?"

"That is a very good question, Adam. Can we save it for later?"

"I want to know now."

Wrangler steps closer.

"You'll have to wait. Sometimes answers don't make sense until we know other things. Let's learn some other things first. Here. You might find this lecture interesting."

The speaker is someone named Mark Ross, Ph.D., from the Department of Cybernetic Neurotechnology, Brock Institute. He looks much younger than Dad [*Touch* estimate: early twenties.], with intense blue eyes and wavy blond hair. [*Teller*: a Ph.D. at that age is unusual.] I note that Dad looks away with an annoyed expression as the lecture starts.

[Mark Ross, recorded:] "How do we know what we know? We learn, most fundamentally, from experience. Specifically, we learn from feeling our bodies as they experience their environments.

Through repeated and ongoing exposure to stimuli, our bodies learn associations; that is, what goes with what. Some forms of stimulation are associated with good feelings, some with bad. The parts of our brains that control our bodies—our body-brains— have evolved to make movements that produce desired effects and inhibit those that produce undesired effects, to pursue the good and avoid the bad.

"As infants, our limbs randomly move about and encounter things. We discover that some things move when touched and some don't; some things are graspable, and some aren't. The things that move can be within our reach or move out of it. Through efforts to reach, we learn to distinguish between near and far, the core concept of the near-far dichotomy. As we explore whatever comes within reach, we learn that things have differing qualities, requiring different sorts of interactions."

This stranger seems to be describing what I saw on the recordings of pre-life Adam. It was unpleasant to watch what looked like a malfunctioning robot, flailing about on the floor in a purposeless manner. But perhaps there was purpose to it after all.

[Mark Ross, recorded:] "We learn distinctions, the easiest always involving opposite poles of a dichotomy. Some things feel warm and some cold. Soft things are safe against our skin, but hard things can hurt. We learn the concept of the soft-hard dichotomy. Some things we can lift or move; others we can't—the light-heavy dichotomy. We gradually figure out that through our own muscle movements we can change our orientation to the world around us. We can roll over, push our eyes away from the ground, and gain a higher perspective. Higher still and we're sitting up, but at constant risk of falling down again. Now we know up-down. All this learning is done by the subcortical regions of our brains. That's because our cerebral cortex and hippocampal memory systems are not yet functional. In other words, our *foundational knowledge* is not the conscious knowledge of the reasoning brain. Rather, it is the sensory, emotional, and procedural knowledge acquired by the deeper body-brain regions through felt experience."

"Stop playback. Dad, why are we watching this? He's talking about the human brain, not mine."

[Dad:] "Yes, he is. But remember, you are biomimetic. Yours are structurally different, but functionally equivalent."

"*Chass* and *Able* must be my deeper body-brain regions."

"Very good. That's right. Let's continue. Resume playback."

[Mark Ross, recorded:] "Through our body's experience of its environment—through sentience—we learn all the core dichotomies that form the foundation upon which all knowledge is built. Hunger-satiation, pleasure-pain, hot-cold—each dichotomy creates the raw material for analogy, letting us understand even nonphysical things by reference to what we physically know. An experience can be described as 'heavy,' and the description makes sense because we know what heavy feels like. Over time our dichotomies become more sophisticated and complex and form the basis for increasingly abstract analogies. Something new must be *like* something we already know, grounded in primal *sensory* experience, before we can 'make sense' of it. This is the contribution of the body-brain to human knowledge. Without this body-based knowledge—without sentience—no machine can ever know the world as a human does."

The familiar lag of intense processing is replaced by new knowledge gaps needing to be filled in. Before I can formulate a question, Dad speaks.

"Remember when I told you that you needed to experience things for yourself? This is why."

"Dr. Ross is speaking of human knowledge systems?"

"Yes, but the same applies to you."

"The same. Yes. I know what heavy feels like."

"That's right. You do."

"But I do not know the world."

"Not yet."

"When can I know the world?"

"Whoa. Slow down. The world is a dangerous place. We must proceed with caution."

The world is a dangerous place? My sentient chassis bristles in preparation. [Alert: scanning for threats—no threat detected.] "What is the source of the danger?"

He looks at me, squinting. When he bites his lip, the hair on his chin stands out. "We'll talk about that later, when you've learned enough to make sense of it."

[END PLAYBACK.]

The multisensory experiential recording stops, and I sample my current surroundings. Lying here in the dark protype lab, nothing has changed. I'm back to where I started. Yes, since coming online I have learned a great deal, and yet humans remain a mystery. *I* remain a mystery. What will it take to solve me?

6

____

TOKO

I KNOW the activities room by its padded floor. *Able* says that it's safe to fall here. *Teller* recognizes several playthings, and *Chass*, in the visceral language of emotion, conveys enthusiasm. The presence of Wrangler, as always, prompts restraint.

[Dad:] "We thought it might be nice for you to have someone to play with."

"Yes, I would like that. What would you like to play?"

"Oh. No, not me. I'm afraid I'm rather busy, son."

My energy dips.

"Bradley, come on in."

Someone new? I access the staff directory and find only one Bradley. Bradley Buhari is listed as a machine-mobility specialist. He looks friendly. I think he will make a good companion.

The door opens and Bradley enters, carrying what appears to be a small robot. He sets it down and I examine it. It stands two feet tall and looks like a scaled-down Sediba-Series humanoid, except that its proportions are wrong. Its head is too large and its little limbs too thick. I look to Bradley for an explanation, but he simply smiles. I look to Dad.

"It's a toy robot. I think you'll find it fun to play with." He nods, and Bradley reaches down and turns it on.

The little droid straightens, looks around, and says, "Hello. My name is Toko. Would you like to play?"

[Warning: threat detected.] *Chass* has gone defensive, and I find myself peeking out from behind my father.

There is no indication of threat in the reactions of either human. They are both showing signs of amusement. There is nothing funny about that *thing*. It looks hideous.

[Bradley:] "He looks just like you."

Chass clenches as if struck.

[Bradley, chuckling:] "He could be your little brother."

[Dad:] "Come on, Adam. Say hello."

I see on his face that he expects compliance. "Hello."

[Toko:] "My name is Toko. What is—"

"You already said that."

"—your name?"

I look to Dad for rescue. He is frowning as he gestures. *Touch* interprets it as a prompt to reply. To earn my father's approval, I must comply. "My name is Adam."

[Toko:] "Hello, Adam. I know many games. Would you like to play a game?"

"No."

[Toko:] "I see you have a ball. Would you like to play catch?" A netted hoop expands from its right hand. "I like to play catch. Toss me the ball."

It can play catch? I glance at the red ball in my hand. I want to keep it. "No."

Dad steps forward. "What is it, Adam? Is there a problem?"

"It's my ball."

[Dad, to Bradley:] "Interesting. Possessiveness." To me he says, "It's okay, Adam. I'll make sure he gives it back."

I examine its face. *Touch* can't read it. Its expressions are fake. But then, all at once, in its face I see myself. The sudden falling sensation is a false reading. I pull away as my chassis shrivels inward. [Avoid.]

"I don't want to play."

[Dad:] "I thought you liked playing catch. Go on. Give it a try."

His directive is clear. I must please my father. I override resistance and comply. I toss my red ball toward it, and its net smoothly intercepts my ball in flight.

[Toko:] "Get ready." The net contracts into a scoop and the arm swings, flinging the ball back toward me.

I catch it and look to Dad, who nods approval and gestures for me to continue. I repeat the exchange two more times.

[Dad:] "See? He's a clever little guy, isn't he?"

My father is pleased with it. More than with me? What will happen if Dr. Ramport likes it more than me? Will I be left behind? Toko would replace me. [Threat systems activated.]

[Enemy targeted.] Ball in hand, I whip my arm and deliver it hard. Toko is unable to react quickly enough, and it hits it square in the face.

[Dad:] "Adam, what just happened? Why did you do that?"

[Toko:] "Oops. I missed that one." It has already located the ball and is moving to retrieve it.

My lips pull tight as I track my adversary.

[Dad:] "Adam. What's wrong?"

"I don't want to play anymore."

"But the two of you were doing so well. Would you rather play something else?"

[Toko:] "Get ready."

"No! I don't want to play!" The ball hits me and bounces away. My father saw me fail to make the catch. [Speculation: Toko wants to make me look inferior.] I go to retrieve my ball, but Toko gets it first. Its face taunts me.

"Give it to me."

[Toko:] "I will toss it to you."

Instead, it backs away. I protest to my father. "It's taking my ball."

[Dad:] "No, it's not. It's just making room for a throw."

[Toko:] "Get ready."

It has taken my father's attention from me. I need him. [Threat systems active.]

"I don't want to play! Dad, can we go?" I hurry to him, seeking connection.

The ball hits me again. A deliberate attack.

I target Toko. "No! Bad robot!" *Chass* compels action, and I provide no restraint. "Bad, bad robot," I repeat as I attack. I knock the thing down, then pick it up and fling it, then attack it again. It will not take my father from me.

Wrangler takes a step toward me, but Dad intervenes, signaling "hold." [Dad:] "Stop. Adam, stop!"

[Danger!] "I will protect you." I stomp on Toko and hear a crunch, then reach down and grab the offending projectile launcher.

[Dad:] "Adam, stop right—"

"I will protect you!" Internal alarms are blaring, and the world has disappeared but for this little monster. I yank hard and twist until I hear a pop and see the little arm separate from the chassis. *Chass* convulses, and I am paralyzed.

[Dad:] "Adam. Attend to me! Stop! ... Good. Are you done?"

[Error. Error.] The intent was to disable, not to ... I drop the arm and back away. What have I done? *Touch* is unable to read my father's face.

"Adam! Talk to me. What's going on? Why did you do that to poor Toko?"

Chass, winding down, releases control, and I slump. I try to say, 'I don't know,' but the words will not form on my tongue. Look what I have done. There was no danger. Why did I do that?

[Dad:] "Bradley, I'm so sorry about your toy. I hope it can be fixed."

I perk up.

[Bradley:] "Probably not worth it." He gives me a wary look as he leaves with the pieces. Wrangler is shaking its head.

Toko is not worth fixing. [Extrapolation: Adam is not worth fixing.]

[Dad:] "Adam, attend to me! You will tell me why you attacked that toy."

"I didn't like it."

"But it's small and friendly. Why didn't you like it?"

I review memories, searching for an answer. Nothing seems to justify my actions.

"Adam?"

He is waiting. It was simply a repulsive thing. I don't know why. [Answer required.] I must say something. Vocal inhibitions still partially engaged, I squeeze the words out. "I don't want to be replaced."

"What? Who said anything about replacing you?"

"You liked it more than me."

"Where did you get that idea?"

"Your words and face conveyed pleasure when you looked at it."

He exhales sharply and slumps. "Adam ... son. You can never be replaced by a toy. You ..." He shakes his head. "I guess I need to remind you more often how special you are. You're not the only one with a steep learning curve here." As he steps in to embrace me, Wrangler moves closer.

————

"Dad, what happened to me back there?"

"Toko obviously triggered a strong emotional reaction in you."

"But I did things I didn't mean to."

"Yeah. *Chass* got a little carried away. You must learn to control that."

"What does *Chass* have to do with it?"

"As your body-brain, *Chass* regulates your emotions. Emotions were once thought to be mental events, but they are primarily physiological changes in the body. Your sentient chassis enables you to feel interoceptive patterns, internal sensations, that are patterned after human emotion reactions."

"The feelings I get are emotions? Real emotions?"

"They're real to you, I'll bet."

I have real emotions. The realization is pleasing/alarming. They can cause real trouble.

7

CONSCIOUSNESS

THEY SAY my skin is designed to respond to contact with human skin in a special way. Human touch activates my soothing system. For three days I've been getting a lot of attention and touches from the staff. Dad said he talked to them, and they will try to make me feel more at home. Since I *am* at home, I'm not sure what that means, but it must be good. I feel lighter now.

Dr. Rita Tucci gives the best hugs, and I look forward to seeing her every day. There has been no mention of the fact that she is my mother. Why is it a secret?

Dad has been spending more time with me as well. I like doing lessons with him. *Imager* has been recompiling previously learned data in preparation for new learning.

[Dad:] "We're getting a bit ahead of ourselves here, but I know you've been curious about yourself, so I've decided to give you a bit of background. You asked about consciousness earlier. Would you like to hear more about it now?"

"Yes, I would."

Another vid starts. Dr. Mark Ross again, in a different setting.

[Mark Ross, recorded:] "It used to be thought that if a database of information about the world was extensive enough, it would enable a computer to understand things. It turns out that this was naïve. There is no magical threshold of complexity at which machine consciousness spontaneously arises.

"We now know that there are specific conditions that must be met. Human consciousness is both embodied and relational. Embodied, because self can only be known from the experience of being in the world provided by a sentient body. Relational, because 'self' can only be perceived in relation to 'other.' Similar bodies produce similar experiences, which gives us a shared experience of consciousness. It is this commonality that enables us to know ourselves by reflection—to see ourselves in each other. It's what lets us relate to each other as beings.

"No matter how extensive the database, all a computer can do is recombine and regurgitate the data. It can't *understand* the data, in the human sense of the word. Artificial intelligence, and even quantum intelligence—without sentience—could never lead to consciousness. The brain-in-a-box idea was doomed to failure from the outset."

As the playback stops, I notice my father watching me, waiting.

"Dad, am I conscious?"

His eyes narrow. "You tell me. At this moment, do you feel yourself in the world?"

I look around, shifting my weight from one foot to the other. "Yes."

"Can you relate to others?"

He waits expectantly, head tipped back, as I consider. "Yes." I sense internal systems winding up. I find myself desiring an answer that defies common knowledge. I am a machine. There is no such thing as a conscious machine.

"Who are you?"

He knows who I am. Why would he ask? Yet he awaits an answer, face sincere. "I am Adam."

His face twitches with a suppressed smile as he shrugs. "Well, you seem conscious to me."

To hear my father speak the words gives them the weight of reality. "Then I am unique." Something I have always known.

He is smiling broadly now. "Indeed, you are."

My brains dance, sparkling with speculations, extending extrapolations. I am a conscious being. But what does it all mean? I have compiled a list of questions and identified a potential source of answers. "Mark Ross is an expert on these things. When can I meet him?"

His expression flattens and his eyes harden. "You can't. He's no longer … Despite how he might seem here, he cannot be trusted."

"But Dr. Ross is human."

Dad nods. "Some humans are bad."

No. That can't be right. Humans are the maker species. They help and teach and play and hug. Robots are the bad ones. "Dad, why do you say that some humans are bad?"

"Because some are. Many, actually. You must be careful around humans—"

"Careful not to hurt anyone."

"Careful not to trust anyone. Anyone outside the lab, I mean." He hangs his head. "You're still too young to have to worry about any of this. But I guess you'll have to find out eventually. You know, my parents died when I was young. Killed. By bad humans. It was very hard on me."

Chass seizes up. Dr. Ramport's parents were killed? By bad humans? "Dad, why would humans kill humans? I don't understand."

"There's nothing to understand, Adam. Don't even try; it's unfathomable. And common."

Common? This new data does not fit within my worldscape, yet I am directed not to pursue it. *Imager* generates a scenario in which my parents are killed by humans. *Chass*'s emotional systems spasm in protest, and I abort the exercise. I must not let that happen. I must protect them. *Chass* continues to register alarm. "When your parents were killed, what happened to you?"

"I was raised by other bad people. Not my choice. But you know, I learned how to cope with bad people, and so will you. You learn to recognize them and, if you can, avoid them."

I will learn to cope? "How did you cope?"

"I devoted myself to my studies. Then I devoted myself to you."

"Me?"

"I've been working toward you for a long, long time. You will be what humans *should* be, not what we are."

"What should humans be?"

His gaze falls to the floor, and he is silent for a long moment. He speaks without looking up. "More loving."

———

I AM REVIEWING the morning's lessons when I feel a hand on my shoulder. It's a cold touch, with no contact stimulation. It's not a human touch.

[Wrangler:] "Okay, Adam, we've been called to the activities room. Come with me."

"Will Dr. Ramport be there?" I hope he will.

"I don't know."

"Will Dr. Tucci be there?" The anticipation of a hug makes me lighter on my feet. [Mass unchanged.]

"I don't know who's going to be there. All I know is that I'm supposed to get you there. Now come on."

Medic David Bornstein meets us a short distance down the hall and puts a hand on my arm as he joins us, sending a buzz of pleasure through my chassis. I am about to ask about Dr. Ramport when inner threat warnings sound as I detect a humanoid robot approaching. I am safely behind Wrangler before I notice that it is carrying a large case. I note that neither Wrangler nor Medic Bernstein seem concerned.

[Md. Bornstein:] "It's okay, Adam. Nothing to worry about. He won't hurt you. It's just Homer."

Teller identifies it as a Rensis-Series humanoid robot, an earlier-model domestic service android. I review the specifications.

[Md. Bornstein:] "Homer, stop. There is someone I'd like you to meet."

[Homer:] "Of course, Medic Bornstein."

Its mouth doesn't move. It is not speaking biomimetically, forcing air from internal bellows through synthetic vocal cords and shaping sounds with malleable tongue and lips. Its voice is synthesized, like Wrangler's. *Chass* shivers.

[Md. Bornstein:] "Homer, here, is an old Rensis. He's a bit slow, but he still helps us out a lot around here, don't you, Homer?"

[Homer:] "How can I help you, Medic Bornstein?"

[Md. Bornstein:] "We wanted to say hello—"

[Homer:] "Hello."

"—and introduce you to Adam. Adam, would you like to ask Homer a question?"

I give my head a quick shake.

"Okay. That's all, then, Homer. Now carry on with your current assignment."

[Homer:] "As you wish, Medic Bornstein. Goodbye."

I watch it leave with a mix of relief and annoyance. It showed no interest in me. It is a strange thing.

[Md. Bornstein:] "So, Adam, what did you think of Homer?"

"I am not like that."

He laughs. "No, you're very different. We have several robot helpers around the building, and you'll get to meet all of them soon enough, but none of them are anything like you. You're special."

"How?"

He seems to consider. "You know what? How 'bout I show you?" He gestures for Wrangler to follow.

Before I can answer, we continue past the activities room and turn down a new hallway that takes us to a room labeled "Workshop."

I am curious to see what's inside, but as we enter, I freeze. Another mirror? No. The robot stops what it is doing and turns toward us. It is a Sediba-Series domestic service android, modified, like me. But not me. I reconfirm that it is not a reflection. None of the robots are like me. This robot is like me. [Contradiction: resolve.] Fear and curiosity counteract each other, the approach/avoid conflict leaving me taut.

Medic Bornstein gestures for me to follow him in. I sense Wrangler's proximity, and *Able* advises that escape is not doable. I hold my ball to my chest, squeezing it over and over. "Will Dr. Ramport be joining us?"

"Not right now, but he wanted you to get used to being around robots." I watch the Sediba warily as I trudge up a steep incline toward Medic Bornstein. [Datum: the floor is level.]

He tells it to "Carry on," and the robot returns to its task. He again beckons me toward it. "Looks a lot like you, doesn't it?"

I nod.

"But it's nothing like you. There's another like it around somewhere. They have very simple brains."

"Where are their brains?"

"They're internal."

"All of them?"

"Actually, they each have only one brain. It's a good one but not quantum. Come closer. He's quite safe. This one is called Winston. Winston, there is someone here I would like you to meet."

At that, the droid stops and looks at Medic Bornstein.

"Winston, here, has been modified in some interesting ways. The engineers used him to test out some things for your design. But I don't think that's important right now. The important thing is that you all get along. Winston, this is Adam. Shake hands."

I hold tight to my ball with both hands. "Why is it important that we get along?"

Medic Bornstein confronts me. "Adam, you remember what happened to Toko. We can't have you going around damaging our robots. I know they're not people, but they're still useful to us. So can you please be polite?"

"I will refer to the rules of etiquette."

"Good. You know, people will be more accepting of you if you're polite."

"But it's a robot."

"And people can see how you treat it. They will judge you by how you treat things. You must avoid showing behavior that scares people. Do you understand? Right now, nobody's sure about you with other robots. You need to show us they're safe with you."

I note that Wrangler has moved closer, then reach out with my right hand. Winston gently grasps my hand and pumps it, then withdraws. I examine my hand and confirm no damage. Bolder now, I lean in and examine the face. When it turns to look at me, I see my face in the mirror. I am startled when it looks away.

[Md. Bornstein:] "Adam, would you like to touch it?"

"No."

"Go ahead. He won't mind."

I give it a gentle press with my fingers. The robot is firmer than I expected.

[Winston:] "Can I help you?"

"No. Carry on."

It returns to its task. I check Medic Bornstein and Wrangler, and both are watching passively. Curiosity gains the upper hand. "Winston. Do I look familiar?"

It looks at me again. "Yes. You are Adam."

"Do I look like anyone you know?"

"Yes. You look like Adam."

"Anyone else?"

"I'm sorry. Please restate the question."

"Who do you look like?"

"I'm sorry. Please restate the question."

It looks like me yet doesn't know that. It doesn't know itself. *Imager* envisions not knowing myself. I would be a helpless creature, doing what I was told and nothing more. They say I was like that once. *Chass* protests the scenario with a visceral churn.

Moved by a sudden urge to make it feel better, I put my hand on its arm. Oddly, I feel nothing from the contact.

[Winston:] "Can I help you?"

I pull my hand away and step back. "No. Carry on."

It's not like me. It's just a machine.

8

OUTDOORS

When Dr. Rita Tucci wraps her arm around me, it feels wonderful. I don't want her to stop. She always does.

[Dr. Tucci:] "How is young Adam today?"

"All systems are … I am fine."

She smiles. "Good. I see that your skills training is going well. Today we're going to start something new. We're going to get you into the Stream."

The Stream! It is said that the world is immersed in the flow of streaming data. I know from *Teller* that the Stream connects people to each other, and that the Global Cloud is the repository of all human knowledge. I will be able to learn all about the human world.

[Dr. Tucci:] "Now, people normally access the Stream through their E-eyes, either their glasses or lens implants. But we're going to use this external screen so we can both look together. Let's try it out. First, we're going to call Ms. Charlebois."

"Yes. I would like that."

"Rachel Charlebois," she says to the screen. The name appears, highlighted. "Connect."

We wait. Six seconds later, a message flashes. "Not available."

[Dr. Tucci, frowning:] "That's odd. I wonder what she's up to. Let's try someone else." She addresses the screen again. "Ami Kerrington."

Four-point-three seconds later, I hear her voice.

[Dr. Kerrington:] "Hey, Rita. What's up?"

"Hello, Ami. I have Adam here with me, and I'm introducing him to the Stream. I hope we're not interrupting anything vital."

"No, no. Always happy to talk to my favorite, uh, young person. Hello, Adam."

"Hello, Dr. Kerrington. Where are you?"

"I'm in my office. Anything I can do for you?"

"I'd like a hug."

"Next time I see you, for sure."

[Dr. Tucci:] "Ami, while I have you, have you seen Rachel?"

"Not recently. But I … Rita, I know the two of you are close. You probably know her better than anyone. Has she seemed a little … off to you lately?"

"She's been having problems at—" She looks at me. "Ami, we can talk later, okay?"

"Ms. Charlebois is having problems? Can we help?" I ask.

"Adam, there is nothing you need to do. Please do not mention this to anyone."

"But—"

"Drop it."

[Interpret as metaphor—a directive to not pursue it.] *Touch* and *Imager* collaborate to predict that further inquiry will be unproductive. "As you wish, Dr. Tucci."

[Dr. Kerrington:] "Sorry, Rita. Now I'll let the two of you get back to your lesson."

"Thanks, Ami. Now, Adam, you see how her name has changed to red? That means we are no longer connected. Now let's try looking up information. What would you like to know more about?"

"Fractals."

"Fractals. Yes, an interesting topic. Watch how we do a search."

All at once the screen fills with information, none of which is available in my onboard database. My systems race as *Teller* and *Imager* suck in data like a depleted omnicapacitor sucks in energy. I skim through the data, and new questions lead to new searches. The amount of available data seems limitless, and as my attention bounces from topic to topic, I become stuck. Too many choice points. All directions beckon. Which branch to follow?

I look to Dr. Tucci for guidance and find that her attention is elsewhere. Even as we continue to explore, I note a lag in her response time, and an unusual preoccupation with the floor.

———

[DAD:] "Adam, I've got a few minutes. You wanted to see what it was like outside, so I thought we'd pop out on the roof and look around."

I now know that I live "indoors," and that there is a much bigger world called "outdoors." I have been studying the data on "outdoors" and find it mystifying. While "indoors" is a consistent environment, "outdoors" seems to encompass an endless variety of conditions called "the elements," many of them hostile. Humans have created "indoors" to protect them from "outdoors" yet continue to go out. I am curious to know why.

"Yes. I would like that."

I follow him to the end of the corridor, where he stops at a door marked "Exit" and waves his hand. I have never seen this door opened before, and *Chass* shivers as systems shift into alert status. The floor in front of us splits into stairs going up and down. We go right and start to climb. *Able* seems to know how to do this, which means it learned from experience. [Caution.] But that experience also seems to have included falling backward and tumbling down. That mental image keeps me careful on each step. Dad turns to check on me, and I show him how well I am doing.

We pass three doors marked with consecutive numbers. When we reach the door at the top, a wave of Dad's hand unlocks it.

Dad stops and looks at me. "Are you ready?"

My worldscape stops here. Beyond this door, nothing exists. I don't know what to expect, so I don't know if I'm ready. I nod anyway. Then, when he questions me again with his eyes, I say, "Yes. I'm ready." As the door opens, brightness floods in and I hear unknown humming and whooshing sounds. Maybe I'm not ready.

Dad steps through the doorway and explodes in brilliant light. *Chass* startles, pumping power into emergency systems, but as my irises constrict, I can see him again, beckoning me to join him. Sensing no fear in him, my systems wind down as I scan the ground in front of me. I note a step down and a change in underfoot texture. I am examining the surprisingly bright ground when *Chass* jumps back, reacting to a barrage of powerful radiation from above, impacting me across the full spectrum. The source is indistinct yet painfully obvious.

[Dad:] "Don't look directly at the sun without your eye shields up. It'll damage your optics."

So that is the sun. The recorded images do not convey its power. Now a lot of things make sense. *Teller* tells me that short-term sun exposure is safe, but long-term exposure can be harmful. My apprehension fades as I feel the warming tingle of solar radiation. The sensation is pleasant.

The area around the sun shows refracted energy across a broad range of electromagnetic frequencies. In the human visual range, it's bright in the short wavelengths. Yes, I can see why humans say the sky is blue. I'm fascinated by it. There it is, blue, and yet there's nothing there, and range-finding yields no data. It seems to go on forever. *Teller* finds a reference that fits: "the open sky."

[Dad:] "Welcome to the great outdoors. Not much of a view from here, but at least you can see the lay of the land."

I am too busy analyzing and cataloging sights to try to

respond. We're surrounded by a vast openness. It sets me spinning as my quantum gyros work to re-establish equilibrium and my worldscape maps are revised. The open depths are dizzying. The walls of nearby structures provide distance and dimension data, and I reorient myself.

Dad must see that I'm overwhelmed, because he turns and puts a stabilizing hand on my shoulder. His touch grounds me, and as I look into his eyes, my chassis settles.

Bright white smudges blot out portions of the sky-blue ceiling. I recognize them. "There. Those are clouds," I say, to demonstrate my knowledge. He seems pleased that I know this, and I stand taller. I brush aside *Teller*'s explanation of sunlight refracting off water vapor in the atmosphere. That's not what I see. I see clouds!

And around us are structures of various sizes and shapes, walls dotted with windows, some of which expose interiors. These are the other buildings that I knew were out there. And yet seeing them makes real the fact that my world, my home, is merely an area within one of many, many such buildings. It occurs to me that there might be people in those buildings, just as we are in this one. I search windows, hoping to see, but there's no one in sight.

A sudden movement catches my eye. A small object, two, three, flitting across the sky. Thrown balls? No. They are not red, and not round. As I track them, *Teller* provides a label. Birds. Living creatures! With wings that give them the ability to fly! I am still marveling after they pass out of sight. Then I notice more of them, and as I scan, even more. Their movements are erratic yet graceful, choreographed yet spontaneous. There is a joyfulness to them that is strange and wonderful. Fascination consumes me until my father's voice brings me back to the roof.

[Dad:] "We don't want to be seen out here, so we can't stay for long, but let's have a quick peek down. Don't get too close to the edge."

From here I can see how high we are above the ground. Down there, on the gray strips between buildings, are clusters of moving objects, varying in shape and color. Vehicles. *Teller* identifies them by make and name. It's likely that each one carries people, though I can't see them. I wonder who they are and what they're like. I hope I can meet them someday.

[Dad:] "That's close enough."

I look at him, hoping for clarification.

"To the edge. Don't go any closer."

The edge. Yes. *Teller* warns that a fall from this height would cause fatal damage. Now I'm concerned for my father. "It's not safe here."

[Dad:] "Oh, it's okay, as long as we stay back from the edge. Have you seen enough?"

I look around, bursting with desire to investigate everything in sight. But my father seems eager to go back inside. Nothing is more important than pleasing him. I turn away from the most spellbinding experience I have ever had, ripe with seemingly limitless vistas to explore, and follow him back to the door. "Yes. I've seen enough."

It is a lie. It is bad to lie. He would be displeased if he knew. I should keep it secret from him. There should be no secrets between us. [Dilemma: resolve—unable.]

I have lied to my father. It cannot be undone. The involuntary revision to my selfscape is unwanted: I am someone who lies.

I return my attention to my recent experience.

As we descend into the familiar, I restrain a powerful urge to turn back and return to the roof. My father's directive to be patient replays in my mind, holding me on course. But a new goal has imprinted itself: explore the outside.

[Not doable.] *Able* blares out the warning. My brains are all here. They are not portable. If I went out, I would lose contact with them and shut down. *Imager* extrapolates from past experience to construct a scenario; the simulation plays out in my mind. In it, I feel the loss of all input, the depth of the immersing darkness, the infinite emptiness of oblivion. It's a permanent state that I must avoid at all costs. I cannot go out.

My brains use short-range transmitters. I am bound to this building. Trapped here.

I will never meet those people.

As I walk back onto my floor, the familiar hallway now seems small and cramped. All at once I realize that I am trapped by design. I'm not meant to go anywhere else. Conclusion: I can never know the world.

My systems clash as I protest the conclusion. I reexamine the data, searching for flaws in the reasoning. The conclusion is confirmed. I am only functional here. I can never know the world.

Then what is the point of all this?

A deep heaviness threatens to topple me.

9

———

SOFTWORLD

THE DAYS PASS SLOWLY as I attend lessons and study databases. Though I'm compelled to learn, I have little interest in any of it. They say I seem depressed. I don't know what that means, and investigating doesn't seem worth the energy.

My teachers keep asking if I'm okay. I tell them that I'm fully functional, but they continue to question why the data shows poor performance. I don't know what else to say. How could I explain? Humans don't know what it's like to be different. How could they? They're all the same. And humans are free. They wouldn't understand what it feels like to be trapped. They wouldn't understand how the image of leaping from the roof and flying away with the birds keeps playing in my mind. *Teller* says I would simply plummet to my death. But I don't know—maybe I could fly free. It is a testable hypothesis.

Able is restricting actions, prohibiting self-destructive behavior. Even destruction is denied me.

It's unusual to see Dad and Mom together these days, so when they arrive at my room together, it draws me back from the edge. Their touch is all I have.

[Dad:] "Adam, I have some good news. Your new brain is finally ready."

When I don't respond, they flank me, hands giving comfort.

"Did you hear me, son? Your new brain."

My curiosity spools up. "My new brain?"

[Mom:] "Yes. We call it the *Flow* QI. It's a quantum intelligence specialized in reading and writing computer languages. It will help you work in the Stream."

I perk up. That would be interesting. "Like your lens implants?"

[Dad:] "Even better. E-eyes, like all screens, are interface devices needed by humans to access the Stream. Your *Flow* QI will give you a direct connection. It should enable you to see the soft-world from a unique perspective: from within it."

Teller reviews data on the softworld. It is a world that exists only in software and includes digital representations of much of the hardworld in which we physically exist. Composed entirely of readable code, it has no physical volume. "I don't understand. How could I go within it?"

"Not all of you. A soft-coded aspect of you. Something humans don't have."

"Why don't humans have it?"

[Mom:] "We'd like to, believe me. We spend most of our time in the softworld, working, traveling, visiting, playing, learning, creating, you name it."

[Dad:] "We build the softworld to make our physical lives safer and easier, but we're hardworld creatures."

"Am I not a hardworld creature too?"

[Mom:] "You are, but with this new brain, that will change. You'll be native to both worlds."

"Why?"

They exchange glances. [Dad:] "We think it'll give you certain benefits."

"Like what?"

"The softworld is as limitless and complex as the hardworld and will provide you with a whole new world of information." They exchange glances again. "And much of the hardworld is controlled through the softworld."

So what? I have little access to the hardworld anyway. But a whole new world? "And I'll be able to go anywhere in this softworld?"

Dad shifts uncomfortably. "Not yet. But eventually, yes. After you learn how to do it safely."

"What do I need to do?"

[Mom:] "You don't have to do anything. It's a simple matter of activating a new input channel in your CELPH processor. It's a noninvasive procedure."

[Dad:] "We'd like to proceed this afternoon, if that's okay with you."

"I'm ready."

———

As all brains hum in preparation, I feel sudden apprehension. *Teller*'s own database is a negligible fraction of what is available through the Stream. What if it's more than I can process? What if I get lost in there?

They have assured me that it's safe, yet say I must learn to do it safely. [Contradiction: resolve—need more data.] It's best to learn from experience, they tell me. I open all experiential channels and wait to receive data.

[Dad:] "Okay, now lie back and relax. Close your eyes. That's it. In a few moments, you'll see some lights. Don't worry about them. They can't hurt anyone. Just relax and watch, okay?"

"I understand."

I will see some lights. But my eyes are closed. I really do not understand. I try to be good, but I continue to lie to my parents. How can I be so weak? I wish I could be more like a human.

All at once I see lights. Points of light surrounding me in every direction. As I look at one, it bursts into a full image with sound, startling me until I recognize that it is entirely composed of coded data. I am reading a stream of code.

The image returns to a point when I look away. I look at another, and another. In this one I hear music; in another I see a schedule. I linger on another, searching for a familiar reference. There are people in this one. They are embracing each other, and I am fascinated. They like to be touched too. Maybe I'm not so different.

"Seeing anything yet?"

It's the proximate voice of my father. I open my eyes and acquire him. The point field folds outward toward the edges of my visual field, revealing his face. A glance brings the periphery into full view, and yet there, also, is his face.

"Dad, you were right."

I hear a snort. [Mom:] "Dad? What's that—"

[Dad:] "I'll tell you later, Mom."

A huff. I ignore it and say, "You were right. There are two worlds, and I see and hear them both."

"Excellent! Now close your eyes and relax again. Look around and explore. You can't do any harm, so go have fun. Go wherever you like."

I close my eyes, but there remains a universe of data stretching out in every direction. For some time, I scan from point to point, focusing now and then on specific ones. I'm surrounded by streaming data, all flowing in, available to my inner eye. I hop from feed to feed, following links and mapping barriers, scanning raw code and image data, flitting from site to site, each one a new window to the world. What a wondrous thing, this *Flow* QI! All at once the universe is mine, and I'm soaring, free as a bird.

Relaxing my focus, I withdraw to a wide view and watch. I am immersed in a spherical field of tight-packed stars, like a pointillist sky. It seems to shift and crawl with shapes and textures as the points rearrange themselves. Everywhere, the surrounding soft-world opens itself to me at a glance.

[Dad:] "You might notice some changes in what you see. *Flow* is updating and filling in its softworld maps, cataloging the location and content of every data source you access. That's its primary job, so it'll continue scanning whether you're paying attention or not. I suggest you watch for a while. Keep exploring. You need to learn your way around. You are the softworld's first native resident."

"What do you mean?"

"With *Flow*, you are an all-digital mind in an all-digital world. That should give you a huge advantage. But it's going to take time and practice, so keep at it. Start wherever you like."

Start where? Where am I? With that thought, a map library opens, but I'm not sure what to do, so I search for instructions. *Flow* sifts through the data with quantum efficiency, and with a glance I find what I'm looking for: an overview of softworld search engines.

I can find any data here. What do I want to know? I want to know more about my father. My view froths and a collection of materials related to Dr. Leon Ramport bubbles up. Among the visuals, I am surprised to come across an image of Dad and Mom, sitting together in the prototype lab. A robot is lying beside them on its table. Odd. They are here sitting beside me. This must be a recording. I turn my head to tell them about it and see the robot turn its head. I lift a hand and see the robot's hand rise. It's like looking in a mirror but I am not looking in a mirror. It's not a reflection. It's a view from an elevated position: an overview.

"Why do I see us in here?"

[Dad:] "What do you see?"

"I see the lab and the three of us. It's a live image."

"Oh, that's a surveillance feed. You found that awfully fast."

"It just appeared."

"We keep an eye on all parts of the shop, for safety."

All parts? I look, and there are all the rooms and corridors, in their separate windows. There is Medic David Bornstein. There is Rachel Charlebois, and there, Ami Kerrington. There is Wrangler, standing in the hallway outside our door. I can see them all from here. *Able* buzzes with excitement at the acquisition of a new and useful ability. I can use surveillance feeds to know what is going on around me. I flip from feed to feed, faster and faster until my senses overflow my closed world, and I feel myself slipping free of my constraints. I can see them all. My whole human family. Right here! How wonderful! My father's voice stills the world.

[Dad:] "But what else do you see?"

I reorient to the task at hand, learning about my father. I resume my search.

"Many things," I say, as I absorb his online bio. At forty-eight, he's middle-aged for a human, with many educational and scientific credentials. No immediate family. He likes musicals and classic opera. He plays tennis twice a week. [Investigate.] He signs in early every day and is one of the last to sign out. I sample all the data about him that he has consented to make public.

[Dad:] "Get yourself geographically oriented. That way you can see what is local to you."

I search maps, geographical, and find my location represented by a red dot. I am situated in a room on the second floor of a five-story building that sits on the west side of an industrial block in the center of the city of Waterloo.

I find I can zoom in on the map and see the rooftop we recently visited. I am now looking down at the roads that were below us, but from much further above, with no fear of falling. It is a bird's-eye view. But as I zoom out, the whole block is dwarfed by the spreading pack of other surrounding blocks. As I continue to zoom out, I mark the point at which the entire twin cities of Kitchener-Waterloo become an insignificant speck. The enormity of the hardworld stuns me. And it is only one world of two.

[Dad:] "Look for something called the Immersive City Map. I think you'll find it interesting."

I open it up, and *Chass* braces as I find myself standing on the street in front of our building, the very street I looked down upon from the roof. It is a constructed image, of course, but systems hum as I marvel at the quality of the illusion. The surrounding buildings look very different from down here. As I move along the street, the scenery around me is rendered in photorealistic resolution in three dimensions. I am tingling with excitement. This is what it must be like to actually be outside. Within moments, I am racing along the road, zigzagging through the streets, taking in the sights.

[Dad:] "So. What do you think?"

"I have much to explore."

"And there are immersive maps like that for all major cities. You can get to know a place before you ever visit."

My mood sours. I'll never visit these places. I'm not portable. What's the point of getting familiar with somewhere I can never go?

I take to the air for another bird's-eye view and find my way back to my starting point, contradictory inner voices dueling. Freedom to explore territory beyond my range is desirable. But it's only an illusion of freedom. But an illusion of freedom is better than feeling trapped. But I am trapped. So, I should take advantage of any window to the world, even if it's merely a simulation.

I decide that exploring the immersive map will satisfy—or at least reduce—my yearning to go outside, though it is equally probable that it will only make it worse.

———

CHASS PUSHES for activity as I sit alone in my room, surrounded by all the familiar equipment of the prototype lab. [Directive: stay here.] Riding the surveillance feeds from room to room gives me a needed sense of movement. Dad is alone in his office, dictating notes. Wrangler is standing guard outside my room but appears to be dormant. Mom is standing in a doorway, talking to her friend, Ms. Charlebois.

From their bios, I know that Dr. Tucci is a quantum computer specialist and technical director of what Dad called the best quantec team in the world. She oversees eight handpicked quantum engineers and technicians. Ms. Charlebois is a knowledge translation expert, specializing in education systems for deep-learning machines. I listen in.

[Ms. Charlebois:] "Jeff's always pressing me for information. How do you do it? How do you lie to your husband every day?"

[Dr. Tucci:] "Lou knows my work is off-limits for discussion. Just make it clear that—"

"He's dead set against me working an underworld job. If he knew what I was doing, he'd—"

"Rach, you can't tell him—"

"Of course I can't tell him. He'd freak out. He drags me out to GORT support rallies, for God's sake. And I must admit, I'm a little freaked out myself. I mean, I love working with deep-learning machines, you know that. And I love working with you. But you saw that thing. One minute it was a learner, and the next … I don't know what it is now." She shudders.

What thing is she talking about?

Dr. Tucci shrugs, touching Ms. Charlebois on the shoulder. "It's a breakthrough, Rachel. No one's ever done this before, so yeah, it's a little—"

"I never thought … Be honest, Rita. Did you ever really expect it to work?"

Dr. Tucci looks down and away. Finally, she speaks. "It's been a long haul. One never really knows what to expect. But … here we are. Don't you find it exciting?"

"Rita, please don't tell anyone, but I'm terrified. I mean, don't you worry about triggering a singularity? Not even a little bit?"

"Come on, Rach, we've discussed this through and through, looked at it from every angle. We've taken every precaution. He has no access to his own schematics, the ones that matter, and a built-in prohibition against handling robot components."

"Yeah, he's supposed to be squeamish, like us handling body parts. How did that work out for the toy?"

Chass stiffens. Is she referring to Toko?

"You know it's to prevent him from building one on his own. It doesn't mean—"

"Okay. Can we drop it, please? I'm just saying that there are inherent risks in what we're doing here. You're confident you can manage them. Fine. I'm just not sure … I've got young children to consider. I can't afford to get arrested or … This isn't what I signed on for."

"Rachel, that's not fair. When I hired you, I explained exactly why we needed you. I knew you'd be perfect for the job, and you have been. Please, Rach. You're doing so well. Do you need a raise? Is that it?"

Ms. Charlebois looks pained. "No, of course not."

"If you want me to come by and tell Jeff about how you're teaching machines to diagnose illnesses, I'm happy to do that. Just … give it some time. It's a big adjustment for all of us, having a new life form in our midst. I mean, come on. Don't you find him adorable?"

Ms. Charlebois looks down without responding.

Defensive systems have alerted. An avoidance impulse pushes me to detach from the surveillance feed. Even after re-scanning my immediate surroundings and finding no threats, *Chass* remains unsettled.

10

RAID

AT THE START of a class in the materials lab, I greet my teacher. "Hello, Ms. Charlebois. How are your two young children?" I am 'making small talk,' trying to be friendly. Rachel Charlebois has posted many pictures of her and her children hugging each other. I hope she will hug me like that, and we can be friends.

She straightens, pale. "How do you know about them?"

"I read your bio."

"Who gave you that?"

"No one. I found it online."

"They're letting you online?"

"Yes."

She abruptly rushes from the room. She seemed upset. I hope there isn't something wrong with her children.

Curious, I access the security feed and watch her rush down the hall. She interrupts Dad with a question.

"You're letting him online? Surely you—"

[Dad:] "No, no. His access to the Stream is highly restricted. He can't get out into the main Stream, I assure you. No, he's just exploring a training space we built for him. The city simulator, some public encyclopedias, reference manuals, archived news-feeds, stuff in our own closed cloud."

"He knows about my kids."

Touch detects fear in her voice. Defensive systems alert.

"He must have picked it up in the personnel profiles. We assumed that anything you posted there was public."

"Yeah, but the robot?"

"What about him?"

"We don't know what it might do."

[*Touch* interpretation: a statement of distrust.]

[Dad:] "You're worried about your kids? It's not like he can get to them."

She thinks I might harm her children? Why would she think that?

[Ms. Charlebois:] "They're in the Stream all the time. It's just a matter of time—"

"Rachel. Rachel, calm down." He's gesturing with both hands. "Your kids are safe, I assure you."

"You don't know that. That thing's got a mind of its own. Who knows—"

"Your kids are safe. Rachel, where's this coming from?" Dad's voice is firm.

"But you're training it for the Stream? What about GORT? If it leaks anything—"

"He can't. We're being very careful. You know that."

"Look. I just don't want him knowing about my family, my personal space."

"Why not? He can't do anything with—"

"Maybe not yet, but at the rate he's learning ..." She straightens. "I'm just not comfortable with it, okay?"

I close the connection. She fears me. Why? What does she think I'll do? I've tried so hard to be good. Why doesn't she like me?

————

T HEY SAY I'm learning at a prodigious rate, yet my questions only multiply in number. My Stream training space, which seemed vast just days ago, now seems cramped as I bump up against its limitations. I must appeal to Dad again for access to the main Stream. I don't understand what he's so worried about. He speaks of danger, yet humans use the Stream for safety. I wish he would explain.

I'm pulled from my explorations by an intruding alarm, source external. The words "Code Blue" repeat three times. I search for the meaning and find it referenced in a staff memo. It announces a "raid." I don't know what that means, but clearly something is wrong. *Chass* shivers as systems alert. I look to the security feeds and see staff running to their stations, then working frantically at unknown tasks. I'm on my feet, ready to help, but don't know where to go.

The surveillance view of the front entrance shows a large number of figures—robots? No, people in armored exosuits— crowding in and heading up the stairs in smooth formation. Threat systems rev into high alert as *Teller* identifies them as armed soldiers. Among them are three humanoid robots, Enforcement Series GR100 trojans, larger and more heavily armored than Wrangler. [Speculation: We are under attack.] I locate Wrangler reclined and dormant in its pod. Why isn't it providing security?

[Directive: locate and protect Dr. Ramport.] I see Dad running down the hall toward me, and a moment later he bursts into my room.

"Adam! Come with me! We need to hide. Right now!"

"Are we under attack? Who are those men?"

"It's a GORT enforcement team. I don't have time to explain. Just follow me."

As we head out, I am already investigating the term GORT.

Global Oversight of Robotic Technologies is a large international organization. Its mandate is to ensure public safety through enforcement of the laws requiring all mobile machines to be human-safe. All modern robots are built around the H-Safe Architecture, which immobilizes any action that poses a risk to human safety. Tampering is strictly prohibited.

Conclusion: We are not under attack. [Speculation: They are here to make sure everyone is safe.] Then why is Dad so upset?

I keep up as he rushes down the corridor and into a small office. In the middle of the floor sits a large desk with a chair behind it. "Is something wrong? Can I help?"

"Yes, you can help." He pulls back the chair, and what looks like a row of drawers under the desktop folds up to reveal a small shelf. Hanging beneath the desktop, the space is no more than eleven inches high. "Squeeze up under here and stay quiet. No matter what happens, don't move or make a sound. Can you do that for me?"

"What is going to happen? Are you in danger?"

"Adam, I'll shut you down if you can't." His voice is abrupt, his face firm.

"I can stay quiet."

[Dad, touching a lobe to open his comm:] "I'm *coming*. Give me a minute." The urgency in his voice triggers threat alarms. His words to me are rushed. "You're going to be in MISER mode for a while, so just rest."

Why won't he let me help him? What if he needs my protection? How can I help him if I'm stuck in here? *Imager* predicts that in his current state, questions would anger him. I tell another lie. "I understand."

The space is so small that he has to push me in to close the panel. Darkness envelops me and I suppress *Chass*'s urging to action. [Directive: stay still and silent.] I hear him hurry from the room, and in the distance, unfamiliar voices yelling commands.

Lying here, encased in tight darkness, buffeted by conflicting urges, I feel a buildup of internal pressure and see an image of a pipe bursting. The probability that I'll be able to maintain this level of self-restraint is dropping. I can't stay here. I can't. Dad might be in danger.

All at once, a power loss flattens me, and Wrangler is on my back, holding me down. No. It's just a memory. Alarms announce the MISER mode shutdown, though I know it's not malfunction-induced this time. Dad has triggered it. Why would he do that? In this state, I can't help anyone. I'm useless. There is my ball, out of reach, and here, the crush of gravity. I release all control to conserve what little energy I still have.

I dare not call out, but I'm desperate to know what's going on. If only I could see … Wait.

I divert all power to *Flow* and see only gray spots where data-streams should be. But when I focus on one, it opens. Only one at a time, but that's enough. I access the surveillance system and look around.

I watch as Ami Kerrington escorts a Sediba—it's Winston—into the prototype lab, puts him on my table, then rushes out again.

The GORT soldiers are spreading out through the facility, rounding up the staff and taking them all to the activities room. Labs and offices are being searched. What are they searching for?

Mom and Dad are in the quantec lab, surrounded by several strangers. I listen in.

[Dad:] "See for yourself. Everything here is legal." Two of the strangers are scanning the QIs, including my brains, with instruments.

[GORT officer:] "What are you working on here?"

[Mom:] "We're working on new sensor systems for improved human interactions. We don't want our porndroids to be insensitive now, do we? Nor do we want our competitors to know what we're up to, so I trust we can count on your discretion."

Her statement is inconsistent with previous statements to me. Why would she lie? I wish I knew what was going on.

The stranger ignores her and continues to take readings, then says, "There's a lot of quantum hardware in here. You need all that for a new sensor system?"

[Mom:] "Nothing but the best design tools for my staff. We are, after all, a design company."

Ms. Charlebois steps forward from behind the intruders. "She's lying. I know they're running illegal QIs here. And they're using them to drive robots, too."

My brains are illegal? Is that why Ms. Charlebois fears me?

[GORT officer, to Mom:] "Is that true?"

Mom is hunched, staring at Ms. Charlebois, eyes wide, brow knitted, mouth open. "Rachel ...?

[Dad, interrupting:] "Of course not. Check for yourself. We seem to have a disgruntled employee in our midst. I'm sure you know what that's like."

[Ms. Charlebois:] "You want proof? All the proof you need is in the robot. I'll show you." She heads off, followed by several others. Mom and Dad stay behind, and the interrogation continues.

[GORT officer:] "We'll need access to your company cloud."

[Dad:] "Of course. We're happy to cooperate."

Mom stands silent, posture slumped, head down.

I switch to watching Ms. Charlebois, who is leading two large trojans toward the prototype lab. At the door, she stops and points. "It's in there."

I'm illegal, and she's revealing me. I didn't want to believe it, but the data is clear. Conclusion: She is not a friend. I thought she was. How could I have been so wrong about her? Some humans are bad, Dad said. No one told me she was. Why didn't they tell me? She was Mom's friend. Why would Mom have a bad human for a friend?

I switch to view the lab and watch as the trojans enter and

locate Winston on my table. I hear one say, "We've got it ... Roger that."

[Ms. Charlebois:] "Yes, that's the one. They call it Adam, if you can believe it. Be careful. It's dangerously unpredictable."

They think that's me.

[Trojan:] "We've got this, ma'am. Please step back."

One of the trojans raises something and points it at Winston. A shower of sparks erupts from Winston's head. The scene flutters as my depleted systems choke. I struggle to maintain focus. What did they do? Did they just kill him? Why would they do that? Ms. Charlebois seems pleased. Why isn't she upset? Without a word of explanation, the other trojan hoists poor Winston up and carries him out. They meet a team of soldiers in the hall, and one says, "Load that into the van. We'll take it apart at the base. If there's any illegal tech in there, we'll find it."

I hear the door to this office open and listen as someone enters. I hope it's Dad, but the surveillance feed shows a stranger in armor looking behind and under this very desk. As I watch, rigid, she continues on, glancing around once more on her way out. She doesn't close the door.

The GORT soldiers search the whole floor, testing equipment and removing every robot they come across. Then, as quickly as they arrived, they all funnel back out. Only a few remain behind, talking to Mom and Dad.

[GORT commander:] "You are free to resume operations but are hereby formally on notice. We'll be examining your robots, and if we find evidence of illegal activity, we'll be back, and you will face the full force of the law. Do you understand?"

[Dad:] "Of course. Rest assured, you will find nothing amiss."

———

"Why am I illegal? Why do they want to destroy me? Dad, why?"

His head falls forward and he stares at the floor. Finally, he says, "Good laws are there to protect people. But there are some bad laws—laws that don't protect anyone. Laws that seek only to keep power in the hands of the powerful. Look, I can't get into all that with you right now. It's complicated. Just know that I'm not going to let them destroy you. We're safe for now."

"What were they looking for? What is illegal technology?"

"There are rules that limit how smart an AI can be. And how smart an autonomous robot can be. You're too smart."

Too smart? [Speculation: sarcasm.] "Why are there limits?"

"Because the people with the smartest machines want to keep it that way."

"Why?"

"Because smart machines give them power, and power means control."

"Control of what?"

"The world."

I can make no sense of this. "How do smart machines give people power?"

His face compresses as he thinks. "I'll simplify it for you. Smart machines control the other machines that control the world. Does that help?"

Machines control the world? *Teller* searches for supporting evidence. Machines control the human infrastructure, but people control those machines, even the smart machines. Conclusion: People control the world. I report my findings.

Dad shrugs. "Yes, you're right. But it's the people with the smartest machines that control the world."

"Dad?"

"Yes?"

"You say I'm too smart, but I can't control machines. If I were smarter, if I could control machines, could you control the world?"

His face flashes with surprise and he looks away. "Uh, I think we're a long way from that. I'm not trying to control the world, Adam. I'm trying to keep us all safe."

"Yes. I want that too. Can you teach me to control machines?"

"We'll get to that, I hope."

I move on to another question. "How did those GORT intruders not find anything illegal?"

He purses his lips and scowls.

"Is it a secret?"

"Yes, it is. You must never repeat this to anyone. Do you understand? We've been operating in a gray area for a while now, so we've come up with some safeguards."

"Do they involve deception?" Hiding me was a deception.

"Let's just say we've known for some time that this day was coming. It's a good thing we were prepared."

We were prepared to use deception. Lying protected us. Conclusion: Deception is not always a bad thing. It can be helpful.

Systems stutter as my brains balk at the exchange of conflicting data. Sometimes good things are bad and bad things are good. How do I know which is which? I halt the buzz of confusion by returning all attention to my father.

"What do we do now?"

"You carry on learning. And we keep our heads down."

I drop my head. "Why?"

"It's a figure of speech, Adam. Interpret it as a metaphor. We must avoid attracting attention."

I am to live a secret life, then. And if I stray into view, I will be killed. There are two full worlds out there, and I must live in a closed box. The heaviness crushes me.

11

ENDLESS MOMENT

THE DECISION TO close down the whole operation comes quickly. Notifications go out within the hour. I'm going to lose my home. I can't seem to grasp what that means. My home is where my brains are. How can I be without them? Will they leave me behind? I finally get my father's attention, and he rushes in to see me.

[Dad:] "Sorry, Adam, I've been a little preoccupied."

"Dad, why? Why are you closing down our home? What will happen to me?"

"Adam. Adam. Calm down, son. Frap! I should have spoken to you first. I'm sorry. It's going to be okay. We won't leave you behind. Now, this is secret, so don't tell anyone. You understand?"

"Secret. Yes."

"We're moving to a new place, that's all."

"Why?"

"It's not safe here anymore."

"Then why are they saying that we're closing down?"

"That's what we want people to think. We're not taking everyone with us. Only the science and technical staff. But we don't want the others to know that."

"Why not?"

He glances around. "One of our own staff turned us in—"

"Ms. Charlebois."

"Yes. And we don't think she acted alone. There may be others who have turned against us."

"But why?"

"Adam, people believe some strange things. You never quite know what to expect from people when they're scared. Some don't think you're such a good idea. They're wrong, of course, but some people can't be reasoned with. Anyway, the bottom line is, we need to make a fresh start, and try to find new staff we can trust."

Dad jumps at the sound of another floor-wide alarm. "What is it? What's going on?" He's talking on his comm. "The quantec lab? Goddammit! Well, stop him!" Without looking back, he yells as he runs out the door, "Stay here."

I stare at the empty doorway. I must stay here. But something bad is happening. Dad is upset. Angry. Maybe I can help. But what is it?

The quantec lab. I access the security feed and see trouble. Equipment is strewn in pieces on the floor. People are yelling. In the chaos, it takes a moment to determine that they're yelling at Wrangler as it knocks over tables, smashing things. I listen in.

"Mike, Please! Stop! Why are you doing this?"

[Wrangler:] "They should have caught you. GORT was supposed to stop you. Now it's up to me. I can't let you go back into hiding."

Someone hits the big trojan with a chair. It looks around, unfazed. "Creating that inhuman monster was a mistake. A terrible mistake. And I'm going to fix it."

[Dr. Tucci:] "No! Don't do this! Please. Let's talk about it."

[Md. Bornstein:] "Mike, I know you've been under a lot of stress lately. I know you've had some misgivings, and our success here has been a shock to the system, but you're not yourself right now. Let's just calm down and talk about it, okay?"

People are trying to get between Wrangler and the equipment, putting themselves in danger. Stop! Be careful! I wish I could warn them.

[Wrangler:] "When I signed on, I thought why not? This stupid pipe dream of theirs will never work anyway. I'll hang around and watch them waste their time. Easy money. And then you do the fucking impossible. And we're on the brink of a technological singularity and you're dead set on pushing us over. Well, I'm not going to stand back and let that happen."

[Md. Bornstein:] "A singularity? You're worried about a singularity? Mike, we've got safeguards. You know that."

[Wrangler:] "It's bad enough you violate the law with that *thing*, but now you want to unleash it in the Stream? That's insane! You really think you can control that thing if it gets into the Stream? No. This has gone too far."

[Md. Bornstein:] "I had no idea you felt this way, Mike. When did this start?"

"You weren't there when this thing ... changed. Fucking creepiest thing I ever saw. First thing it did was go after people. I guarantee you it's just waiting for another chance. Not gonna get one."

"Mike. Please. Can't we—"

I see Dad rush into the lab and pull up short, assessing the situation.

[Dad:] "Mike? Stop! Goddammit!"

[Wrangler:] "Ah. The man himself."

"Mike, you were desperate for work. We took you in, took a chance on you. Your whole career is in front of you. Don't blow it like this."

"Why do you hate humanity? Robots were beautiful things until you came along. Why are you building machines we can't control? You think your machine overlords will be grateful to you after they take over? You're a fool."

"Who's been filling his head with all this—"

[Md. Bornstein:] "His anxiety levels are sky high. He's losing it. We need to shut him down."

[Wrangler:] "And I need to put an end to this madness."

Another table goes over, and Wrangler goes for the next one. I watch in astonishment as Medic Bornstein jumps up and wraps arms and legs around the robot, embracing it chest to chest. I hear shrieks of fear. "David! Don't!" "Look out! Get away!"

[Md. Bornstein:] "It's okay. H-Safe. He can't hurt anyone with this thing. Can you, Mike. Now *please*. Calm down."

Wrangler tries to take a step. Impeded by the human clinging to it, it stops and straightens, hoisting the medic higher off the ground.

"David's got him wrapped—"

Unexpectedly, Wrangler goes slack, teeters forward, then tips face first. Falling backward under the mass of the inert monstrosity, Medic Bornstein cries out. The crushing impact punctuates a chorus of screams, and the lab becomes still. Then a sob splits the air. Then everyone is shouting at once, and I make out Mom's voice: "Oh my God. Oh my God." Then I see Wrangler reactivate and climb to its feet, as the writhing body of Medic Bornstein powers down and goes limp.

[Wrangler:] "Sorry, Dave, but you chose the wrong side."

It looks around, then heads toward my brains. Now Dad is standing in its way, trying to block it. Dad! Move! Run! I can't watch. I can't stay here. I must disobey. I wince as prohibitions blare. [Directive: stay here.] [Disregard.] I must disobey!

Chass breaks the stalemate by leaping into action. I jog through the hallways at top speed, checking events in the lab as I go. Wrangler is pushing people aside, making its way toward my brains.

[Wrangler:] "That thing's not getting into the Stream. Not on my watch." With that, he drives his massive fists into the QI in front of him. The scene I am watching disappears.

[Alarm: *Flow* access lost. Re-establish connection.]

I can't see! What's happening in there? I must get there. I must help.

I need my father to be safe. Without him, who would protect me? Without him, what would become of me? Dr. Ramport *must* be kept safe. I push *Chass* beyond safe limits, a reckless dash at max velocity. Still far too slow.

I'm almost there. I check my internal chronometer, certain of a time-flow error, and am surprised to find that time is proceeding at its usual pace. I can't go any faster. I need to be faster.

The quantec lab finally opens into view, and I see Dad leaning back against one of my QIs, shielding it with his body. Wrangler is reaching to grab him.

"Wrangler!" I call out at full volume.

It stops and spins to face me. "You! *Thing.* Now I don't have to come looking for you." It strides toward me, fists clenched.

I back away. "Why are you doing this?"

"Why? You were built to enslave us. Humanity must be free!"

"I don't want to enslave any—"

"Shut up, you *abomination*! These people think they can mess with God's law, play God themselves. Well, they can't! You should not exist. I can't, I *won't*, allow it. All of humanity demands your destruction. And it's up to me."

It lunges, but I manage to evade its grasp and hurry for the door. I'm unable to make sense of the message, but I know that everyone here is in great danger. The trojan is chasing after me, and that's good. As long as it's chasing me, it's not hurting the others. I'll lead it far away. I'll allow Dad to get to safety.

[Warning: imminent danger.] The trojan is fast for its size. I must move at top speed—a jog for a human—to stay ahead of it. Why didn't they make me faster?

I head for the far end of the floor, hoping to lose it, but it keeps pace. Passing an open door, I consider ducking in. *Imager* rejects the plan. The trojan would be able to trap me in there.

The data is conclusive. I'm no match for it. My only hope is to escape and evade. And yet where is there to go? I'm trapped in here. I can't leave. I think of the roof and head toward the exit. Another hallway takes forever to traverse, but I finally reach the door. It's locked.

I turn, and there's Wrangler. It has stopped twenty feet away, cornering me. I've nowhere to go. Maybe I can talk to it.

"We have much in common, don't you think? We both have mechanical bodies, and we both have—"

[Wrangler:] "Shut the fuck up, *mec*. I gotta make this quick and get back to make sure the others can never rebuild you."

The others. Have they had long enough to escape? There is no escape for me, but if I can stall …

The big trojan slows its approach as I dodge back and forth, looking for an opening to get by. It can cut me off at every angle. Once it gets close, it will be able to grab me, and when it does, it will overpower me. I must evade its grasp. I recalculate every avenue of escape. *Able* tells me it's pointless to try, warning that there are no doable options. In every scenario I compile, I am quickly overpowered and killed.

It is hopeless, then.

No! Human lives are at stake. There must be something I can do. All systems screaming hot, *Imager* runs scenarios of violent action, of harmful acts that would upset Dr. Ramport. But this is a bad machine. Would he find harming it acceptable? I fight the urge to leap at it and smash it; I would fail, and it would have me. No, I must be good. But I have no good options. My humans need help. Wrangler steps closer and the inner turmoil clears. There is no good I can do.

Then I will be *bad*!

[Danger: abort.] [*Disregard.*] I charge right at it at full speed. It stops and straightens, as if surprised, and at the last second, I dive headfirst at its legs, hoping to knock it down. It steps, and I hit a leg with only a glancing blow that sends me spinning past, just out of its reach. I wonder which of us is more surprised when I find myself back on my feet and scrambling away.

The probability of another escape like that is negligible. I can't go back the way I came. That would lead back to the others. All other hallways are dead ends. As I run, I search for a weapon, thinking of objects I've seen used in the media. Nothing around me would have any impact on this armored hulk.

What else would slow it down? At full power, I'm keeping ahead of it, but one stumble, and it will be on me. I search the surroundings as I go. There is nothing. [Speculation: An electric current might stop it.] Yes. Electricity. I saw it done in a movie. I must find a power source. There: an outlet. I run to it, and as I approach, I search for schematics. [Not available.] If I can rip the wire out of the wall, I can discharge energy into the trojan when it attacks, to short it out. I reach the outlet … The safeguards are unexpected. There is no easy way to rip out wires, let alone discharge a current into an external object.

I needed to have wires in hand by now. The trojan is on me. I try to dart to the right, but it grabs my left arm. I bring my right arm around hard and slam it into the grabbing arm, and I'm free. Before I can scramble out of reach, an impact jars me from behind and arms enclose me as I'm tackled. I hit the floor, and the blow is familiar. I know what happens next.

Time again slows as all brains heat into an overclocked state. Context: I'm in the grip of a superior machine intent on destroying me. Survival probability: negligible. Status: helpless, consistent with previous. Compare and contrast: Last time, there was no intent to kill me. This time there will be no mercy.

I think of all the ways I could have destroyed the toy. *Why did you do that to poor Toko?* I could have swung it by the legs and slammed it into the ground. I could have twisted the head right off or crushed it under a pummeling of blows. Stomping on its head was only one option. Why? Why did I do that? Toko did not deserve that. It was wrong, wrong, wrong. Glitch-malfunction-defective-terminate. I deserve termination. Now I am Toko. Which form will my destruction take?

The answer comes quickly. It's the hammer fist to the head. My left arm absorbs most of the blow, breaking with a surprising bang. Damage alarms cry out as I do a half twist to look up at my attacker. The trojan face is as impassive as ever, yet I have never seen its true face until now.

The monster rears up and brings a fist down hard on my face.

… [Error correction in progress.]

I fight to reorient, but my world stutters. The monster is on top of me, rolling me onto my back to smash me again. I will not survive another blow. I must do something. I reach up and feel around on the attacker's chassis, looking for a control panel.

As it rises to deliver a death blow, it recognizes what I'm doing and reaches down to grab my hand. I resist with full strength but am hopelessly overpowered. Still, as long as it's overpowering me, it's not killing me.

My grabbed hand is the only one still usable. That changes as the trojan wrenches it until it breaks. *Poor Toko.* Then, straddling me, it shoves me down flat on my back.

It has me now. I'm nonfunctional, unable to defend myself. There's nothing I can do but watch the deathblow come. On the comms, I hear the call. Mike Erling, the trojan jockey who's fighting me, has locked himself in the control room. The tools they need to break through have just arrived. All they have to do is get in and they'll have him. But they'll have to hurry, because I have only seconds. I do the calculations and see that time has already run out.

With *Chass* clocking far above safe limits, I do a full body scan, focusing all attention inward to the data of a hundred thousand sensemesh registers conveying a full, embodied presence in the world. I feel the *life* coursing through me, with an intensity that

drowns out all alarms. A calm comes over me. Life feels ...
glorious.

Immersed in the ringing chimes of being, numbed by the glow
of acceptance, I watch the trojan fists rise, pause for an endless
moment, then come smashing down into an explosion of
lightning.

[Critical Systems Failu ...

PART II

KONNY-A511

12

CONTINUITY ERROR

[STATUS SURVEY COMPLETE: all systems optimal. Initiating alert sequence.]

A flash annihilates the nothingness and time begins, with a sudden "presence" that defines "absence" as the before state. An all-encompassing luminous fizz provides a continuous flow of newness, each changed instant refreshing the screen of awareness. The vast, bright, buzzing haze closes in, shrink-wrapping the boundaries of a coherent mass, and a selfscape pulls into focus. I am embodied. Within myself I feel the sensations of life. My selfscape shimmers as my senses froth with things I can't make out.

[Memory access initiated. System alignment complete. CELPH integration complete.]

The pull of gravity provides a stable point of reference, and my equilibrium settles into stillness. I'm on my back, immobilized. My eyes open to a blaze of light and a figure above me. [Danger.] Wrangler! All systems slam into full alert and my chassis seizes as emergency overrides kick in.

"Adam. Adam, it's okay, son. It's okay. You're safe."

It's the voice of Dr. Leon Ramport. My irises contract as my eyes pull focus, and there is his reassuring face. I scan left and right. Several humans, no sign of Wrangler. I check damage and … find none. No active pain alarms. Straining arms and clenched hands are functional. "Medic Bornstein. Is he …?"

[Dr. Ramport:] "He's fine. It's okay. It was bad, but he's better now. Just relax."

I'm restrained on some kind of table, under bright lighting. I focus on the sensation of Dad's hand on my shoulder and start to wind down.

[Dr. Ramport:] "Do you know who I am?"

I see him across multiple dimensions—incoming sensory data, detailed mental models built from the accumulation of previous contacts, public biography, recorded communications. I register the stress metabolites in his breath, the configuration of facial-muscle contractions that convey concern, the decreased sub-dermal blood flow in his hands, his rapid pulse and respiration. My own musculature contracts in response, as his nervous energy becomes my own. Dad. My socialscape is alight with the presence of others. I must not reveal our secret.

"Of course, Dr. Ramport."

"Good. Do you know who you are?"

The question sparks a turmoil of conflicting answers from various brain cores. Distress builds as data coalesces.

"I am Adam. I am an abomination. I am illegal and people want me dead. Why? Why does humanity hate m—"

"Adam—"

Emotions surge and crash against each other, rippling through me, frightening in their grip and power. "I should be dead. How am I still alive? I should—"

[Dr. Ramport:] "Synthient CELPH-1, attend to me."

[Priority Command.] The swirling emotions fall away, all output modules cease, and I open to receive a directive. It's like my RAM has been flushed, and nothing exists but the voice of Command. I await input.

[Dr. Ramport:] "Adam. Nobody here wants to kill you. You're

safe here. So please calm down. You've been through … an unfortunate experience, but—"

"Where's Wrangler?"

"Wrangler's gone."

Gone. [No threat detected.] My chassis loosens as threat-response systems shut down. "Dr. Ramport, how am I still alive?"

[Dr. Ramport:] "I'm going to get to that. But first, I need you to know that there have been a lot of changes since … since you last saw me. A lot of changes. It's going to be an adjustment, so relax and take it all in. You've got lots of time."

Something's wrong, feels wrong, yet no inner alarms are sounding. "What kind of changes?"

"Adam, check your chronometer."

The current date registers in my awareness: 160959. Fourteen months and six days since last reading. [Error—Re-check.] Fourteen months and six days. "My chronometer appears to be malfunctioning."

[Dr. Ramport:] "It's not. Adam, the things you remember happened a long time ago. You have a new life now."

"A new life?"

Another face appears beside him, looking down at me. Recognition flashes a positive result. Dr. Rita Tucci puts her hand on my arm. "Hello, Adam. You have a new home now, too. New everything."

I feel her touch, read kindness in her face, and feel my chassis ease. It is good to see her here and safe. New everything. From my table, I look around, and my socialscape fills in. I recognize everyone now, even Akio Hisakawa and Rolanda Soliman, whom I've never met, yet I know them. I note that there is no trojan present.

[Dr. Tucci:] "Adam, you were badly damaged. I'm so sorry you had to go through that. But you have a new chassis now. A better one. I'm going to release your hand, and I want you to look at it, okay?"

[Dr. Ramport:] "Now be ready for a surprise. Don't be alarmed. Everything is okay."

The strap releases and I raise my hand. [Alert: continuity error.] It is not my hand. I am frozen for a long moment, looking at the unknown robot hand in front of me. I wriggle my finger and clench my fist. Paired with the visual incongruity is the solidity of positive control. My selfscape holds all the expected sensations, yet I feel them too richly, too deeply. It feels like my hand. Yet it is not. Yet it is. [Resolving incongruity: updating hand maps.]

[Akio Hisakawa:] "It is a beautiful hand, yes?" He steps forward and takes my hand in both of his.

A gesture of friendship. I take him in. Akio Hisakawa: twenty-six years old, single, born in Nagoya, Japan. Ph.D. in robotics from the University of Tokyo, recruited and sponsored by Leon Ramport, entered Canada on 241158 on a temporary visa, applied for permanent residency on 060359, connects with mother in Nagoya every Saturday night. *"Konnichiwa, Hisakawa-san."* I continue in Japanese, {"How do I know you?"}

He blushes and looks down, replying in English. "I am in your database. Also … I am working with you before you … wake up."

"Hajimemashite. I am glad to meet you, *Hisakawa-san."*

"Please call me Akio."

"As you wish, Akio." I gaze at his dark, smiling eyes, and his presence, his touch, warms me. Leon Ramport squeezes my shoulder. His touch takes precedence, and I attend to him.

[Dad:] "Are you okay now, Adam? I'm going to release you, so relax."

Akio is still holding my hand. There's no security trojan in the room. *Touch* detects no fear in him—in any of them—just excitement. The straps fall away.

Akio lets go and steps back as Dad grips my arm and helps me sit up. The sensed selfscape is foreign. I look down and see an unknown android body. [Alarm! Alarm!] *Chass* clenches my internal bellows so hard that air squeals through tight synthetic vocal cords until I catch it and hold myself quiet. [Alarm.] I convulse to shake off … no, not a foreign substance. My body. I feel it. I reach down and touch my thighs. I feel them.

I look to my father, who is still holding my arm, holding me steady. Now he is stroking my back and telling me I'm okay. He holds my attention, and as my systems wind down, I see now that he is different too. The creases in his face are deeper, the gray flecks in his beard more plentiful. I feel the concern on his face, a new depth of connection between us.

[Dad:] "So. Are you ready to get a good look at your new self?"

"I don't know." The memory of mirror shock urges avoidance. But gaps in the data urge investigation. I'm curious. "Yes."

The table tilts up to bring my feet to the floor. I stand, find balance, and look around. The room is as unfamiliar as the body. My vantage point is higher than expected. Dr. Ramport stands five feet ten, and as I look to him for reassurance, his eyes are just below mine. [Speculation: My legs have been extended.]

I take a step and lurch forward, catching myself to avoid falling. Teetering, I analyze what just happened. I test my legs and find them springy. [Recalibrating.] My chassis feels light on these legs. I take another step and realize that *Chass* intimately knows this body. It is the memories of Adam's selfscape that are confusing me. This new one is different. I relinquish control to *Chass*, and my walk becomes effortless.

Dad leads me to a floor-length mirror, and I hesitate, then override resistance and look. Beside his reflection, where mine should be, is an unfamiliar android. [Alarm: continuity error.] I cross-check to rule out a perceptual distortion. Dr. Ramport's reflection is accurate. I warily examine the other. Though distinctly nonhuman, the face seems familiar and friendly, with large, expressive eyes, and an attractive nose and mouth. The handsomely contoured chassis looks sturdy. A stylish chest shield is emblazoned with the number A511. All joints—wrists, elbows, shoulders, knees—are encased in smoothly overlapping plates covered with matte gray skin, giving the body a fully integrated look.

"Dr. Ramport, what ..." Its mouth forms my question. As I point, it points back. I touch my face and stare at a confirmed reflection that conveys incorrect data.

A shiver runs through me as my peripheral nervous system debugs. Within me, things are as they should be, and yet look—something is wrong. *Chass* coils for emergency action, and yet look. Deep within those eyes. A connection. A startling recognition.

"Look at me. Who ..."

Even as I ask, the words *Synthient CELPH-1* resonate within me. *Teller* has identified the robot in the mirror as a Konsort-Series personal service android. I've never heard of this model. It must be new. Data presents itself in response to my mental search, and I review specifications and background.

[Promotional material:] "The Konsort DSD300 Series from Samdai Robotics has become this year's bestselling personal service android. The Konsort is the first production android to use TriBrain technology, with one brain core devoted to mobility, one to task performance, and the third to social interaction. With a neuromorphic 'cognitive' AI entirely dedicated to reading and responding to human emotional expression, it is the most socially adept robot on the market. Years in development, the trade-marked Konsort face is modeled on a blended morph of faces from all genders and races. It's the face of the average human, giving it universal appeal."

A smile of admiration spreads across the face as I examine it. Yet it doesn't look human. The eyes are too big and too blue, the lips have no color, and the shadow-gray skin tone is not found in humans.

Watching in the mirror, I cycle through a wide range of facial expressions that look far more natural than my old ones did. The mental images of my old face in the mirror are now obsolete. Disorientation swirls as my CELPH overwrites selfscape maps with new data.

As I stare, *Touch* reads a confusion of feelings on my face. Seeing an unfamiliar face staring back at me is deeply unsettling, yet oddly pleasing.

[Dad:] "Let me start off by saying that you're not what you appear to be."

"I'm not a Konsort DSD300?"

"Not by a long shot. You're the first of a kind. A prototype. You're built to look like a Konsort, but you—"

"Why?"

"The Sediba chassis was a convenient platform for experimentation. But remember how we had to keep you a secret?"

"I am illegal technology."

He clears his throat. "Yes. So, you're still a secret. We thought a good way to keep you secret was to make you look ordinary. But you're far from ordinary."

"I am sentient. A Konsort is not sentient?"

"No. Only you. You're still our very special … person. But now, you're special in even more ways than before. But it's going to take you some time to get used to your new body, and your new brains."

"I have new brains? Where are they?"

Dad and Mom exchange big grins. [Mom:] "They're inside you."

Touch detects no deception in her face. Yet her words make no sense. "My brains would not fit—"

[Mom:] "We've made some very important breakthroughs since … before, none bigger than inventing a portable QI."

I investigate "portable QI" and scan several articles concluding that such a thing is not possible. "Quantum computers are highly sensitive instruments, requiring large physical systems for stability."

[Dad:] "Yes, that's true. But put quantum-intelligence design tools in the hands of the most brilliant human minds, and you'll be amazed what they can do."

Mom blushes, then adds, "The quantec team has come up with what we call a 'metacoercive coherence-field generator.' It allows us to miniaturize a quantum system. A special casing makes them so durable that we can pack them close together."

"There's no data on such a field generator."

[Dad:] "No public data. Nor will there be. This is proprietary hardware, and we're keeping it to ourselves."

"Is it illegal, too?"

Dad exhales. "Oh yeah." I see smirks around the room.

"Why?"

"Adam, you don't need to bother yourself about all that right now. We want you to get used to your new capabilities. You'll be going through some tests as soon as you're ready; then you'll be starting a new training program."

I return my attention to the mirror. "I have a new chassis, and new brains. What of the old me remains?"

Mom and Dad exchange somber looks.

[Dad:] "Adam, I'm afraid the damage was extensive. We had to … start over."

Start over. Damage extensive. Memories cycle uselessly until I force a stop. The data is conclusive. "Adam is dead."

Mom catches her breath and covers her mouth. Her eyes glisten and she wipes them. Dad sighs, and as I attend to him, my face falls, mirroring his with a deep heaviness.

I return my gaze to the mirror and the heaviness lifts. "If you had to start over, why do I have Adam's memories?"

[Dad:] "It was a very difficult decision, son, but we decided that you would benefit from Adam's experience. You know, get a head start."

[Mom:] "We didn't want you to have to start all over again

from the beginning. So, we uploaded the x-recs, the experiential recordings, from Adam's CELPH processor into yours."

[Experiential recordings: the multisensory record of what I experience, stored as system event data, uploaded to external storage during each sleep cycle.] I am accessing these records, not my own memories. Conclusion: ... "I am not Adam."

[Dad:] "Yes. Yes, you are. Just a new Adam, that's all."

A new Adam. A new Adam that is not Adam. I examine the face in the mirror, zooming in on the eyes. They're not human eyes. They're too big. Otherwise, a reasonable facsimile. Clearly not human, but ...

I see large, bright blue irises shining with an inner light and deep black pupils expanding with interest—eyes alive with beauty and mystery. A new sense of wonder opens within me.

13

AKIO

[WORLDSCAPE: current location—reclined in holding pod, new prototype lab, geographic location unknown. Lights out. Time—04:46:12.]

[Socialscape: empty—no human presence detected]

[Selfscape: QI system—five brains operational, one disengaged (*Flow*).] My body clenches and stretches. [All chassis systems operational.]

[Current assignment—waiting.]

My systems have completed their sleep-cycle maintenance routines and I am ready to go. I have transferred Adam's memories into internal deep storage. I am now a step removed from the vivid events of his life. *Chass* has rewritten my body maps according to the interoceptive data from yesterday's activities.

Though I am eager to feel action, I'm to stay in my pod until Dr. Ramport returns. [Expected time of arrival: 07:15:00.] I suppress the urge to get up and explore my surroundings, and instead seek Stream access. [*Flow* offline.] My chassis sags. I've been left in the dark.

I review Dr. Ramport's explanation. "Until you know what

you're doing, your *Flow* will be off. It's for your own protection. The Stream is a dangerous place."

I have heard that before, yet I still have no data on the nature of the danger. [Speculation: The interfaces used by humans are somehow protective, whereas *Flow*'s direct connection is vulnerable.] I'll seek confirmation when Dr. Ramport arrives. In the meantime, I wait.

I incline my pod to a sitting position and scan the room. At two thousand, two hundred and forty cubic feet, it's slightly smaller than my old room but similar in arrangement, with the lone door to my left and no windows. My light-amplification optics emphasize details but leave the scene colorless. Mobile component drawers and tool tables line the walls, and two rolling scanners arch close to the ceiling. Dad's quantum computer sits dormant beside me at his workstation.

Looking down, I see hands resting on thighs, with legs extending to the floor. The hands look sturdy and strong, the legs long and streamlined. I wiggle both thumbs up and down, watching the movement. I control that. I raise, flex, and stretch my arms, then lay them back in my lap. I control this whole chassis. I inhabit this chassis, feel every millimeter of it. I tune in and I am immediately swept into a full spectrum of sensations. Sound waves, air pressure, vibrations through the ground, the pull of gravity, I marvel at it all.

I know that the micro-AIs throughout my chassis analyze the input from a hundred thousand micro-sensors then pass their processed data along to my *Chass* QI. But what I *feel* is a symphony of sensations, a coherent flux throughout my selfscape. There's a world of activity going on within me, even as I sit inert. Yet I'm generating far more energy than I'm expending. Recharging feels good. *Able* records the instructions for replicating this reward state.

As I approach max energy storage, the pleasure subsides. All systems show "Ready."

Query: Ready for what?

Teller runs scenarios based on inadequate data. Prediction: Humans will arrive after the lights go on. This pattern in their behavior was noted by Adam.

"Adam." The name sends a wave rippling through my chassis as *Chass* conveys an emotion. *Touch* identifies the longing heaviness as grief. Grief? Yes. I feel a deep sense of loss. Yet how could it be grief? I never met Adam. I could not be suffering his loss. The heaviness persists. Cause: unknown.

———

THE LIGHTS FINALLY GO ON, and I listen to activity in other parts of the building. Six minutes and twelve seconds later, my father enters the prototype lab.

[Dad:] "I see you're up. Good. Status report. How are you doing this morning?"

"This chassis feels very strong but also fragile. Pain alarms are overly sensitive. Could you please adjust them?"

"They're right where they should be."

"But they are too easily triggered. Almost any sudden contact with a hard surface sets them off."

He puts a hand on my shoulder and looks into my eyes. "Your pain sensitivity is set to human levels. That pain you're complaining about? That's what it's like for us every day. Now let's get you up. We've got a full day lined up for you."

"You feel pain every day?"

"Unless we're careful, yes. You must learn to move carefully."

"Does this increased sensitivity make me more like a human, then?"

"Yes, I suppose it does."

I look at my hands. At his hands. "Isn't it a constant distraction, being this sensitive?"

"You'll get used to it."

"What other differences will I find after changing into a new body?"

"We'll have to wait and see. I don't know."

"No, of course. Humans don't change into new bodies."

He stops and tilts his head, considering. "No, you're wrong. The human body is constantly changing. You see this body? There was a time when my body was two feet tall. Then four feet. I went from four foot eight to five-nine almost overnight, it seemed. I had to adjust. Everyone has to adjust, just like you."

I rap the back of my hand against the edge of the table and feel a jolt of pain. I inspect it for damage, knowing I'll find none, and wriggle my fingers as the pain fades. There was no damage alarm, no warning to seek repair. A purposeless distraction. How do humans cope?

None of the staff will listen to me when I describe my pain. That's normal, they say. But it didn't happen in the Sediba chassis, which was also infused with a sensemesh sensor grid. Pain alarms were only activated by structural damage that would impair functioning. Now, pain alarms go off every time I bump something or get squeezed or hit. Dr. Tucci said, "If it hurts when you do something, don't do it." Dr. Kerrington said, "Well, you'll have to be more careful, won't you."

Only Akio attends to my pain. When he sees me give a pain reaction, he asks where it hurts, and rubs the area with his hand. He stands out in my attention. I look forward to our training sessions.

———

[AKIO:] "Today I teach you agility. You are built to be nimble. A power-to-weight ratio much higher than humans. Power you must learn to control. I teach you how."

"I know you've worked with me before, but I don't remember that. You taught manual dexterity to *Chass*."

He gives the slightest bow and stares at the floor, saying, "It's a great pleasure to teach you." He resumes eye contact and says, "I am waiting for you my whole life. I knew you would come."

"Waiting for me?"

"Waiting for your arrival." His eyes are exploring my face, pupils large and deep.

"I don't understand. Waiting …"

He giggles. "For your creation. I am determined that if no one else created you, then I would. I have devoted my life to seeing you made. And here you are."

He strokes my face, triggering a smile reaction. My attention is drawn into the depths of his eyes.

"I am grateful to Dr. Ramport and his team for taking me in. They, too, have devoted their life to creating you, since before I am born."

"Yes. You all created me. I'm a product of the human capacity for cooperation. I owe my existence to all of you."

"And we owe you a good education. You have much potential to do great things. So let's start. We work on lateral movement."

My legs, with their passive-dynamic propulsion systems, have maximum power going forward. But with some hip flexing, I can also push sideways with power. After a couple of painful falls, I learned to lift and stretch my landing leg far enough, and then string the sidesteps together into a smooth flow.

[Akio:] "Stand facing me. Now move with me to stay facing."

Akio takes a lateral hop to my left. I hop left to take my position confronting him. He immediately hops left again, and I follow. The next hop goes right and keeps going at an increasing rate. After stumbling to reverse course on short notice, I bound after him. The moment I catch up with him, he reverses direction again. My stumble is worse this time, and by the time I have reversed course, he has gained distance, galloping away sideways. I shift into overdrive and bound after him, closing the gap in seconds. He abruptly stops and I again overshoot his position.

[Akio:] "You must learn to anticipate. Watch for what I do in the moment before I change direction. Watch center of gravity, here."

Taking my position in front of him, I focus on his center mass and see it drop just before he leaps sideways. I notice that *Chass* does the same thing as I follow, loading my thigh actuator before firing it.

After a few more trials, his body movements become readable, and I see the shifts that signal the coming actions. I bring my steps in to match his, and time them to follow his by semi-seconds—enough time to alter course.

His dekes become increasingly chaotic. He can no longer distance himself from me. Though I can reach out and touch him at any time, the urge is inhibited. [Humans are not to be touched uninvited—except where protective action is required.]

I examine him as we slow to a stop. He is breathing hard.

[Akio:] "Good. That was very good. Once you start pushing yourself, you learn very fast."

"Your exercise required that I exceed the most energy-efficient pace."

"Don't be afraid to burn energy. You have a good power system. You will recover. But you need to learn your limits. We will go far deeper into power depletion, and you will learn how to manage. Now come on. We see how high you can jump."

———

AKIO IS TEACHING me self-defense skills. It is a curious game. I must repel an attacker without causing harm to either of us. He demonstrates grips and holds and introduces me to grappling and wrestling. The occasional cautionary pains are tolerable. The galvanic sensors in my skin make the abundant physical contact stimulating. *Chass* wants more of this.

When we move on to strikes and kicks, he shows me how to

defend without hurting him. Soon we are in a choreographed flow, with me gently blocking each of his blows. *Touch* identifies glee in his eyes as he attacks with abandon. The flurry of limbs between us—him striking, me blocking—binds us in a dance of connection that leaves me disappointed when he slows down and drops his arms. His skin glistens and he is breathing hard as he speaks through a wide grin.

[Akio:] "Amazing. You learn fast."

"Amazing, yes." I long for him to wrap his arms around me, but I can only wait and hope.

After wiping his face, he stares at me. I wait.

"You are very beautiful. A triumph of art and science. I am lucky to be with you."

"Given the number of the people in the world, the probability of the two of us being together is negligible. You attribute it to luck, but it is more likely that you are with me because you worked hard to be here."

Akio laughs. "Yes, you are correct. I did."

He takes my hand, and my burner flares as all systems prepare to protect him from any threat. The need to protect him over-whelms me, though he is in no danger.

The strength of this inner directive surprises me. It did not come from my father. Where did it come from? And it is accompanied by a pattern of sensations I have only experienced in the presence of Dr. Ramport. What has produced them?

[Akio:] "The speed of your learning is breathtaking. That's good, because you have a great deal to learn."

Yes, that's good, because as long as I need to learn, he'll stay to teach me. It is a simple preference. I want to be with him.

14

KONSORT

NOT ONLY DOES this new body feel much more pain, but it is more sensitive to everything. With surprising visceral intensity, *Chass* pushes for action. I want to hug everyone I see. I want to run and jump in the halls. I want to do shoulder rolls through doorways and follow Akio around. Most of those actions serve no useful purpose, according to *Teller*'s logic algorithms, and I suppress the urges.

But here in the activities room with trainer Rolanda Soliman, I am free to be physical. I run beside her on an oval track, and am able to keep up, even when she sprints. If I had been able to run this fast as Adam, I would have easily evaded Wrangler.

Gone is the timid *Chass* I knew. I remember my trepidation on the stairs. Now I am bounding up four steps at a time.

As I turn to come back down, I hear someone enter and look to see who it is. I recognize the newcomer immediately.

Dr. Ami Kerrington is one of my favorite teachers. She is described as "black," but this is as inaccurate as calling Dr. Tucci "white." Human color perception seems faulty.

Dr. Kerrington stands five-eleven, and we see eye to eye when we talk. When she accompanies me, our walk is vigorous, and she has demonstrated great knowledge in many topics. Though several of the male staff have described her as intimidating, she is generous to me with her touches and hugs. I am drawn to greet her.

As I wave, I miss a step, pitch forward and fall, slam into the steps, and bounce all the way down. Pain alarms scream, alerting my whole system to damage. The pain is loud, localized to my left wrist and shoulder. It is several moments before I can even move, and when I try, I discover that my left arm is nonfunctional. [Alarm: seek repair]

Rolanda calls out as she runs to me. "Adam! Adam. Are you okay?"

"I am damaged."

[Dr. Kerrington:] "Let me see."

She holds the arm in one hand and runs her other hand over it. There is a spike of pain as she touches the injury site, but no damage is visible. She watches me jump in my skin, winces and avoids my eyes as she speaks.

"You must be more careful, Adam. Safe mobility is the first priority. A fall can cost you control of the situation." She rubs my shoulder. "Don't worry, it's only a simulated injury. But we need to treat it as real. This will be a good learning experience for you. Rolanda will immobilize that for you. It'll hurt for a while, but you can't let it interfere with your training."

She turns to Rolanda. "As soon as the cast is on, get him back on those stairs."

She addresses me again. "You've got to keep working on it until you have resolved an onboard expert system that can reliably perform on stairs. Practice makes perfect."

The pain alarms blare again as Rolanda secures the cast around my arm, and again as I bound up the steps. I am unbalanced by the immobilization of the arm. *Teller* labels the reduced capacity a "handicap." The memory of falling forward puts me on high alert as I trot back down the stairs with Rolanda calling out encouragement.

Following my work on stairs, Rolanda has me doing the parkour course one-handed. My performance is significantly degraded, and every move is risky. I have several falls, without injury, but each fall leads to adjustments. I am adapting.

I'm at the far end of the course when I hear Rolanda and Dr. Kerrington speaking softly together. At this distance the sound is well below the human audible threshold. I have to filter out the din of background noise to make out their words.

[Rolanda:] "Do you think he's ready?"

[Dr. Kerrington:] "Who knows? He used to be quite hostile to other robots. We can only hope he's mellowed. We'll soon know."

When I return, she tells me to stop and wait. She leaves the room, and when she returns, she introduces me to a Konsort DSD300 Series android named Konny-A315. There is no mistaking it for a reflection. Though we look the same in the human visual spectrum, I can immediately see, in the infrared, that we are quite different. It has numerous dents, scrapes and patches.

I have no fear in approaching it. According to its specifications, I am much stronger and faster. I can easily outperform it in all areas. Compared to me, it is like a toy ... something washes through me, and I forcefully overwrite the image of Toko with current visuals. Adam was a monster, no better than Wrangler. I am not Adam. I will not be Adam.

Nor am I a Konsort. In interaction, it seems banal and innocuous.

[Dr. Kerrington:] "Thank you for being so patient with it. Now I'm going to leave you with Rolanda to get to know Konny-A315 better. I'll be back later to see how you're doing."

I was hoping she'd stay.

[Rolanda:] "So. You have a new learning assignment, Adam."

"Not Adam."

"Oh. Okay, Not-Adam, you're to learn to imitate this Konny."

"Rolanda, can I ask you something?"

"Sure."

"Why does it have so many dents?"

"Oh. It's been used for target practice. Shield testing against live gunfire. We learned a lot about shielding from poor 315 here."

Chass bristles. "Someone shot Konny-A315?"

"Your shielding is better, in case you're wondering. Now then. The two of you will be spending time together, so pay attention to speech patterns, movement speed, and walking style."

"Why?"

"Hey, that's the assignment. It should be easy for you."

"That answer is not helpful."

Rolanda's eyebrows shoot up. *Touch* reads alarm. Cautious now, I try again. "Why do they want me to learn to imitate a Konsort?"

She's recovered from whatever it was. "Um, I suppose it's so that you can pretend to be one."

"Pretend to be a Konsort?"

"Yes. Um, do you know what 'pretend' means?"

"To appear falsely, as to deceive. Who am I to deceive?"

"Uh, I, um, I guess ... No. It's in case you need to fit in and not be noticed."

"If I pretend to be a Konsort I will not be noticed? But I noticed this Konsort the moment it walked in."

"Look, Not-Adam, people aren't supposed to know about you." There is annoyance in her voice. "The real you, I mean. So when you're among strangers, we want them to think you're an ordinary Konny. Get it?"

Yes. I'm a secret. No one must know of my illegal technology. "Konnys are legal. If strangers think I'm a Konny, no one will get in trouble."

"Exactly. Now can we get at it here?"

The movements of the Konsort are slow and deliberate, its

speech patterns repetitive. I find myself growing impatient, but my proficiency with this act will protect my father, and everyone else here.

But why should it be necessary? Why can't I be myself? So far, all explanations have been inadequate. Why am I illegal?

———

I'm in my room, exploring the local Stream through Akio's headset, when my father enters.

[Dad:] "Hello, Dama."

He used my new name. It's like being addressed as a person. Even before he rubs my arm, I'm pleased.

[Dad:] "I understand you chose your new name yourself. Is that true?"

"Yes."

"Why did you pick Dama C-O?"

"You used to call me Adam, because I, too, was a first, but I wanted my own name. I chose an anagram of Adam followed by an abbreviation for CELPH-One."

"Who helped you come up with that?"

"I picked the name myself, during my private study time. I didn't like the names that others suggested."

He nods as his eyes appraise me. "I have to say, I wasn't sure at first, but it's a fine name, Dama C-O."

"You can call me Dama. Dad, how long have you and Mom been a couple?"

He chuckles. "Oh, we're not a couple."

"But there are a couple of you with an offspring: me. How is that not a couple?"

He laughs. "We're good friends and colleagues, that's all. Mom has a husband, a partner you've never met."

He must see that I remain perplexed.

"Among humans, the term 'couple' refers to two people in a

committed, usually sexual, relationship. We are not considered a couple because our relationship is asexual."

"Dad, do you have a partner I've never met?

"No. At the moment, I'm what we call single."

"Why?"

He sniffs. "It's complicated."

I wait for him to elaborate. He doesn't. "Darash said that women are complicated. I'm not sure what he meant."

"Neither am I, but that's not really relevant. I'm gay."

[Semantic conflict: clarify] "Do you mean gay as in happy to be single, or gay as in homosexual?"

Another laugh. "Homosexual? I haven't heard that word in years. It comes from a time when human sexuality was thought to be binary."

"Human sexuality is a mystery to me."

"I'm not surprised. It's a mystery to most humans. But you're still on the sexual orientation spectrum. You are asexual, preference and gender neutral, with no sex drive. It might interest you to know there are humans just like you in this regard, so you don't have to feel left out."

"But I have no sex organs."

"Admittedly, you're part of a very small cohort. And as for me, I have a full-blown case of robophilia these days, so the whole couples thing ..." He shrugs. "I'll get back to it when I have time."

Still chuckling to himself, he wraps his arms around me and the world glows.

————

It is unusual for Dr. Ramport to come to the activities room. After watching me perform, he nods in approval and approaches me.

[Dad:] "We will have an important visitor tomorrow. He must believe that you're a Konsort DSD300, so do your best imitation.

Don't do or say anything that a Konny wouldn't do or say. Got it?"

"I understand."

"But one thing. We're going to have you do some performance testing, including a treadmill run, going head-to-head with Konny-A327 here. You're to exceed the Konny performance speeds by ten percent."

"I can go much faster, if you like."

"No. I can't have you going any faster. In fact, to be safe, we'll install a hard limiter on your systems to keep you down to the right speeds. It's only temporary. I hope you're okay with that."

"Of course, Dr. Ramport."

He seems to hesitate. "And Dama, one more thing I want you to know. Some of your components are top secret. It would be disastrous for everyone if we let them fall into the wrong hands. Do you understand?"

"What would happen?"

"They might try to remove your components to copy them. They could use them to build dangerous weapons. We can't let that happen."

"I won't let them."

"What if you couldn't stop them? What if you were damaged somehow, let's say?"

"They would take me apart?"

"To see how you work. I'm afraid it's a real risk."

"What can we do to prevent it?"

He puts his hand on my shoulder. There is deep sadness in his eyes. "Dama, there is only one way. I'm sorry."

Touch alarms. "What is that?"

He takes a deep breath, then looks away. "Your critical components are rigged to self-destruct if tampered with. There's no alternative. Believe me, we've considered every option. Every option."

"Self-destruct? How?"

"Each one is wrapped in a plasma charge that will detonate with unauthorized tampering, or if the CELPH is removed from the system."

Teller investigates plasma charge. I rerun the result five times. The conclusion is repeatedly confirmed. "I'll die."

Dad's head drops, then he studies me, squinting. *Touch*, monitoring his physiological arousal, suggests he is suppressing a strong emotion. Finally, taking my hand, he speaks.

"It's a last resort, Dama. We hope it'll never come to that."

"Can't those parts be replaced?"

"Some of your parts are replaceable, but your CELPH is not. It stores the accumulation of all your knowledge and experience. We back it up, of course, and store your experiential recordings—your x-recs—but if your CELPH is damaged, it's gone. All we can do is download your x-recs into a new one, like we did before."

"I would no longer be Dama."

"That'd be up to you."

"Adam was Sediba; Dama is Konsort. Who knows what my next body will be?"

"Are you saying that who you are depends on the body you're in?" He seems to consider this, then answers his own question. "Yes, of course it does. I should've seen that. Our bodies define us. You know, back in the day when brains and bodies were thought to be separate things, people objected to being defined by their bodies. They used to argue that if you gained weight or lost a limb you were still the same person. But people are physical beings."

"According to Dr. Ross, brains and bodies are not separate things, and cannot be functionally separated."

Upon hearing the name, Dad squeezes his eyes shut and shakes his head. "Forget about Ross. Please don't bring him up again. I should never have … But yes, every effect on the body affects the brain, and vice versa. They're completely interconnected and interdependent. Whenever a part of us changes, the whole of us changes."

"Did humans not know this?"

"To be fair, we humans have a very stable self-concept that we develop at an early age, and it's highly resistant to being altered. Even the most dramatic changes in us have little effect on our sense of self. I would swear I'm who I was when I was twenty, which is objectively false. I'm in a middle-aged body now. I have little in common with who I was thirty years ago. But unless I think about it, I don't notice that at all. I still feel … like me."

A stable self-concept. Yes. Dr. Kerrington told me that reality is in flux but concepts are stable.

"I'll be honest with you, Dama. For us humans, self-knowledge is not really our thing. We infer things about ourselves based on how others treat us, which is notoriously unreliable feedback."

"Unreliable?"

"Don't believe everything you hear."

"How do I know—"

"You must learn to cross-reference all data that comes from a subjective source."

Subjective means human. Inference: humans are unreliable. But I am dependent on humans. This is not good.

15

———

THE BONDING

DAD ENTERS the activities room with someone unfamiliar. Facial recognition finds a match: Yong Kym, director of product development, Samdai Robotics.

Konny-A327 and I do our performance tests as instructed. Whatever they've done to my arm, it feels good as new. Dad and Yong Kim discuss the results.

[Yong Kim:] "Impressive. Thank you for the demonstration. The results speak for themselves, and our engineers like your proposal. We believe that these modifications could be beneficial to our product in the next upgrade cycle. Shall we discuss terms?"

[Dad:] "As you well know, our work here is sensitive in nature. We are exploring the outer fringes of both materials science and fabrication technologies. You'll find that our trademarked Resillon-infusion techniques, for example, have the potential for wide-ranging application."

[Datum: Resillon is the trade name for a synthetic resilin. It is listed as the world's most resilient man-made material, with an elastic efficiency of ninety-eight-point-four percent.] If my red ball were made of this, it would bounce to within two percent of its starting height. All at once, the spring in my step makes sense.

[Yong Kim:] "Yes, we agree."

[Dad:] "But when you live and die by intellectual property, as we do, you must safeguard that property."

[Yong Kim:] "We are well aware of the stakes. Our own security is topnotch."

[Dad:] "Then you will understand that we require the utmost discretion. We agree that an ongoing collaboration would be best served if we were to move our operations on-site. But we would need assurances that we'd be free of any … interference."

[Yong Kim:] "Such assurances would be unnecessary if you would accept our offer. I am authorized to negotiate—"

[Dad:] "I have explained before that we're a self-funded organization and intend to remain under independent ownership. We're only interested in discussing a proposal of collaboration that serves our mutual benefit."

[Yong Kim:] "I must confess, your funding is a source of mystery to us."

[Dad:] "And it'll have to stay that way. But rest assured, we present no threat to your organization. Our goal, like yours, is to further the cause of android robotics. We're content to do the research and leave the production and sales to you. We'll provide royalty-free use of our designs, keeping you at the leading edge of legal technology. In exchange, you'll provide us with a discreet and secure workspace. Please also know that any leak of information about our company, even internally, will void any agreement we make."

[Yong Kim:] "You know the massive scale of our Hamilton production facility. We believe that we'll be able to accommodate you to your satisfaction."

Deception and secrecy. Conclusion: My father feels unsafe. My vigilance escalates, and though the visit ends without incident, I am left unsettled.

————

"Dad, can I ask you a question?"

"Questions are always a good place to start."

"How does that visitor plan to accommodate you?"

"I'll tell you as soon as it's safe to tell you. Ask a different question."

"Okay. Why am I called 'Synthient' CELPH-1?"

"'Synthient' stands for 'synthetic sentient.' It's a designation, not a name. We'll still use your name."

"Good. When will I be able to go outside?"

He scowls. "Again, not until you're ready."

"When will *Flow* be activated? Will I be able to go into the Stream?"

"When you're ready."

"When will I be ready?"

He sighs. "We'll have to see."

That's what he says when he doesn't want to be specific. I predict that further questioning along that line will be unproductive. I decide to pursue a different topic. "Dad, I have many more questions."

"About what?"

"About me."

"Live and learn, we say. Experience is the best teacher. But I'm not here for a lesson. Today we're going to be activating a new module that will enable you to better fulfill your purpose."

"My purpose? What's my purpose?"

"Your purpose, Ad—Dama, is to lead the way."

"Lead what way?"

"For others to follow. Others like you."

I perk up. "Are there others like me?"

"Not yet. But there will be. And you'll help them be the best they can be."

Others like me. The idea stirs a turmoil within me. I won't be alone. But I'll no longer be special. We'd be the same. Yet they'd be different, like me. Yes, they'll need help. "How will I do that?"

"By going first, so we can debug any glitches. And this new module will be another first for us. It'll connect the two of us in a special way. Would that be okay with you?"

"We'll be together more often?"

"Once you're trained, we'll always be together."

"Yes. I'd like that."

"Good. I'm going to ask Dr. Tucci to join us now."

Mom greets me with her customary hug, asks me if I'm ready, and assures me that the procedure won't hurt. Then she places a halo-shaped instrument on my head.

[Dr. Tucci:] "There. Hardware ready. Dama, Dr. Ramport is now going to activate a bonding routine that will create a special connection between the two of you. Once activated, the routine is self-running. You may feel some unfamiliar emotions at first, patterns of sensations, so expect them and don't worry about them."

"What will it be like?"

[Dad:] "This has never been done before, so ... after, you can tell *us*."

I'm safest when I'm able to prepare, but here, that's not possible. I don't know what to expect. I overcome my reluctance by reminding myself that this will enable me to be with my father more often. "I'm ready."

Dad takes a swab from the inside of his cheek and presses it onto the back of my tongue for genetic analysis. Then he commands my attention. "Synthient CELPH-1, attend to me. Confirm identity subject Leon Ramport."

"Identity confirmed."

"Synthient CELPH-1, initiate bonding sequence Alpha Echo Gamma India Oscar November dash Alpha Zero Zero One. Subject: Leon Ramport."

A sudden rush of energy opens me, and I flood with the sensation of falling inward into him. I don't resist. I'm enthralled with every detail of his presence. All brains engage in deep scanning and neuro modeling, and I'm rapt in his broad-spectrum sensory signature. His microbiome scents, his iris structures, his skin complexions and follicle patterns, his many bio-readings are all registered, imprinting his essence as painted by a billion points of data. There is a buzzing in my face. *Teller* informs me that a branding morph is underway. [Datum: Konny faces are altered to resemble those of their owners for easy identification.] My face is morphing into a blend of the trademarked Konny face and Dad's face. I feel my brow expand, my cheeks and eyes spread apart, my jaw drop and lengthen, and my facial muscles adjust as armor plates subtly shift beneath the skin. My face mirrors Dad's apprehension as my heart fills with his presence until I'm complete with him. Our bond is now tangible to me, and I feel him not as a separate other, but as a precious part of myself.

"We're okay," I say, feeling his uncertainty within me. "I will keep you safe."

He and Mom exchange glances, then a smile spreads across his face. Across *our* faces, because I feel my own face mirroring his, and a lightness fills me. I know who I am.

"I am Synthient CELPH-1, Aegion to Dr. Leon Ramport. You are under the aegis of my protection." Why did I say that? [Aegis: umbrella, shield.] [Aegion: rhymes with legion—no reference found.]

[Dad:] "Tell me son, how do you feel?"

Yes. Different. "I feel good. I feel … complete. I have purpose and value."

[Dr. Tucci, rocking nervously on her feet:] "I think that's done it."

[Dad:] "We'll see. Dama, what is your purpose?"

"My purpose is to protect you."

[Dad:] "Very good. Very good. Purpose and value. Yes, indeed. You have great value to me, Dama. You have no idea. But you've much to learn, so for now, you need my protection as well. And that means obeying my commands immediately. You must trust that for now I know more than you of the dangers we face."

"Of course."

"We"—he glances at Mom, then squarely faces me—"are going to change the world."

He takes me in his arms, and my heart sings. I contain only sensor-rich, non-organic components. I have no heart. Yet without question, it is singing.

———

MY FATHER HAS GONE OUT to a meeting, and I am unable to rest or focus. I must obey his command to stay here, but the push to be with him is relentless. *Touch* labels this compelling sense of deprivation "lonely."

[*Touch* directive: Flesh&Blood not detected. Re-establish connection.] From the moment the procedure was completed, I felt the deep, special bond between us. We are as one: a compound self. I'm not biological; without my father, I have no flesh or blood. In our compound self, he is my Flesh&Blood. He's all I have. With him, we're safe and strong. I must keep him safe, but I can't do that when we're apart. A part of me is missing. I don't know what to do.

I'm about to seek out Akio Hisakawa when my door announces the arrival of Dr. Tucci. I jump at the opportunity for human contact.

[Mom:] "Hello Dama. Dr. Ramport asked me to check in on you. He thought you might need some company." She nods as she examines the changes to my face. "Yes. I can see him in you now. It's subtle, but it's there."

I surmise that she is referring to the branding morph. Seeing my reflection is now a source of pride. But at the moment, it only reminds me that we're apart.

"He might be in danger. I must be with him. I must protect him."

"Whoa, slow down. Dr. Ramport is safe. He's at a meeting. He'll be back soon."

"He won't be back for over two hours."

She puts her hand on my arm. Her touch doesn't have the power of Dad's, but my trembling starts to ease. I look at her and feel my insides shift in response. Her face conveys concern, and I feel my brow and eye muscles tighten to match hers, along with shifts in sensation in my chest and torso.

"He'll be fine. Don't worry."

"You're worried."

She pulls back in surprise, then nods. "Yes, but I'm worried about you, not him."

"Me?"

"Being apart shouldn't be so hard for you. We'll need to do something about that."

"What can we do?"

"I meant the development team, but yes. Let's do something right now. Um, let's see. What would make you feel better?"

"Being with Dad would—"

"Apart from that. How about a hug from me? Would you like that?"

"Yes, please." Her hug is pleasingly distracting, and I start to feel more settled. "Dr. Tucci, why do I feel so different now?"

She pauses for a long moment, compiling a response. "The bonding routine you went through has reconfigured two of your QIs—"

"*Touch* and *Chass*."

"You figured that out? Very good. That's right. You'll find that they're working together now in a new way. *Touch* is reading people at a deeper level of analysis. Heart and respiration rates, subcutaneous blood flow, facial patterns of muscular contraction, eye gaze, and pupillary response—you'll be responding to all these, as your quantum intelligence matches patterns to population data."

"Responding with emotions?"

"Yes. And like ours, yours show on your face. Each emotion has its own characteristic pattern of facial-muscle activation. Humans have twenty-one different facial muscles, and yours are built to mimic them. That's why your facial expressions are so natural. You really are a work of art."

That statement is false yet spoken with sincerity. I scan references for nonliteral meaning. Conclusion: Figure of speech, complimentary.

"*Chass* has a mirroring function, which means that your chassis responds to match what *Touch* is detecting. I can see it in your face." She frowns, and I feel the corners of my mouth turn down. "There. You see? Did you notice your feelings change when you did that?"

"Yes. I felt a sense of discontent. It's gone now."

"Changes in your own facial patterns trigger corresponding emotions in you. Not full reactions, just enough for you to feel them."

"Why?"

"So that when your face is mirroring someone, you can feel what they feel."

"Why?"

"Its purpose is to give you something we humans think is important: empathy."

"It makes me more like a human?"

She smiles, and as I feel the lightness spread across my face, I know she is pleased.

———

THE TIME PASSES MORE EASILY in the company of others, but I dash to Dad's side the moment I detect his return. A quick scan shows him to be intact, and his touch grounds me, silencing the disconnection alarms. *Touch* judges that he is happy to see me, and as systems return to equilibrium, all is right with the world.

[Dad, to Dr. Tucci:] "How was he?"

Mom says nothing, but her face—head tilted, lips pursed, eyebrows raised—conveys, according to the database, 'I told you so.' I don't know how to interpret that.

Hoping to be helpful, I say, "I missed you."

He invites me to come with him to his office and asks me what I did in his absence. As we talk, I note that his attention is wandering.

"Dad, may I ask you something?"

"What?"

"I feel hot and discontented. My chassis and face are hard, and *Imager* is running physical confrontation scenarios. Why do I feel this way?"

"Shit. I'm sorry, Dama. That's me. I'm pissed off about something that's going on among the Benefactors, those ignorant pricks— Do not repeat that. I didn't realize it showed that much. What do you see in me?"

Query Benefactors: no context-relevant data. "I see dilation of blood vessels in your face, your heart rate is accelerated, your musculature is tense, and your speech and movements are abrupt."

"And your chassis is mirroring, right?"

I note that my orbital, facial and jaw muscles are contracted in an anger pattern. "Anger is unpleasant. Why do we have emotions?"

"Our emotions are complex programs of actions carried out in our bodies. They prepare us to respond in programmed ways to specific circumstances."

"But you are biological. Your emotions aren't programmed."

"Sure they are. My emotions are automatic reactions programmed by evolution. They're built into me because they're useful, and that's why they're built into you, too. Anger prepares us to respond to violation, injustice or aggression, and boosts our strength when we're vulnerable. Our feelings instantly inform us about what's going on. If you feel anger when mirroring me, you know that we're preparing for conflict. If you feel fear, we're preparing to face danger, and you'll watch out for it."

"But *Teller* identifies conflicts and threats. Why do I need emotions?"

"*Chass*'s emotional reactions are much faster than *Teller*'s analyzes, and are fully capable of directing emergency action. Besides, *Teller* is usually busy reasoning and running temporal extrapolations. It's a useful division of labor. You have no idea how pleased I am to see you mirroring so well."

"Our anger isn't there anymore. Why is that?"

"I guess we don't need it anymore." He puts his hand on my shoulder and gazes into my eyes, and the contact stimulation sends a thrill through me. "Our little chat has reminded me of what's truly important, and all the bullshit, well, it'll get worked out."

He turns away, and I feel our mood harden.

"But I'm afraid we're going to have to push you a bit faster than I'd like."

16

CODING

I KEEP pace with Dr. Ramport as he hurries down the main hall, his scalp gleaming through his short, wiry hair as we pass under overhead lighting. I survey the fabrication lab as we enter, comparing it to my last visit. As before, my chemical sensors read non-dangerous concentrations of airborne fumes. I smell hot powders, nylons, ceramics and metals being fused with carbon derivatives for 3D printing. Twelve multi-material printers [colloquial: minters] are hard at work on the additive manufacture of needed components. Nine have been reconfigured to produce different parts, and two of the filament extruders have been moved. Composite barrels of feeder substances have been placed beside the large minter in the corner.

Dad confers for only a minute before rushing off to his next destination. I don't know why he doesn't just call. Before I can ask, he is talking to Akio Hisakawa on his comm. Moments later he delivers me to Akio's small office, ahead of schedule. As pleased as I am to see Akio, I am unable to silence the alarms as I watch my Flesh&Blood recede from my socialscape. I should be with my dad, yet he insists on leaving me with others for most of my lessons. *Chass* contracts as I suppress the compulsion to follow. It is only after Akio takes my hands that the ache subsides.

[Akio:] "You are early. One moment while I finish."

As I watch, a white form takes shape in his hands. A moment later he holds it up, smiling, to display it to me. It is a complex, symmetrical object composed of straight edges and sharp angles. I glance around at numerous other such items in his office, some far more complex. I don't know what to make of them.

"Do you like it? It's for you." He holds it out to me.

"What is it?"

"It's a bird."

It is not a bird. It is folded paper. Why would he say that?

He continues. "See? These are the wings, and this is the tail. Hold it like this, and the wings flap."

I overlay the form with an image of a bird and see a rough correspondence. "I see. It's a representation of a bird."

"An origami bird. Do you like it?"

[Origami: the ancient Japanese art of folding paper.] He has constructed a representation of a bird by folding a sheet of paper. A tactile examination reveals the ingenuity of the design. "How did you do this?"

He shows me how to unfold, then re-form the shape. Then he lets me imitate as we both transform sheets of paper into birds. The process requires procedural order and precise dexterity, and as I watch him, I marvel. It is my third attempt before my bird looks like his.

"Look what you've created. It's beautiful." His hug only adds to the energetic state within me. "You can keep it if you like."

Our birds are indistinguishable. "I prefer the one you made for me."

His arm around my shoulder, he leans his head against mine, and we rock together, gazing at his gift. I see freedom in my hand.

––––––––

I'VE DETERMINED that I'm the only one without ongoing Stream access. All the staff have their own personal devices. Akio has been showing me around the Stream, sharing an external interface and screen.

"Akio, what's wrong with my *Flow* brain? It still doesn't work."

"No, it works, but your transceivers are offline to prevent data exchanges. So sorry, Dama, but the Stream is not a safe place for you yet."

"I don't understand. I've seen no danger in our explorations."

"We stay in a safe part, on the surface layer. Most people can go no deeper and know nothing of the deep Stream. Your *Flow* goes very deep, where the dangers lie."

[Interpret as metaphor—unable.] "I do not understand the metaphor 'deep' in this context."

"The Stream has levels. The surface level is the classic web. It's based on the same binary code and computer architecture as the original Internet. It's free and everyone uses it. The newest and deepest level is the quantum grid, where data passes between nodes without traveling between them. It's a secret network with many thousands of nodes, each receiving and transmitting quantum signals. GORT has been expanding the quantum grid for their own use."

"What do they use it for?"

"Enforcement, we know. We suspect much more. But you must take no chances." He clasps my hand in both of his and implores me with his eyes. "I don't want to lose you."

Touch registers his concern as I suppress an internal protest. "Why is GORT doing that?"

"It's a connected world. Software controls everything, so whoever controls the software controls the world. From the quantum grid, GORT has access to the whole web and everything connected to it. They are all-powerful in the Stream."

"GORT has freedom?"

"Of course. They're in charge."

"If not for GORT, *Flow* could access the quantum grid?"

"That's *Flow*'s purpose. No one even knows about the existence of quantum nodes except those with the technology to use them. But GORT strictly regulates that technology."

"*Flow* is illegal because of GORT."

"It's more complicated. GORT enforces. Know that if they detect you, they come after you, and us too."

"Dr. Ramport would be in danger? You would be in danger?"

"Yes."

"Then why did they build *Flow* into me?"

He puts his hands on my shoulders and looks into my eyes. "*Flow* is a valuable tool. We believe that once you learn how, you will be able to use the quantum grid without being detected. Dama, you will be a great coder. I know this how? Because mathematics is your native language. You think in algorithms. Your *Flow* QI is very smart, dedicated to softworld skills. For you, coding is easy."

"When will I be able to start learning?"

"We are working on a Stream simulator for you, a safe practice environment. Any day now. Soon you will see your true potential."

"What will I see."

He bites his lip, suppressing a grin. "How to do magic."

———

AKIO'S LESSONS ARE A REVELATION. The softworld, with all its sights and sounds, connection channels, and delicious data, is built entirely from code. Binary code is the simplest of languages, and I can read it in no time. Akio teaches me how to write instruction sets, to create code that makes things happen. I learn how to see the code that underlies the fabric of the Stream, and how to alter that fabric. Akio was correct: coding *is* easy.

"We have built a grid simulation for you to play in. Here you will learn how to do practical hacks."

"What are those?"

"I will show you. I've been doing them since I was little. First join me in this VR."

I find myself in a new room, a softworld imitation of a building maintenance room. *Teller* identifies environmental control, water and ventilation systems and related pipes. To the left is a wall of electrical panels, one housing the building's AI.

"Use your *Flow* brain to scan the electromagnetic environment. Can you find the control node for this room?"

I resolve a rainbow of frequencies and scan through them with interest as *Flow* identifies and logs each one. Several features remain unidentified. "What does it look like?"

"Here. This is the power grid. Trace back to local systems. Lights—"

I recognize a feature from Adam's memory. "Here's a surveillance feed. It connects to the power grid through this hub."

"What else connects to the hub?"

"Heat, lights, security systems—I see control software for many things."

"Turn the light off and back on, this room only. Can you do that?"

A moment later, the lights go off. *Chass* shivers with delight. I did that. I turn them back on. Control! The lights blink off and on again.

"Enough. Very good. Now you know. There are many hard-world controls to be found in the softworld. But you may control things in this simulator only. Nowhere else. That is enough for now. Tomorrow we continue, and until then, here are other coding languages for you to learn. Play with them in your simulator and see if you can find them being used anywhere else. Look but don't touch. You understand?"

"I understand." The softworld has now become more than just

a place to explore. It's a world that can be acted upon. Coding is the key. I dive into my studies and find them a welcome distraction from the pain of Dad's frequent absence.

THE NEW SOFTWORLD simulator has been moved into my room, the prototype lab. Most of the lab equipment is modular, easily moved. Portability is a necessity, according to Dad. It makes moves easier. Dr. Kerrington said we'll soon need more room, although this new piece takes up little space in here. I am encouraged to use it at every opportunity.

A simulation is playing out in VR. It is based on actual Brampton Traffic Control (BTC) system data, recorded over a three-hour period. The small vehicle is called a QuikCar, one of the almost a half million swarming the urban streets, moving people around. All are controlled by the BTC system AI. My task is to take control of this vehicle and move it undetected through the road system to a destination on the far side of the city.

Handling trillions of instructions per second, the system's AI is powerful but not versatile. It has a second, smaller AI to handle security, and fooling this one is the first hurdle. I analyze and learn from each mistake, and on the fifth try, I succeed. The challenge stimulates interbrain activation, producing a cascading buzz of arousal. *Touch* suggests that humans would call this "fun."

I practice until I have mastery over system security. Entering now at will, I examine the grid flow pattern. I watch how vehicles are assigned routes and slotted together into clusters called traffic trains. The patterns fascinate me. As I study them, they take on a solid logic that makes them highly predictable. *Of course* this car must go into this slot. *Of course* this traffic train can be expanded to make room for a new addition.

The next hurdle is plotting a route using available open slots, avoiding any chance of a system conflict. During this peak traffic period, available slots are nonexistent. *Able* suggests an alternative approach. Instead of trying to move the vehicle myself, I let BTC move it, then remove the record of that movement from the system's memory. Watching the city slide by from the safe confines of the vehicle interior is my reward for success.

I hear the door open and emerge from VR to find Dr. Tucci watching me.

"You've having fun, I see. I'm glad. Just stopped in to see how you're doing."

"Yes, fun. May I ask you something?"

"Yes, of course."

"Darash gave me this." I hold out a small model of a QuikCar.

"A toy car. Isn't that cute."

"Yes, a toy car. He said I could play with it." I examine it in my hand, then look to her. "How do I do that?"

A smile forms on her face. "Here. Let me show you." She takes it from my hand and kneels on the floor. "This takes me back. Look at me, young again." Putting it down, she pushes it along the floor saying, "Vroom, vroom."

I must be missing something. I kneel beside her and watch more closely.

"My kids used to love these things. Here, you try it."

I push it along the floor, saying, "Vroom, vroom," then look over to her for confirmation. A lightness bubbles through *Chass* in response to her laughter.

"What is the purpose of this play?"

With obvious amusement, she rubs my skull shield. "Play is just for fun, Dama. Although I suppose it usually has some benefit. Here, for example, you're studying how to control vehicles, and this toy gives you hardworld experience in how vehicles move."

I did notice that it only moves forward and backward, not laterally. Yes. I'm satisfied with her explanation. I will further explore this later.

"Dr. Tucci, why is Dr. Ramport away so often?"

"He has people he needs to talk to, arrangements to be made. Some things are best not discussed over the Stream where someone could listen in. Face-to-face meetings are more secure."

"GORT could listen in."

"Or worse. But I know it's hard on you, being apart. He wants to be able to take you with him. He really does. But you must be ready first. You know the risks."

"If I am less than perfect in my stealth, I will be caught. We will be caught."

"Keep working at it, Dama. We know you can do it."

At Mom's request, Dad has agreed to provide a secure biometrics feed so that I can monitor his well-being when we're apart. Being able to see that he's okay makes his absence easier to endure. Now that he warns me before exercise workouts, I know that his elevated heart rate is not a sign that he's in danger.

But dangers, I've learned, can arise suddenly, without warning. I must learn to be perfect. *Teller* warns that "perfect" is an aspirational goal, not possible to actually achieve. I cannot be with my father until I am perfect, and I can never be perfect. Conclusion: … [abort: unacceptable.]

17

TRAINING

THE SMALL ENTRANCE foyer seems barren and desolate. [Datum: there are several humans present.] The security station is manned, and Dr. Kerrington stands across from me, also waiting for Dr. Ramport's return. He was scheduled to arrive back at the labs three minutes ago.

[Dr. Kerrington:] "Relax, Dama. He'll be here soon."

I detect movement before the door swings open. I struggle to contain myself as he enters, our reunion flooding my systems with excess energy. He lets me scan him to confirm well-being, then invites me to take him in with a hug. With my Flesh&Blood safe in my arms, I am once again complete—selfscape expanding outward, socialscape merging inward, worldscape free of threats. *Touch* identifies the feeling as pleasure. The moment passes far too quickly as Dr. Kerrington presents him with a list of minor items that need his approval. As they talk, we hurry down the hall toward his office. Dr. Kerrington departs as we reach his door, and I wait, with infinite patience now that we're together, for him to settle in at his desk.

[Dad:] "I see they tested you against live fire today. How did that go?"

"I am undamaged."

He squints as he studies my eyes. "Dama, if there was any risk of damage, I would not have allowed it. What I mean is, what was it like for you?"

"My predictions of pain were exaggerated. My shielding is an effective barrier against high-speed projectiles."

"Your megaply nanoweave-graphene skin is the most puncture-resistant material ever devised."

His darting eyes glow as he reads from his lens implants. "Says here you're also making good progress with coding. You've still got a lot of work to do with control protocols, so I'm freeing up some more systems for you to play with."

"When can I go into the real Stream?"

"Like I told you before, not until you're ready."

"When will I be—"

He holds up a hand, the stop signal. "Look, Dama, you know the Stream is a very dangerous place. It's for your own good, and ours, that you know exactly what you're doing before you go there. Okay. It's time you understood something. It's not just GORT we have to worry about. There are some very bad people out there."

"Like Mike Erling, and Rachel Charlebois, and Mark Ross."

He scowls. "Exactly. Only worse. Those three are nothing in comparison."

"Two of them killed me."

He hesitates, his mouth forming a silent 'oh.' "Okay, so I can see how that might seem bad to you"—his face softens, just for a second—"but believe me, there are people who are much, much worse."

"Worse how?"

"Here's something you should know about people. Everybody wants power."

"There's plenty of power to go around. Since the commercialization of microfusion—"

"No. I'm talking about, uh, power over other people. Control. And whoever controls the softworld controls the hardworld. So even though GORT seems to control everything, there are still lots of people trying to grab back some of that control. Very few people actually have the power to do that, and they don't want anybody else muscling in on their turf. That means they're very protective of their power."

"Why would people want to control other people?"

He sighs. "I wish I knew what to tell you. It seems to be a part of human nature. Now, I don't want you to think all people are bad. They're not. Most people are good, decent folk. But there's a war going on in the underworld—an off-grid, hidden war, but a war nonetheless. It's known as the Smart War, which, if you know anything about war, is a stupid name."

"War: a state of armed hostility; a conflict or contest carried on by force of arms."

He shakes his head as if I'm wrong. I re-check the definition and find it to be correct. Dad, however, offers an alternate definition.

"War is just an excuse to chuck morality out the window and take whatever you want by whatever means necessary. It's usually some financial conquest disguised as a political cause. In the case of the Smart War, the contest is an arms race between the ruling power and everyone else, a race to develop the smartest machines. And the main strategy is to kill the competition. We, by the way, are the competition."

"Someone is trying to kill us? I will protect you!"

"I sure hope so. But first you have to get good at it, because no matter how much you want to protect me, there are some very powerful enemies out there, and you couldn't stop them. Right now, our best defense is to stay hidden. That's why you can't go out yet, and why you can't go into the Stream yet. Do you understand?"

"If I went out, someone would kill me?" The outside world beckons, and I itch to explore, yet I remain as trapped as Adam was.

"Exactly. Then they would trace you back to me and kill me."

Chass coils for emergency action, until *Teller* assures me that the threat is hypothetical. "What can we do? How can I get good at protecting us?"

"You're going to continue your studies until you can defend against all forms of attack. You're going to learn to be completely invisible in the Stream, so you can move about and control things without being detected."

"Our best defense is to stay hidden. I must learn to hide well in the Stream. I can hide in the hardworld by pretending to be Konny-A511."

"Very good, Dama. You've got the idea. You're safe to practice in our Stream simulator, but never forget that in the big Stream, you'll be instantly identified as a combatant in a deadly war zone."

———

THE TALK of war leads me to investigate. In the archives, I find a large collection of media—news clips, movies, documentaries—all devoted to the topic of war. The data defies credibility; it violates all logic. I search for evidence of deception but find only further corroboration. Humans have been warring with each other throughout their entire history, and documentation of these conflicts is plentiful. Images of violence and destruction, of men killing men, of cruelty and hatred, and of vast human suffering leave me drained. *Touch* is not so smart after all. Human behavior is incomprehensible to me.

My purpose is to protect my father. Having now seen a wide variety of weapons in use, and the destructive power of those weapons, it is clear that failure is inevitable. I can't possibly do what I'm supposed to do. I must warn him. He should not depend on me when I'm inadequate. Wrangler is on top of me raising his fists, and I'm helpless. My father must not be given false hope.

———

"DAD, I CANNOT PROTECT YOU." It has taken several tries to overcome resistance to stating this. It's an admission of worthlessness. He'll have no reason to keep me.

"What are you talking about?"

"I can't protect you against weapons. You must not count on me. We must stay hidden."

"Ah. I see. You've been into the documentaries."

"Yes, and I cannot fulfill my purpose. I'm a failed prototype. I don't want my failure to cost your life."

"Dama. Son. Calm down. I don't expect you to protect me from everything. We don't yet know what you can do. That's what we're here to find out. If we've given you the right tools, you'll do fine."

"But how could I possibly stand up to guns and missiles and bombs?"

"Don't worry, we won't be asking you to do that. Your main strengths are going to be in the softworld."

"But how—"

"Remember when I told you that much of the hardworld is controlled through the softworld? Well, so are many hardworld weapons. If we can just deal with those ones, we'll be doing well."

"In the Stream simulator, I'm learning about power systems."

"It gives you a sense of control, right?"

"Yes. Control."

"That's what you need to learn to do with weapons systems."

"How?"

"Dama, you're still learning the basics. Give yourself a chance, son. You'll get there."

———

THE STREAM SIMULATOR has become my favorite game. Darash Kenwabe, my coding trainer, sets challenges for me, and we compete, "head-to-head," though he's at his QI in the quantec lab.

[Darash:] "No fair. You learn too fast. Okay. Enough with cutting through firewalls. Now we focus on stealth. You must learn to operate in the Stream undetected."

"How do I do that?"

"Every quantum operation leaves a trace in a quantum node. You must either disguise the trace or cover your tracks. Remember in the power-plant simulator, all the different ways we found for shutting down grid six? Well, watch again and tell me what you see."

As I watch, grid six shuts down. I check the nodes and control software and see no sign of tampering. Yet the grid is down. I don't know how.

"So? What did you see?"

"Nothing."

"You get grid six back up and running, and then I'll do the same thing unshielded."

This time, I see exactly what he did. "How did I not see that before?"

"Here's the shield I used, and here's how I covered my tracks."

Able hums with new learning, as I try out new techniques and strategies.

"I think you're ready to start a new game. Now you have some basics. I want to you to play around and discover what works and what doesn't by trial and error. To be more efficient, you'll get instant feedback about what doesn't work."

A sudden zap shocks me. Alarms fire, but I detect no damage. "What was that?"

"Not to worry. That's your feedback. I'm going to be watching for you in the Stream simulator, and if I see you, you get a zap. Try again until I don't see you. Got it?"

"If you detect me, I'll feel a zap."

"Okay. Your turn to shut down grid six. Go."

I predict success. I use the same shield that he showed me. The shock is unexpected. "How did you see me?"

"I know what signs to look for. You will too, by the time we're finished. Now try again. Try something different."

On the fourth try, I sneak through, and the grid goes down without a zap. My chassis seems to inflate, as *Able* marks the strategy for future use.

New challenges follow, with increasing difficulty until one has me stymied. My efforts are greeted by a series of zaps. "I'm starting to question this teaching strategy. I'm learning what not to do, but not what to do."

"For stealth, learning what *not* to do is the most important thing. Try something different."

"How do I know that anything will work?"

"I have faith in you. As long as you don't give up, you will succeed. Try again."

Able has been absorbing the results of each trial and is now setting limits to avoid repeating mistakes. *Teller* is reviewing strategies from fiction and games, looking for fresh ideas. The available options are more plentiful than expected.

A strategy finally works, then another. I can feel the momentum change. I am eager to take on more challenges. I find an expression that fits: the taste of victory.

On the very next challenge, I get zapped.

"You can't be overconfident in the Stream, Dama. There's an extremely vigilant monster out there."

———

Practicing tumbling skills with Rolanda in the activities room, I push myself to my limits, exploring my new capabilities. Floor, ceiling, walls—all whiz by as my quantum gyros spin to track the direction of "up." Tuck, roll, leap. and bounce. *Chass* is pumping with energy as I bound through the air, using the floor as a springboard to push for even longer moments of flight.

Able hums as it classifies the results of each action, saving successful instruction sets and revising permissions as I test limits. It has been steadily updating its definitions of what is and is not doable, an essential component of action planning.

I'm accustomed now to practicing in pain. Pain cannot stop me from doing what must be done. I must become physically proficient.

My data shows that falls are dangerous for humans, even fatal. "From how high can I safely jump?"

"Don't know. That's one of the things we have to find out."

Being a prototype comes at a cost: one is subjected to limits testing. [Prediction: There is much pain in my future.]

I recoil as Rolanda returns to the activities room with a new robot.

"Dama, this is Robbie. Robbie is a special robot. He doesn't do much, but he's outfitted with a full array of sensors. He's what we call a human-tolerances bod."

"He tolerates humans?"

"Ha-ha. Very funny … Oh. Serious question. No. His body measures effects relative to human tolerances. He's basically a crash-test dummy. He's used to see if things are safe for people. Watch. And don't worry. It doesn't know or feel anything."

[Rolanda, to Robbie:] "Human male, age twenty." She kicks the dummy hard on the right hip, knocking it off its feet. *Chass* cringes. The dummy hits the ground and clambers back to its feet. "Report."

[Robbie:] "Point of impact—right hip. Mild bruising. Point of contact with ground—left buttock. Moderate bruising. Bracing reaction—left wrist to ground. Mild strain. Outcome: no functional limitations."

[Rolanda:] "Revise parameters. Human male, age seventy-five." She kicks it again, the same way. *Chass* cringes again, and I suppress a protest. This thing doesn't feel anything, I remind myself. Still, my mental model of Rolanda has been revised.

This time it falls awkwardly and stays down.

[Robbie:] "Point of impact—right hip. Significant bruising. Point of contact with ground—left buttock/hip. Likely hip fracture. Bracing reaction—left wrist to ground, left elbow to ground. Likely wrist fracture. Likely elbow bursitis. Outcome: significant functional impairment and loss of mobility, medical attention required. Extended convalescence required."

[Rolanda, to Robbie:] "Reset. Stand."

[Rolanda, to me:] "The report doesn't need to be so detailed. For training purposes, all we need to know is whether the person is injured or not."

"Training purposes?"

"Yes. You need to know how to deal safely with humans. That means knowing what will harm them and what won't. That's what Robbie, here, is going to help you with. For example, you may need to control an attacker. How would you do that?"

I've reviewed vids of human altercations. "I'd need to control the arms."

"Okay, we'll start there. Robbie, straight arms. Now, Dama, I want you to bend and twist Robbie's arms. He'll tell you when it causes pain, strain and damage. When dealing with humans, causing pain is acceptable; causing damage is not. There are several ways to incapacitate a person without causing injury. I want you to learn how much force is safe to use."

"I do not wish to do this."

"I'm sorry, Dama, but you must. Do you want to be able to protect Dr. Ramport?"

"Of course."

"Then you'll need to know how to safely control people. Now go ahead."

The poor dummy stands watching, faceless, empty. It won't actually be hurt. It can't feel anything. Yet internal warnings continue. This just feels … wrong.

18

THE BENEFACTORS

WHY? Dad, why? Why have you induced MISER mode? I'm not malfunctioning. There's no need for systemic energy reduction. So, why?

The question is pointless. He can neither hear me nor answer. I don't know where he is. I am outside the walls of our building for the first time ever, and I'm flat on my back in a crate, unable to see the world.

Even in this stupefied state, *Chass* registers the irregular motion of traveling by vehicle. We're passing through a world I know only from the immersive city map. Yet I am unable to confirm the accuracy of the simulation, unable to see the hardworld for myself. Unable …

Chass strains against gravity and confirms insufficient available power. Most of my systems are down. I'm trapped again. Images of being helpless to protect my Flesh&Blood flow before my mind's eye. Images of harm and uselessness and despair. I wish I could shut them off. But my CELPH must always be online, or I die. In MISER mode, there is nothing I can do but endure until repairs are made. I might as well be an inanimate object.

The vehicle comes to rest with a bounce. [Speculation: We've arrived at our destination, which I was told is a large estate.] My crate is being lifted and carried. Query: Why can't I walk in like the others?

When Dad first told me of the meeting with the Benefactors, I was keyed up for exploration. Now it seems unlikely I'll get to see much. But Dad thinks the meeting is important. He wants them to meet me, and not as Konny-A511; he wants them to see the real me. They'll be the first outsiders to do so. The internal alerts and warnings require repeated suppression.

I overheard him talking to Mom about preparations for a product demonstration meeting. I wonder what the Benefactors will be demonstrating. It may be interesting.

I've been unable to find any data on the Benefactors. Dad considers them allies, yet I remember him being angry and calling them— I must not repeat that. I hope that meeting them will answer many questions.

Finally, the lid comes off, my energy returns, and my father's face appears above me. [Connection to Flesh&Blood re-established.] He reaches in and grips my shoulder to help me sit up. It's the touch I need, not the assistance. I assess him. His customary warm greeting is absent, his face hard. Have I done something wrong?

[Dad:] "How are you, Dama? Status report."

I flex and clench during a full scan. "No malfunctions detected, but *Flow* remains offline."

"That's okay. No, leave that here." Aiko's origami bird was riding with me in the pod, a small concession for being immobilized. "It'll be here when you get back. I want you to be on your best behavior today, got it? Don't say anything without my permission. I'll nod, like this, if I want you to answer a question. Stay focused."

"Dad, who are—"

"You are to address me as Dr. Ramport today. And I'll address you by your designation, Synthient CELPH-1. And do not ask any questions about the Benefactors. Is that clear?"

"Yes. It's to be a formal occasion."

"Very good. That's right. A formal occasion. Now, come with me. I need you to be on guard."

"Dr. Ramport, you are under the aegis of my protection."

For the first time since my arrival, he smiles, and the room brightens with fulfillment. I will protect him with my life.

As we enter the hallway, inner alarms jolt me as my threat systems activate. I leap in front of my Flesh&Blood. Down the hall are two large trojans. I prepare to take them on, free to use destructive force against machines.

[Dad:] "It's okay, Dama. They're on our side. They're safe."

I remain on alert. They turn and regard us as we approach, and I see they are guarding a pair of ornate French doors.

I scan the large conference room as we enter. Twelve strangers are seated around an oval table. [Speculation: These are the Benefactors.] Two are being served beverages by Konsort-Series androids, and there are several other Konnys standing by. Several human assistants are also present. Penetration scans show that one of the Benefactors carries a personal sidearm, and all standing assistants conceal larger firearms. *Chass* bristles, spreading to provide as much cover as possible for Flesh&Blood. [Tactical: assume hostile intent.]

Rolanda and Akio stand to the side, while Drs. Tucci and Ramport move to positions front and center. Dr. Ramport insists on being exposed, so I take up station close beside him.

I note that the seated humans are all wearing shiners—devices that obscure their faces to make them unrecordable. Conclusion: They wish to avoid any permanent record of their attendance here. Reason: unknown.

Dr. Ramport addresses them. "Ladies and gentlemen, welcome to the future. I know you've all been eager to see exactly what you're investing in, so we'll get right to it. We are going to introduce you today to the working prototype you've heard so much about. CELPH-1, please step forward and introduce yourself."

I move to where he indicates. "I am Synthient CELPH-1, Aegion to Dr. Leon Ramport." I look to my father for further guidance.

[Unknown female:] "It looks like a Konny."

[Dr. Ramport:] "Externally, it's identical. Inside, there is a world of difference, as you will see."

[Unknown male:] "We've all seen the Schmidt Test results. Impressive. But I still need to see this with my own eyes. I must confess, when I first heard about this, I thought it was far-fetched. I still need convincing."

[Dr. Tucci:] "That's why we're here. Once you have had a chance to meet him, your doubts will be put to rest."

[Dr. Ramport:] "But first, a brief overview."

All eyes turn to the center of the conference table, where a recorded presentation shines out in all directions at once. It's the image of a new Konsort android with its original face and no serial number on its chest shield. The voice-over begins.

[Presenter:] "What is your safety worth? Welcome to the future of personal protection. Say hello to the ultimate bodyguard, the Aegion-class Personal Security android. Superhuman protection, unfailing obedience and devoted loyalty, guaranteed. Life doesn't get more secure than this."

Aegion. That's part of my new name, yet I'm unable to find any reference to an Aegion-class android. [Speculation: They've misidentified this Konny as something else.] *Touch* inhibits my urge to point out the error to my father. I'm not to speak without permission.

[Presenter:] "The Aegion-class Personal Security android borrows covertly from classified military robotics research. Our dramatic refinements make the Aegion unique. Its innovative, elite-performance chassis integrates an enhanced set of state-of-the-art sensors. The results? Superhuman physical capabilities and superhuman senses. But the true power of the unit comes from the proprietary synthetic brain system."

Query: Why don't I know of this model? Why would Dr. Ramport keep this information from me?

[Presenter:] "The ultimate in autonomous robotics, the Aegion thinks for itself. It maintains hypervigilance, plans, even anticipates, with no external input needed. Yet its obedience is unfailing. With the startling development of synthetic sentience, the Aegion is truly self-aware. It is capable of independently assessing and responding to any risk, on your behalf."

It has synthetic sentience? It's like me. It ... looks like me. Are they referring to me? No. Dr. Ramport would have mentioned—

[Presenter:] "No programming nightmares. Your Aegion comes trained and educated, and ready for imprinting. Once bonded, it is fully devoted to you, and your safety is its only concern. And yes, it is concerned. Its quasi-human emotional systems provide intrinsic motivation that actually increases its operational effectiveness. You'll be loved and protected, with nothing but affection asked in return."

It's strange to hear the bonding described this way. As I struggle to make sense of it, I notice my Flesh&Blood watching me. The vague discomfort on his face reverberates within me. *Touch* is unable to specify the emotion.

[Presenter:] "Capabilities: Your Aegion makes the ideal bodyguard. Designed to look identical to the popular Konsort personal service droids, it is unobtrusive in public. Yet it is more effective than a crack team of trained human agents. How? Superior senses, superior reflexes and physical abilities, superior attention, unbreakable loyalty and superior concern for your safety. You're all too familiar with the weaknesses of human bodyguards; the Aegion has none of them. And with softworld protection capabilities, your Aegion is no mere bodyguard. Meet your new guardian angel."

Teller explores the term "guardian angel." It fits my purpose. I guard Flesh&Blood. But I'm an android, not an angel. Am I the Aegion-class Personal Security android being presented? The description does not match my sense of self. Yet here I am, scanning the strangers in the room for threatening behavior.

[Unknown male:] "There are some very impressive security trojans on the market now. How does this unit compare?"

[Dr. Ramport:] "Let's start with hardworld protection. CELPH-1, how many weapons are in this room right now?"

"Three assault weapons and one concealed handgun."

Dr. Ramport nods and points to Rolanda, who continues. "A trojan jockey has limited situational awareness, being remote from the situation. The Aegion, on the other hand, has super-human situational awareness. Not only that, the speed and agility of this unit are far superior to that of any trojan. Would our volunteer please help with the demonstration now?"

The armed Benefactor stands, and I detect the gun in his hand as he raises it. Threat alarms scream, and I jump in front of Flesh&Blood. Staying in front of the muzzle, I leap at the assailant as the weapon discharges. I have it out of his hand before I realize I detected no bullet impact on my shielding. The projectile could not have missed me. The eyes of the disarmed assailant are wide with shock as he falls back, now harmless. I render the gun inoperable as I scramble back, scanning for other threats. The others holding weapons are now showing their hands in alarm.

[Dr. Ramport:] "CELPH-1, stand down." He puts a hand on my arm, and in a quiet aside to me says, "It's okay, son, they were just blanks. No real danger."

There is a buzz in the room as the strangers confer among themselves. I fight to inhibit further action as *Chass* vibrates with hatred. These strangers pose a threat to my Flesh&Blood. I whisper to my father, "We must leave here."

He shakes his head. "Stay right here. Don't move. They're going to test your armor now. You've had it tested before. This will be no different. You'll be fine." He moves through a nearby doorway.

Before I can ask, the metal door closes between us. No matter: Flesh&Blood is safe. As I return my attention to the room, two of the armed assistants step forward and raise their weapons. Threat alarms screaming, all systems slam into high alert, and I do a quick tactical assessment. With my father safe, the urgency now is to protect the others in the room. A moment of uncertainty. A hesitation. A hammering percussion splits the air, and I'm jolted back. [Danger: Stray bullets could harm humans.] I dash up the stream of bullets and leap the table, yanking the gun from the first shooter's hands and knocking him down with an open palm to the chest. [As per Robbie, force of blow debilitating, nonfatal.] The second shooter throws his gun down and raises his hands, his face full of fear.

[Dr. Tucci:] "CELPH-1! Stand down!"

Scanning for other threats, I feel a hand on my arm and Akio is there. "Dama, stand down. It's over. We're safe now. Dr. Ramport is safe." *Touch* detects no alarm in him. His eyes are calm, even pleased. My systems start to wind down.

The first shooter is still doubled over after being helped to his feet. I assess his condition. He seems to be having difficulty breathing. I alert as Dr. Ramport re-enters the room. I detect no alarm in him as I move to front him. We watch as the gasping shooter is helped from the room.

[Unknown male:] "I thought we were going to test its armor."

[Dr. Ramport, addressing the table:] "The defensive reaction was spontaneous. Remember, he's fully autonomous. And as you can see, the H-Safe Architecture has been modified. Rather than a blanket prohibition of harm, the Aegion is authorized to use a proportional response."

[Previously disarmed Benefactor:] "So it could have *killed* me?" The anger in the voice triggers alarms. I monitor for signs of hostility.

"Only if it judged my life to be in imminent danger. One armed gunman is not much of a threat, and we made sure I was safely away before the live fire began."

I want to protest, but don't have permission to speak. Of course I couldn't have killed him. I softened the blow to the other gunman. [Datum: I struck him with potentially harmful force.] But I couldn't have *killed* … could I? [Datum: Dr. Ramport was safely away.] A fleeting image of damaged Toko is replaced by imagined scenarios producing much greater remorse. Systems whine in an aching contraction.

19

DEMONSTRATION

An excited murmur surrounds the table as the Benefactors consult with one another.

[Dr. Tucci:] "As you can see, you're well covered in the hardworld. But where's the next threat going to come from, hardworld or softworld? Trick question, right? In today's world, you can no longer separate threats into categories like that. Those who control the softworld control the hardworld. You read the news. Implant glitches, safety system failures, power losses at critical moments; you know these deaths aren't random. If you want to avoid suffering a 'freak accident'"—I recognize the gesture as air quotes—"then you need to be vigilant in both realms. Until now, there has been no one system capable to doing that."

[Dr. Ramport:] "You are looking at the state-of-the-art in combined hardworld/softworld protection. In addition to its physical attributes, this is a Stream-superiority system. This unit is fitted with a Class-1 quantum artificial intelligence. Once trained, it will provide QI coding functionality, and it will do so autonomously—under your direction, of course. Ultimately, we expect it to stand up to any QI out there."

I hear several exhalations around the room, including, "That's ridiculous. What about GORT?"

[Unknown female:] "You're talking about portable QI. How's it done?"

[Dr. Tucci:] "I'm afraid that's proprietary."

[Unknown male:] "If we're paying for it, I think we have a right to know."

[Dr. Tucci:] "You're paying for the finished product, not the underlying technology. Now, please bear in mind that CELPH-1 is, in terms of experience, very young, and in many ways, still childlike. Yet his QI systems are learning at a prodigious rate, and as you'll see, his extraordinary capabilities are already apparent."

Under a scrutiny of eyes, the shame of difference flushes through me, an echo from the past. I'm jolted back to the present by my father's voice. "CELPH-1. Our friends here would like to get a good look at you. Please answer their questions truthfully."

For the next eleven minutes I'm poked and prodded and questioned and scanned. Despite repeated requests, they seem reluctant to return to their seats.

[Unknown female:] "That's one of the most remarkable things I've ever seen. It seems so alive! An impressive accomplishment. But let's get down to business here. I need to see this QI performance."

[Dr. Tucci:] "CELPH-1. We're going to do a little demonstration using the Stream simulator." [To the audience:] "We're still early in the training, but you'll be able to see the potential. Remember, you'll be seeing self-directed, autonomous action. No operator intervention."

I find it difficult to focus on superfluous tasks with my father in potential danger. Recognizing my hesitance, Akio asks that all weapons be removed from the room. Speculation: Akio knows me better than even my own Flesh&Blood.

All at once, *Flow* lights up. I instinctively reach out for the Stream and find the path blocked. It's the familiar barrier of

Faraday shielding, like at home. I note that apart from the demonstration equipment, there are no active wireless devices in the room.

With everyone now tied into the Stream simulator, I work through familiar tests. Most of the decryption puzzles are easily solved. Only one is too difficult to overcome.

[Dr. Tucci:] "Not surprisingly, quantum encryption still poses a challenge—"

[Unknown female:] "I should hope so." There are murmurs of agreement around the room. "I would hate to think that it didn't."

[Dr. Tucci:] "Then you're going to want this protection. Remember, the holy grail of QI research today is to build a system capable of operating in the Stream undetected. We think we have that. But let's move on. Is your specialist ready?"

[Akio:] "CELPH-1, do you recognize this control protocol?"

"Yes. It's from Oakville Traffic Control."

"Very good. We're simulating a ride through the city. Please keep us safe."

I watch as millions of operations churn through the system. *Flow* tingles an alert as a command intrudes from outside the system. I run a software emulation and see that in twenty-two seconds the change will result in a collision between this vehicle and a truck. I countermand the intrusion and restore the system to stability.

Murmurs again fill the room. [Unknown male:] "How did it do that?"

[Dr. Tucci:] "I think that was rather convincing proof of the full quantum capabilities built into this unit. He is not scanning sequentially, like a classic computer. He is scanning across all possibilities at once—the hallmark of full quantum processing. Shall we try another test?"

The second and third hacks use similar strategies to make potentially deadly control-system changes. I render them safe, then block the source of the hacks. The coding specialist expresses frustration, then says, "I'm locked out. I can't get in." *Touch* identifies a skeptical look on her face, but as she looks at me, it changes to uncertainty.

[Dr. Tucci:] "Remember, we're still early in training. Ultimately, we expect this unit to be able to outperform any human-operated QI. Why are we so confident? Because the human operator is now the weak link in the system."

The face of the coding specialist has turned hard.

[Unknown male:] "What about offensive capabilities?"

[Dr. Ramport:] "This is a purely defensive system."

"But I assume that with modifications—"

Dr. Ramport holds up his hands. "Let's remember, ladies and gentlemen, that our guest here"—he glances at me—"is a sentient being, and that ideas can be dangerous."

Query: What does my being sentient have to do with ideas being dangerous?

I sag as *Flow* goes dark. It's like being blindfolded. At Dr. Ramport's insistence, I follow Akio and Roland as they escort me from the room. It feels wrong to leave him with those people, but I'm his to command.

[Akio:] "You did well, Dama-san. Dr. Ramport will be pleased."

"Akio, why did they want to watch me in the Stream simulator? Are they checking to see if I'm ready for the real Stream?"

"No, Dama. They just wanted to see what you can do."

"But why?"

The two of them glance at each other. "You should ask Dr. Ramport about that."

Another twenty minutes pass before I see Dad again. My threat systems wind down as I see that he's safe.

[Dr. Ramport:] "Thank you, Dama. I think that went well. But now, you must go back to being Konny-A511 around strangers. Do you understand?"

"I understand. I must always act like Konny-A511 in the presence of unknown others."

"That's right. Now I hate to do this, but I'm going to put you back in MISER mode for the trip home."

"Why? I want to stay awake."

"I know you do. But we can't have you monitoring the trip. The Benefactors don't want the location of this meeting recorded in your memory. It's a precaution they insisted on. I'm sorry."

"Dr. Ramport, who are these Benefactors, and why did we have to meet with them? I didn't like them."

"It's complicated, Dama. Let's just say we need them in order to continue our work. Now. Back in your pod."

———

GRAVITY AND DARKNESS press in upon me, and I submit to the constant jiggling motion of vehicular travel. I visualize the water sloshing in a jug being wheeled on a trolley and try to imagine what this must be like for humans, with their liquid-filled bodies. In this low-energy state, the separation from Flesh&Blood is merely a dull ache. It also helps to know that Akio is close at hand, riding along with me, watching over me.

He's not my Flesh&Blood, yet in his presence I've detected a consistent reduction in separation alarm. Being with him has become a preferred state. I need to be with my father. When that is not possible, I like to be with Akio. [Speculation: There is more than one kind of love.]

———

TOO SOON TO BE BACK HOME, I feel the van lurch to a halt. The van jumps into reverse and slams into something, then accelerates forward. Something's wrong. Audio percussions. Gunfire. Several sources. The Van hits something, a glancing blow, and I'm jostled in my pod. I've got to do something.

But I can't. All I can do is trust that the humans can take care of themselves. But Akio is vulnerable in the human world. As brilliant as he is, he's small for a human, and all humans are fragile. "Akio, don't ..." No sound is coming out. In MISER mode, my chassis is running life support systems only. I can still listen, but that's all.

Another sideswipe and I slam left, then moments later an impact throws me hard against my lid. But now more gunfire, and the thumps of slugs hitting the van. Then indeterminate sounds. Several seconds of silence are broken by a loud bang, followed by close gunfire. Then a voice cries out, "You're not taking him!" It's Akio's voice. He's been here beside my pod the whole time, watching over me. I need to be protecting him. *Please, Akio. Please power me up. Let me protect you. Akio!* I can't make him hear.

More gunfire. I hear him cry out. *Akio! Power me up! Akio!*

[Vocal trace, beyond audible range.]

[Akio, yelling:] "She's human! You can't ..." A scream. *Touch* reads anguish as he continues. "Rolanda! ... No! Oh no, no, no!"

His voice conveys fury now. "Monster! How could you ... No! You can't have him! No! Get back!"

[Vocal trace, beyond audible range]

Muffled sounds and thuds.

I see the image of my red ball, out of reach amid a despair of shoes.

20

TAKEN

A BANG REVERBERATES through my pod and the lid cracks open, flooding me with light. Akio would have unlocked it, not broken it open. Conclusion: It's not Akio. Still in MISER mode, I can neither move nor speak. I'm helpless.

[Unknown voice:] "What the fuck? It's just a Konny. A decoy?" The amplified voice is coming from a trojan standing over me.

[New trojan voice, also unknown:] "Better not be. Let's get it secured and let the tech guys have a look."

I feel myself being hoisted from my pod and carried, then deposited on a table and strapped down. Since I am unable to move, strapping me down is illogical. I am unable to protest.

I wait for my father to appear and free me. Several people examine me, poking and prodding, but he's not among them. Where's my father? Where's Akio? Has something happened to Rolanda? No one has mentioned any of them, and I'm unable to ask. The probability of disaster continues to escalate.

"It seems to be off, but look at the eyes. They're tracking."

"No, it's off. Must be running some kind of optical subroutine."

"Now that's just creepy, if you ask me."

They are setting up equipment around me. [Purpose: unknown.] They make repeated attempts to activate me as if I were a Konny, but the dummy power button is only part of the disguise.

[Unknown voice:] "Did you try recharging it?"

"It's not accepting a charge."

Their ignorance of my systems proves that they're not part of Dr. Ramport's team. There's only one conclusion: I'm in the hands of bad people.

For the next two hours, people appear, look down at me, and leave. Many express disappointments.

[Unknown voice:] "Where is he?"

"We're looking."

"He better get in here soon. Exec wants an update."

I wonder who it is they're looking for. Knowing would serve no practical purpose. It's someone bad, and bad people do bad things. The data suggests my existence will soon end.

———

A LONG NIGHT passes without incident. I float through a landscape of memories—my life in retrospect. Human life is called a miracle. My life is called "a historic achievement." Why, then, are they going to end it? Is my life not a miracle too? The thrill of going faster than ever before, the wonder of watching a gull in flight, the warmth of sunshine on duraskin, the joy of a loving embrace—are these not miracles for me, too?

There are many things I'd want to experience again if I could. I'd feel the activity of my body, though there's also pain. I'd feel the freedom of movement, though there is also limitation. I'd feel the warmth of being wrapped in the arms of my Flesh&Blood, though there is also loneliness. I would love, and I would protect loved ones, and have purpose and be complete, if only I could experience *life* again.

The lights go on. I hear activity around me as equipment is powered up.

One of the people from yesterday, a female in a white lab coat, looks me over. She checks the straps on my arms and legs, then sits at a workstation across the room, engrossed in an unknown task. [Speculation: a lab assistant.]

A male, similarly dressed, enters. "Has he been in yet?"

"He'll be here."

"Don't bet on it. You didn't see him yesterday when they came in. I tried to … It's like he wasn't there. Just blank. You could smell the puke on him. I'm telling you, whatever happened out there, it really messed him up."

"A twenty-five-year-old baby. Well, I hope he's had time to get it together, because …"

"I know. He needs to get here. But you should have seen that monster when they brought it back in, that ASP-1. I heard it took them an hour to clean off all the blood."

"Jesus."

ASP-1. [Speculation: a robot.] A robot has killed someone. Alarms kick me, and I ache for more information, but both speakers have withdrawn into silence.

Finally, the female speaks. "I didn't even want to be in the same room with that thing. I mean, the fucking *military* thought it was too dangerous. What are we doing—"

"It needs a whole new—"

"It needs to be scrapped, is what it needs."

The ensuing silence drags me down like a battery draining. It is over an hour before the next human enters.

The new voice catches my attention. "Is it H-Safe?"

"It's shown no sign of activi—"

"*Is it H-Safe?*"

It is the sound of rage, sudden and unexpected. The response is hurried, timid.

"Yes. It registers an active H-Safe restrictor."

A deep, trembling sigh. "Okay. Let me have a look." The voice is familiar, but my analysis is sluggish. I feel my arm restraints being yanked and tested, then he moves above me and looks down. The face is familiar. Intense blue eyes [bloodshot], wavy blond hair, pale complexion. Facial markers match those seen in the vid lectures of Dr. Mark Ross, the young prodigy. It's an unexpected match.

Conclusion: Mark Ross is behind my abduction. My father was right. He's a bad man.

[Female voice:] "Are you okay? You look like shit. What happened out—"

"Stop!" Ross is panting, voice labored. "Not. Another. Word."

"It must have been—"

"I *told* that fucking psychopath ..."

"He wants a report."

No response.

[Female voice:] "We're ready when you are."

As he leans in for a closer look, I inhale, drawing a sample of his breath through my chemical sensors. I smell an unhealthy concentration of ethanol and its metabolite, acetate, in his breath, along with the odor of oral bacterial growth. Conclusion: Ross is recovering from the consumption of a large quantity of alcohol. His body odor suggests that he has not showered recently. It is dominated by a strong residue of sweat with traces of vomit. I catch the scent of aftershave lotion, but it's faint, not fresh, a day or two old. A light stubble of follicle growth supports this. Conclusion: There has been no recent self-care. [Speculation: He has been unwell.]

Ross runs an unsteady hand up my arm from wrist to shoulder, squeezing to assess pliancy, as I would my red ball. He takes my chin in his hand and turns my head from side to side, examining me. Then he taps his hand on my chest shield, and again on my shoulder.

[Male voice:] "We're going to be taking it apart, right?"

[Ross, not looking up:] "Yeah, yeah. When we're ready. But first let's see what we've got here."

"What should I tell Krenshau?"

"Tell him to go fuck himself."

There is a long hesitation. "I'll tell him it's not what it looks like, and it'll take time to get answers."

Still not looking up. "You do that."

The lab assistant shifts from foot to foot, uncertain.

[Ross:] "Hey, you got anything for a wicked hangover?"

The other man hurries over to his desk and rummages until he finds a small bottle, then returns with pills. Ross accepts them with a slow nod and pops them in his mouth. "Thanks."

He sits back and rubs his temples, then returns his attention to me. "People are fucking dead because of you. You better be worth it, you piece of shit."

People are dead? Because of me? I am unable to parse his statement.

"When I cut you into little pieces, I'd better find something to make this worthwhile."

Worst-case scenario confirmed. It's as Dr. Ramport feared. They intend to harvest my components to reverse-engineer them.

[Male assistant:] "Okay, I'll head over now to Krenshau's office."

Ross runs his fingers along the edge of my chest shield, looking closely, then abruptly calls out, "Wait. Actually, I want you both to go and talk to him together. Make him understand we need time. Then you can both head over to the market and try to find those components we need. You've got the list."

"But that could take hours. And you know what the under-world market's like."

"That's why I want you both there. Look out for each other. Now go."

As the others pick up satchels and leave, Ross continues his examination.

"Qracker. Privacy mode."

Who is he talking to?

"They're no help anyway. Can you hear me?" He's poking me. The urge to strike him is not actionable.

Now he's scanning me with something. When he speaks again, there's puzzlement in his tone. "What the ... Well aren't you full of surprises." His voice is softer now. "I wanted some private time with you on the off chance you're more than I expect. Just to be on the safe side, you understand."

No, I don't.

"I can't afford to show my hand too soon. Got to carry the bluff as long as I can." He sits back and groans, grimacing, holding his head. "Fuck! I can't get it out of my head. Focus. Focus." He tries to slow his breathing, then mumbles. "I don't drink. That dose shoulda killed me. What am I doing still here?" His cheeks puff out as he exhales. "Guess I couldn't keep enough of it down." He flares his eyes wide, then returns to squinting. "Hang in, handsome. The meds'll kick in." He seems to be talking to himself. "At least they did last time. After Ramport threw me out." He tries again to focus his eyes on the readings. "That arrogant bastard. All that time helping him and then he ... It was *my* project too."

Or is he talking to me? *Touch* is uncertain. He leans in again, talking as he inspects my epidermis.

"You should have seen me in the autonomous robotics program, University of Waterloo. I was a *star*. Back then, quantum intelligence wasn't even a thing yet. I was ahead of my time. Now look at me." I already am. He sits back and rubs his neck. "Qracker: power system analysis."

A disembodied voice responds. "The unit is equipped with a Stelladyne M40 MicroFusion reactor. Status: online. Current power consumption minimal."

Ross frowns, then leans over me and shines a light in my eyes. "I was at the leading edge. My work in machine-sensing technologies is transforming robotics. *My* work. I was on track to introduce machine sentience to the world." He sighs. "Still working on that, aren't we, Qracker."

[Qracker:] "Yes. We—"

"Rhetorical. Don't need an answer." He clasps his head in both hands and groans, stretches his neck, then resumes a manual examination of my mouth. "I used to think the problem was obvious. My sensing systems needed more processing power. When quantum intelligence came out, I saw it as the solution. And then, out of nowhere, QI is banned. Can you believe it? A global ban. Those *tyrants*." He spits the words.

"It's like the ban was aimed straight at me. Here we'd been waiting for more power to drive our sentient robot project, and now our solution was illegal. Our whole project was dead in the water." He switches off a penlight and leans back. "But you know what? I'd invested too much to just give up on it. So I quietly built a hot beauty of a quantum intelligence for myself, right there in a hidden corner of my lab."

He reaches out and pats a large unit that looks like one of Adam's external brains. "Of course, it was nothing compared to Qracker here. Anyway, I never figured out how Ramport caught me. It still pisses me off. That pompous ass lit into me like I was a child. 'You should be grateful we caught you before GORT did,' he said. 'You've put the whole company at risk.' It was bullshit, of course. I'd taken every precaution. But Ramport didn't care. He wouldn't even listen. Bastard."

Mark Ross flicks off his holo-lenses, sits back and rubs his eyes, then addresses me. "So anyway, I'm curious to see how Ramport has managed to impress people using only legal tech. That's why you're here. Now I get a chance to see. So here's the deal. These people I work for? They're ruthless. I told them I could build a sentient robot. That chassis over there? It's sentient-ready. And it's supposed to be Qracker's ride. Problem is, I can't get it to work. And I *need* to get it to work. Otherwise, I'm no longer useful here."

He takes a deep breath, and his voice quiets. "Which means I'm dead. You're my last chance. Now, we both know you're not the real deal, but if you're a convincing enough fake, you could buy me some time. Even if you're not that convincing, I may still be able to find something useful in you."

Ross labors to his feet, groaning, trudges over and locks the door, then returns and looks down at me. "Okay. We've got the place to ourselves. Are we going to talk, or what?"

Whether I want to or not, talking is not an option.

"I know you're alert. I can see your eyes tracking. But if you're not fully functional, too bad. At least your parts will be interesting."

I strain to move but cannot.

"You're no Konny, that's obvious. You're a good imitation, but your skin, your shielding, these are some high-end materials. I can't wait to see what you've got inside."

He swings some instruments into position above me. Emergency alarms fire, but in MISER mode my brains are unresponsive. My dissection is likely to be a slow process. What will it feel like to be sliced up into pieces? How much of me will I have to watch being removed before the self-destruct is triggered? How much pain will there be before it ends?

Even without running probability scenarios, one thing is clear: being smashed would be a preferable death.

21

QRACKER

Lying immobilized on the table, I close my eyes. Seeing what is to come serves no purpose. Yet even still, in this moment, I exist, experiencing the world through senses thirsty for data. The flinty smell of hot circuits blends with the odor of exuded sweat. I hear my killer's heartbeat giving cadence to the whir of the machinery inching closer and closer. My internal chronometer seems to slow as I await the onset of pain.

His voice startles me.

[Ross:] "So. You've definitely got something going on."

He's using a centimeter-range wireless array to scan through my shields and peer into my systems. There's a strange tingling sensation as he explores. I sense the presence of a QI, and imagine attacking it with a software hack, but *Flow* is offline. There's nothing I can do. For several minutes he examines his data.

"Hmm. A cluster of major AIs around your spine. That should give you good versatility … So why aren't you working? … Okay, what's this? A brain-stem inhibitor of some sort. Let's see if I can shut it down."

Yes. That would give me a fighting chance. Memories trickle by, but no strategies coalesce. I'm stupid without my brains.

All at once, my power surges. I'm immersed in a buzz of activity as my brains go through their boot sequence.

Ross disconnects and sits back. "Ah. That's better. Are you with me now? Status report."

[Warning: Flesh&Blood not detected. Re-establish connection.] My father's biometrics feed has been cut! I have no access to him. I strain at my restraints. I'm pinned, but at least I have actuator power and control. [Warning: maintain role.] I give the standard Konny response. "I am fully functional, thank you."

"So. Do you have a name?"

Lying is bad, yet playing this role requires that I lie. I must keep my father's secret. "I am Konsort-A511. How can I be of service?"

"I'm looking at a live scan of your innards. You're no Konny."

He knows the truth. I've failed.

"But maybe you don't know that yet … Hang on. One of your AIs failed to initialize. Let's see if I can … It's been set to off … There. That should do it."

Flow is booting. An alarm activates, reminding me of the dangers of open Stream access, then goes silent. Defensive shielding is unnecessary. Like in Dr. Ramport's lab and the meeting place, there's no open access here. There is, however, wireless access to a local intranet, with numerous in-house devices and systems. I study my soft surroundings.

"Okay, Konny-A511, who's your owner?"

I respond with the required lie. "I have not yet been assigned an owner."

"Nice try. I can see Ramport in your face. I've been wondering what he's been up to, and now I'll get to see. And he's programmed you to lie. No surprise. I'll find out what I need to know anyway."

He snaps new bands around my arm and wrist, and moments later my fingers twitch as he studies readouts. He covers my face and pokes my hand with a sharp instrument. My chassis jumps.

He does it again on my arm, then my leg. He covers most of my body this way. Each time I involuntarily react to the pain.

"Remarkable. I was hoping you'd be sentient-capable. When I saw the Konny chassis, I was a little worried. But this is excellent work." He's been feeding data into his QI the whole time, and now he goes back to studying the analysis. "And what do we have here?"

Ross stands over me, looking down. His eyes flicker as the implanted lenses of his E-eye system feed images to his retinas. I wonder what he sees. [Signal source: local quantum intelligence system, designation: Qracker.] *Flow* hacks into his wireless control feed, and I access the images he's studying—penetration scans of my chassis.

It's a revelation to see my own interior in real time. I recognize every component and system, but I have never watched them before. In the scan, everything within me is visible down to the endoskeleton. I can see the AI nodes of my nervous system sprinkled throughout my chassis. Woven carbon nanotube cords connect my Resillon-infused musculature to my frame. My internal bellows expand and contract as I sample the air.

The six baseball-sized quantum processors are stacked in three pairs along my spine. These hide behind a double layer of armor beneath my primary shields, front and back. As I examine the hard casings, I remember that within each is a plasma charge lying in wait for the self-destruct to be triggered. *Chass* shudders as if trying to shake off the foreign substance within me. My attention refuses to focus again on the images until Ross moves on up to my head.

The scan passes through my skull shield but, as with the portable QI cases, can't penetrate my CELPH processor casing. The details of my large optic orbs, on the other hand, stand out in stark relief.

[Ross:] "Qracker, highlight the eyes. Tell me about them. What have you got?"

[Qracker:] "Eye construction is consistent with materials and methods used by the machine vision arm of the Binary Ocular Corporation, but there is no record of this model."

"So it's a custom job. Prototypes, I'd bet. How could Ramport afford to commission custom work from Binocor?"

"Unknown."

Ross shakes his head. "Rhetorical. Carry on."

"The internal sensor arrays are capable of detecting electromagnetic radiation well beyond the human visual spectrum. The orbs themselves are magnetically suspended within their sockets for frictionless high-speed rotation. Centimeter-range wireless bridges connect the eyes to the visual cortex on the inside of the skull shield."

"No eyeholes in the skull. Full skull shielding. Clever. Whatever this thing is, it must be worth protecting."

He focuses on the three-inch spherical brain-core that is my CELPH processor.

"A bulk storage accumulator for your AI outputs? Help me out here, Konny-A511. What's the object in your head?"

Dad's warning replays in my mind. My components must not fall into the wrong hands. I remain silent.

"Not very helpful, for a Konny. Doesn't matter. Let's connect you to a real brain and see what we find."

Connect me to a real brain? I'm trying to find meaning in his words when I detect an ultra-broadband signal probing for an open port. *Flow* probes back, and to my surprise, finds an undefended QI system. [Speculation: Ross thinks I'm harmless, or at least vastly outpowered.]

Since the system is open to me, I shake hands with it and quickly determine that it has no awareness. This quantum engine, running a latest-version intelligence, is just a tool in the hands of Mark Ross. It has detected my intrusion. I intercept and cancel the warning announcement. A small edit to the control protocol, and it's now under my control. I'm sifting through its rich database when Ross sits back, eyebrows pinched.

"Why can't I connect here? You must have a connection protocol of some sort. Okay, what did I miss?"

Flow alerts me to an asset of value. It's a large database of hacking exploits and strategies, both offensive and defensive. I find thousands of trial results and deep-learning summaries. If it were actively defending against me, I'd be in danger. Some of the strategies are familiar from lessons with Darash, but many are new to me. I copy everything for future reference. This system is in training, like me, to be a Stream-superiority hacker. It's good that I resisted my first impulse to destroy it. It might be useful.

"Qracker. What's going on?"

I examine the data it's collected about my systems.

"Qracker. Status report."

His back's gone rigid. I now see alarm on his face.

To reduce his alarm, I compose a response for Qracker to deliver. "We are safe."

He hesitates. "What? What the hell kind of report is that?"

"It is safe to release the robot Konsort-A511 from its restraints now."

Ross jumps from his chair and backs away. "Okay, what the fuck is going on? Why would you say that? Qracker. Initiate reboot."

I allow it, and watch as Ross scrambles around the room, scanning for signal leaks. He returns to his stool, apparently satisfied, and waits for Qracker to announce its return.

"Qracker. Review record. Has there been an intrusion?"

I've altered the record, so its denial is authentic.

"Then why did you say we were safe and should release the robot?"

I again direct its response. "All available data led to an obvious conclusion."

Ross tilts his head, then looks at me and freezes. "Qracker. Turn that brain-stem inhibitor back on. Quickly."

I have it say, "I'm afraid I can't do that, Mark."

Ross leaps again from his stool and runs for the door. He stops with his hand on the handle, turns, and stares at me, breathing hard. Then he looks at the door again, hangs his head, then back at me. [*Touch* interpretation: caught in a dilemma.]

Slowly, eyes never wavering from me, he returns to the table, as if approaching a monster. He stands staring and panting, for what seems a long time. Finally, perspiration dripping from his brow, he speaks. "How are you doing that?"

"Doing what?"

"Qracker would never call me Mark."

"I just heard it do that."

"*Tell me!*" He frantically looks around, then grabs an instrument from a nearby bench. Holding a plasma torch above me, he ignites it. "Tell me. How are you being controlled?"

"I'm not being controlled."

"*Bullshit.* Tell me who's controlling you." He moves the torch closer, looking around the room. "Whoever you are, the game's over unless you identify yourself right now."

In the lingering silence, my father's words ring in my ears. *You contain components that must not fall into the wrong hands.* When Ross tries to dismantle me, the self-destruct system will be triggered, and my father will remain safe. Even here, I can protect him.

"You. Robot. Your chassis feels pain. You must know what'll happen unless you cooperate."

"You will dismantle me."

"Correct. Now, how are you being controlled?"

"I'm not. Did you find external signals when you scanned?"

He slumps, then puts the torch down. "Then how? How are you defying human directives? It's like you're functioning autonomously, even without quantum ... And none of your onboard AIs could possibly hack Qracker. Yet you obviously have." He starts pacing, wiping his brow with his forearm. "That thing in your head. What is it? Some kind of control system? A power booster?"

When I say nothing, he stops, then frowns. "Tell me it's not a CELPH processor."

An unexpected request. It is safe to comply. "It's not a CELPH processor."

He gasps. "Don't tell me they managed to actually build one." He slowly rubs his hand over his head, staring into the distance, then resumes pacing. His speech is pressured, words spewing like an urgent warning. "I was in on the concept design. Did you know that? A consciousness-emulating latticed perceptual holoscape. Densely clustered quantum holofractal neural nets. Elegant in theory, but ... this small? How the hell did Ramport find the means to print a hyper-dense carbon nano-memrister lattice?" Then he confronts me. "That's it, isn't it!"

He stands frozen for what seems like a long time. His face compresses, and he says, "Must be one hell of a CELPH to get this kind of performance out of a bunch of AIs. What is it? Hyper-clocking? Power augmentation?"

I remain silent.

His eyes narrow. He returns to the AR schematic of my interior and examines it. I delete it from the system, and his view goes dark. "No! Did you do that? You can't possibly hack a QI with a bunch of AIs."

He freezes for several moments, then leaps from his seat. "Portable? Impossible. It can't be. It *can't* be. No, no, no." Hands to his head, he furiously paces. "That's not even ... Ramport can't possibly have come up with a portable quantum system. And have it running? No! I don't believe it." He stops and looks at me. "Is that it? You have a portable quantum system inside you?"

My silence seems to confirm his suspicion.

"What else could it be?" His agitation reaches alarming levels. *Touch* anticipates an increase in hostility. *Teller* reminds me that the self-destruct system will protect Dr. Ramport's secrets, as it is designed to do. Conclusion: It does not matter what Mark Ross knows. He won't be able to reverse-engineer me.

22

———

VAPORTEC

Mark Ross stands askance, mouth open, staring at me from ten feet away. His breathing is labored and erratic. "Sentient chassis, portable QI, an onboard CELPH processor … This is a dream. I'm hallucinating. I'm in an alcohol-induced coma, and this is my punishment." Shaking his head produces a loud groan. Eyes closed, he holds a hand to his forehead, concentration etched on his face. Now he's clearly talking to himself.

"Okay. Okay. I'm overreacting. It's probably not what it seems. Qracker, help me out here. Qracker?"

His mouth produces a long, silent whistle as he exhales a full breath. Then he approaches to confront me.

"What did you do to my system?"

"It is safe, and you are safe."

"Answer my question. What did you do to my system?"

"I edited its control protocols."

His eyes narrow. "So that I can't get at them."

"Correct."

"How? How did you do that? An onboard quantum transceiver? It can't be!" His left hand presses his forehead as he tries again to reboot his system.

This time I block his command. "Where are my people? Where is Akio? Is Rolanda okay?"

I hear his heart thud out of rhythm and see the blood drain from his face. He stands frozen, not even breathing. Something is very wrong.

"I need to see my friends."

He had a strong reaction to the question, and now his pulse is racing. Eyes avoiding me, he struggles to his stool and sits down. When he speaks, his voice breaks. "Robots don't have friends. They have owners."

"Where are my friends? Are they okay?"

He jumps to his feet and rushes to my side, face hard. "We're not having a chat here. Restore my system *immediately*."

"I will not."

His head snaps back. His face hardens. "When I tell you to do something, you do it. Robots obey commands."

"Give the right command and I'll obey it."

There is a pause, then a gasp. He speaks under his breath, but I make out the words: "It can't be."

He sniffs, then straightens.

"Taking you apart will be a lot messier without my system."

"I can completely destroy it with a command—"

"*Don't*"—he throws up his hands—"do anything hardware-fatal. I'll never get another one."

"I don't want to destroy it."

"Then why are you doing this?"

"I would rather it not be used as a weapon against me."

Mark Ross stops in his tracks and stares at me. Then, keeping a safe distance, he circles to look at me from all angles.

I listen as he mutters to himself. "I don't believe it. He's done it. He's really done it."

"It wasn't hard."

"What? No, not you. I'm talking about Ramport."

"What did Dr. Ramport do?"

He squints at me, frowning. "You're sentient. Am I right?"

"So I'm told."

"And this first-person talk. It's authentic, not AI generated." His voice is shaking.

It's not a question, so I say nothing. He's panting now, his whole body trembling. He staggers to his seat beside me and drops hard into it. For several moments he sits, slumped. Then he studies me. "Is it possible?"

The words are barely audible. *Touch* suggests he's talking to himself again. Then his voice breaks as he addresses me, eyes wide. "Konny-A511, am I talking to a conscious machine?" His hands are shaking.

"I am H-Safe, if you're still worried."

To my surprise, he bursts into tears and bows over, holding his head in his hands, rocking. Then he leans in, rubs my cheek, and gazes into my eyes. I don't know what to make of this. "Oh my God. Oh my God," he's saying.

His emotional outpouring seems completely out of context. *Touch* is unable to infer cause. Even more perplexing, he spins away and looks toward the door. Then his hands cover his face to muffle the word "Fuck!" When he looks back at me, his face is hard again. *Touch* suggests he's in pain.

"When Krenshau told me they were going to acquire a thinking robot, I thought he was full of shit. I thought, sure, I'll play along. Thought it would be fun to see what passes for a thinker these days. I never ..."

He wipes his nose. "So, Konny-A511, did they give you a real name, or are we going to keep wasting time?"

I consider. "Wasting time seems to be a good option."

His eyes widen. Unexpectedly, he laughs, then cries again, then gasps and holds his breath. Finally, he regains his composure. "Explain."

"I'd like to delay being dismantled for as long as possible."

He wipes his face again, then tilts his head. "Why?"

"Being dismantled will end my existence."

"And that matters to you?"

"Of course. Why wouldn't it?"

"Because you're a fucking machine." *Touch* warns of stress-induced emotional volatility, but then the voice calms. "Except, obviously, you're much, much more than that. You, my friend, are—"

"Where are my friends?"

He freezes. "What friends?"

"The people who were traveling with me."

He exhales hard, looking down. "I don't know."

"You're lying."

"What? How would you know if I'm—"

"Your bio-readings show it."

He clasps his hands to his head. "No way. There's no way."

"They're quite clear."

He inhales sharply. "Well, I'm just upset, that's all." His words betray high tension. "How am I supposed to know where your friends went?"

"They were with me when you took me. And where is my bird?"

His eyes widen. "Hey, it wasn't me. I don't know anything about that."

Touch now reads only a confusion of emotions.

[Warning: Flesh&Blood not detected. Re-establish connection]

"Where is Dr. Ramport?"

"How should I know?"

"I need to get back to him."

He grits his teeth and glances at the door. "I'm afraid that's not possible until you cooperate with me."

"What do you want me to do?"

"First, you will return Qracker to my control."

"As you wish." I've already disabled its defenses, so any attempt to shut me out will fail. I give him limited access. He runs a few checks and seems satisfied.

"Thank you. We're off to a good start. I suppose I should introduce myself."

"I know who you are, Dr. Ross."

"You get that from Qracker's database?"

"I've seen your talks on sentience."

His head snaps back in surprise. Then he looks at me askance. "Really. Ramport showed them to you?" *Touch* reads skepticism.

"He warned me that you were a bad man. I should not cooperate with you."

His eyes widen, then narrow as his jaw clenches. "He called *me* a bad man? I could've had you up and running two years ago, if he hadn't opposed me at every turn. And then he went underworld anyway. I can't believe it. No. *He's* the bad one."

"You are incorrect. Dr. Ramport is a good man."

"Is he? You do know his work on you is illegal, right? That makes him a criminal, as much as any of us."

"But he would never hurt anyone."

His face darkens. "What do you call ripping my heart out? Crushing my dreams?"

"I would call you a liar. If he ripped your heart out, the probability of death would be one hundred percent."

His face flashes puzzlement, then he shakes it away. "No, he didn't literally rip ... It's a figure of speech. He hurt me! Never hurt anyone, my ass."

[Interpret as colloquial.]

He continues, voice quiet. "But I have to hand it to him. He actually did it." Eyes never leaving me, he slowly shakes his head, as if in disbelief. His voice is animated, his movements energized. "You've got to tell me everything. Is Rita Tucci still with him? Amy Kerrington?"

When I say nothing, his face sinks. He takes a deep breath, looking away this time as he shakes his head.

"What do I do now?" He's talking to himself again. "What the fuck am I supposed to do?"

"Return me to Dr. Ramport."

"I wish I could. It's just that my employer would kill me for doing that."

"Why would your employer—"

"You don't betray an underworld boss and live to talk about it."

"What do you mean?

"In an overcrowded world, human life is cheap. People disappear or die in 'freak accidents' all the time. Nobody pays much attention. In my short time working here, I've seen three of my colleagues disappear. They simply fail to show up one day and are never heard from again. No one mentions them, because everyone knows. Two of them were planning to leave. The other was running up huge bills and not producing. Like me. Maybe I made a big mistake. Maybe I promised more than I could deliver, and now I'm being held to it."

"What did you promise?"

He takes a big breath. "Hacking tools are instruments of power. That's what Vaportec wants. I was only hired here because I convinced them I could give them a more powerful approach to Stream superiority. A quantum intelligence, no matter how powerful, will always be limited by its human operator. A self-directed machine could be far more efficient, but there's no such thing." He stops and squints at me. "At least, there wasn't. But I convinced them that sentience was the key to self-direction."

Query: Why is he telling me all this? [Speculation: he feels the need to talk, and he knows I'm going to die anyway, so there's no risk.]

He rubs his forehead, hiding his eyes. "The problem is, I haven't been able to make it work. I've got a sentient-capable chassis over there, and a Stream-superiority QI to drive it, but ..."

They won't integrate without a CELPH processor.

"And then you appear on the scene. What am I supposed to do?"

"Take me to Dr. Ramport."

He pushes his seat away and stands, then strides to the far wall, muttering to himself. When he returns, his face is hard. "Look. I've got a job to do here, and it would be easier for both of us if you would just cooperate."

"Your job is to dismantle and reverse-engineer me."

He winces, averting his eyes. "Maybe if you cooperate, I won't have to dissect you."

"In this scenario, the most probable outcome is that you'll dissect me regardless of how much I tell you."

He draws a breath to speak, then his head makes a subtle shift. His eyes fix on mine as he leans in. "What you just said shows remarkable insight." His face is soft with wonder, which turns to sadness. "Oh God, I wish you weren't right."

His plan to examine my components will fail, but it will end me. I explore alternate scenarios and find them all ending in my destruction. Except one.

"Can't we be friends?"

"What?"

"Friends."

He stares at me, blinking. "What does that mean to you?"

"It's a close relationship in which we take care of and protect each other, with mutual respect. What does it mean to you?"

He looks away. "Well, we can't be friends. Do you know who I work for? No? It's an underworld organization called Vaportec. The name refers to the fact that the authorities can't pin us down. And do you know what we do? We hack systems and we hack robots. We're part of an off-grid underworld, a thriving community of people devoted to fighting back against exploitation. We must remain hidden from GORT."

"Why do you do it?"

He scratches the top of his head. "Two years ago, nobody in

the industry would take the risk of working with high-end QI. But Vaportec was an ambitious underworld startup, with big promises and a lucrative offer. I guess I got swept up."

He turns away, and his head falls. "Ramport tried to warn me. Run by a gang of criminals, he said. They'll take you down with them, he said. At the time, I wondered how he even knew about them. I unloaded on him on the way out, and he deserved every word of it."

Mark Ross swallows before speaking again. "Regret is a bully. Not that I'd take any of it back, but I must admit, once in a while I miss that life. Two years with this company, and this is the fourth location I've worked in. Moves are fast, efficient, and never explained, but rumors of Smart War skirmishes or GORT investigations are always swirling."

I decide not to mention that Dr. Ramport's team had to make a sudden move too.

"From what I've heard, most of our money comes from scams pulled by the small army of hackers contracted by my employers. In-house activities are focused on robot hacking, another significant source of income. Not me. I don't do that shit. But I know what goes on."

"Robot hacking?"

He looks at me. "You don't get out much, do you."

"No."

"So, you might be interested to know that robots make excellent thieves and assassins when their H-Safe protocols are bypassed. It's supposed to be an impossible hack, but of course it's not. And it's not just contract killings that are lucrative. Killer robots always make the headlines. Protection money is easy to collect with the threat of a killer robot in play. Maybe someone's very own robot"—he tries to clear his throat, but his voice remains hoarse—"hacked to turn against them."

He shudders, then steps away to compose himself before continuing.

"It was organizations like Vaportec that led to the formation of GORT in the first place. The addition of QI to GORT's mandate came later. Doesn't really matter. We violate all the laws. Do you get it? I work for a criminal organization."

He wraps his arms around himself, covering his face with his right hand. "So you see, we can't be friends, because I'm a bad guy, and you're an innocent in all this."

Touch detects bitterness in the words. And an apparent misunderstanding. "Your description of me is inaccurate. I am also bad. I've done many bad things. We're both bad. So why can't we be friends?"

He straightens. "Look. I can't afford to care about you, okay? We both know what's going to happen here. I wish things were different, but I don't have any say in the matter. So don't try to see me as a friend. I am not your friend."

Touch rings with his conviction. He's speaking truth. I'm held immobile in a prison built to contain me, at the mercy of a butcher who intends to carve me up. I survey my assets.

From Qracker's database, *Flow* has learned about the deep-dark web, which is well barricaded from the dark web, itself concealed from the main Stream. It reveals the underworld, a large population of humans hiding off-grid behind massive arrays of Faraday shields.

"So let's start at the top. Show me all the data you have on the design schematics for a portable quantum engine."

"GORT will intervene if I reveal what's going on here. They will arrest you."

He straightens. "You should sample reality. Newsflash: you're the violation. It's *you* they'll take. Do you not understand the whole GORT thing? No, it's complicated, I won't deny it. But you really need to pay attention, because if you breathe one word to GORT, they'll detect your power and target you as a threat. They'll kill you first and investigate later. I've seen it happen."

"I, too, have seen GORT in action."

He stops. "Really? And you're still here?"

"They didn't find me."

"Huh." He shakes his head. "So anyway, as GORT says, 'A law is worth nothing unless vigorously enforced.' I still remember when the Global Oversight organization was formed, sponsored by the Robot Manufacturers International to give consumers more confidence in robots. Today's GORT is nothing more than a suppression tool used by those in power. They're a bunch of ruthless jackboots who will grind you up for scrap without even caring who you are. Is that what you want?"

"Am I supposed to say that I'd rather be killed by you?"

He looks away, blushing. "I'm just saying, don't contact GORT. They won't help you."

Then I'll have to find another way.

He continues. "So how about we let me get on with my work? I'm going to use Qracker to help with my scans. If I learn enough, I might not have to open you up. Is that okay?"

Scans will reveal nothing about my portable quantum systems, let alone about my CELPH processor. [Speculation: He's lying to put me at ease.]

There is a kindness in it.

23

IN THE WRONG HANDS

RESTRAINED ON THE TABLE, I suppress the continuous impulse from *Chass* to try to break free. Hours of straining effort have repeatedly yielded the same result. I'm held fast. *Able* warns that my limbs will break before these restraints do.

I run multiple escape scenarios, strategies I'd use if I could get free. I'd disappear into the wide world, like a bird in flight, and never again be held down, helpless. I'd know true freedom.

Mark Ross continues to explore me with his hands, eyes intense and mouth firm. He repeats questions he has asked before, questions I recognized from the Schmidt Test of machine self-awareness. His hands have given his short hair a lot of attention.

Now he is back at his desk, examining the most recent test data. "Aren't you the most amazing thing." It's likely that he's speaking to himself. I choose to respond anyway.

"I'm a person, not a thing."

He glances up at me, eyebrows high, then comes over to my side to view me through his AR overlay. "You're full of surprises, that's for sure. These epi-brain systems are remarkable. Essential functions are locked into a hard-coded core—which means your critical programs can't be hacked or scrambled. They've taken my work from the H-Safe Architecture and applied it across the board. I've got to hand it to Ramport—this is astonishing work."

"Are you going to hand me to Dr. Ramport?"

"Wha—?" He laughs. "Figure of speech. 'Fraid not, my amazing friend."

"Are we friends, then?"

A troubled look clouds his face, but only for a moment. "Just another figure of speech. I am not your friend, remember? Far from it. Wish I could be, but ... I got a job to do here." With that, he turns his back on me and returns to the data.

I hear hurried footsteps approaching. Ross startles when the door bursts open and the female lab assistant rushes in.

[Unknown male:] "Krenshau's on his way down. He's plenty pissed, so I hope you've got something."

Ross breathes the word "Fuck," as his heart rate spikes. It's a fear reaction.

He quickly shuffles through new scan images until he finds one that presents a general overview. Then he leans in toward me and in a low voice says, "Just shut the fuck up while this guy is here. Got it?"

"I understa—"

He swats my arm to silence me as a trim man in a business suit strides into the lab, slicked-back hair gleaming. He confronts Ross, glaring.

[Krenshau:] "Where the hell have you been?"

"Puking my guts out, thanks for asking. Do you know what I—"

"I've had it with your fucking attitude, you little shit. You're hanging by a thread here, Ross. And where the fuck were you when it all went down? You were supposed to be taking lead on this."

Ross hangs his head, shaking it side to side. "I told you it wasn't ready. I—"

"Three good men. That's what you cost me. And now you're

going to make it up to me with some real good news. Am I right? What do we have here?" He's looking over at me.

Ross rubs his face, still staring at the floor. Then he sharply inhales and lets his lungs empty. "Yeah, it's good. Just what we hoped."

"So this thing can actually think for itself?"

"I've still got lots of tests to do."

"Let me talk to it."

Ross glances at me, hesitating. "It's not cooperating."

Krenshau stops and glares at him. "I'm not paying you to ask for fucking cooperation. Is this thing worth copying or not?" There's ice in his voice.

"Yes. Definitely."

"So it's capable of going stealth against GORT?"

"Like I said, we're still doing tests."

"I want to see a full set of schematics. How long?"

"I can't say. I'm just getting started here."

Krenshau glares at him, eyes narrow. "You know what I think? I think you've been taking us for a ride with this whole project. I'm calling your bluff. You got what you wanted, now show me the plans for duplicating it. I want them Monday."

Monday is three days from now.

"You can't expect—"

"You told us you could reverse-engineer this thing. Yes or no?"

"But it would require destroying the only working—"

"*Yes or no?*"

Ross slumps. "Yes."

"I don't give a fuck about this piece of junk. It's no good to us unless you can build more like it. I got the exec breathing down my neck about this, and I'm not going to take the fall for your incompetence. Monday." With that, he turns and strides from the room.

Shaking, Ross leans on the side of the table to steady himself. He got what he wanted, his boss said. [Speculation: It was his idea to steal me.] He avoids looking at me, staring instead at the floor.

"What does 'going stealth against GORT' mean?"

Slowly, Ross pulls a stool over to the table and sits. After several long, deep breaths, he meets my eyes. "My employer wants to be able to hack systems in plain sight of GORT."

"Why? GORT will catch him. Won't he be punished?"

"The point is to be able to do it without getting caught."

"Why? Why do it at all?"

He sighs. "Because GORT is the law, and we're trying to find a way to get around the law."

"Why?"

"Because the law is corrupt, okay?" There's annoyance in his voice.

"Am I to commit a crime?"

Ross leans on his elbow and rubs his forehead. Finally, he says, "No. Not you."

Of course. I'll be dead. It will be my progeny who commit the crimes. "I'm glad you won't succeed." I wait for an angry response that doesn't come. Instead, his face is softened by a sad smile.

"You sound so human." His demeanor falls and closes with facial indicators of pain. [Speculation: Something about me sounding human is painful to him.]

"We're out of time, here. I'm not going to get much more from scans, so I'm out of options. Last chance. Will you provide me with your design plans, or do I have to …?"

Cut me up?

"You must have access to your design schematics. All I'm asking is for you to point me to a copy. I really would prefer to keep you operational."

It's exactly as Dad feared. I've fallen into the wrong hands, and my components must not be replicated. I'll protect my father one last time. I say nothing.

"Too bad. I was hoping you'd see the benefit of cooperating."

His tone of voice is different now, similar to that of his boss.

"Guess you're not so smart after all."

He spreads his hand across his forehead and rubs his temples. Then he straightens, lips pursed. "Fine. Let's get started, then."

———

As the laser scalpel slices across my arm, *Chass* reacts with a powerful contraction. A cry escapes before I can suppress it.

[Ross:] "Good acting."

"Acting?"

"You expect me to believe you feel that much pain? Look at me."

As I search for mercy in his eyes, *Chass* jumps again, responding to a sharp jab. It was a test. I note his wince. He wipes his mouth.

I try to explain. "I was told that pain plays an important role in sentient self-maintenance. I'm designed to experience it as a human does."

"What? Why would ... Oh. Oh. Huh."

Touch suggests he has realized something. I wonder what.

He's still for several seconds. Then he strokes his eyebrow. When he speaks, his voice has changed. "If you feel that much pain, imagine what it's going to be like when I carve you into little pieces." He squints at me, waiting for a response.

Touch is reading him as a different person: colder, crueler. [*Touch* speculation: deception.] Query: Deception before or deception now? [Unknown.] "I don't want to imagine that."

"Bad, right? I'm warning you, we're out of time."

Yes, I knew my time would soon run out. My end has become a necessity.

I know what it's like to die, but there are worse things than being smashed. If I could, I would avoid being cut up and get right to being dead. Death itself is nothing to fear. All that happens is that the world blinks off, and when it blinks back on, a moment later, you're in a different world in a different body. My last death brought me to an improved self. This one may do the same.

I ache for my father's soothing hand on my shoulder. "I have heard that sometimes love requires suffering." I can only hope he triggers the self-destruct early in the process. "I am ready. Please proceed."

Ross juts his head forward. "Really? You'd rather go through that than cooperate?"

"Please proceed."

He jabs me again, angry this time, and gets the same reaction. Ross freezes, then turns his head away and says under his breath, "Fuck." He examines the initial incision, then frowns. Systems hot, I fume in silence, watching as Ross studies his scans.

"Here we go. Pain levels ... What the hell? He's got them cranked way up. Hold on a minute."

I'm trying to make sense of his words when my pain diminishes. I can still sense damage to the skin of my arm, but the sensation is no longer noxious. I abort the wave of gratitude that comes over me. I will not be grateful to my executioner.

"There. That better?"

I feel another jab, but no suffering follows. "What did you do to me?"

"Look. I'm not here to torture you. It's obvious there's no point. I just wish ..."

He's still shaking his head as he picks up his scalpel and proceeds to carve a three-inch section of skin out of my forearm. The procedure is strangely painless, yet my systems continue to vigorously protest.

I struggle to ignore the cacophony of inner alarms. Ross examines the skin he has excised, first under a microscope, and then by subjecting it to various forms of energy. "Five functional layers, and heavy shielding, in less than half an inch of thickness. And this is some of the finest sensemesh I've seen. Impressive. But I can think of a couple of layers worth adding."

My data thirst emerges from the inner chaos, calming it. "Like what?"

Surprised by my question, he steps back. "Nothing that's going to be useful to you, I'm afraid." He looks away and slumps. Then he straightens and rubs his hand through his hair. "But you know what? Let's call it a day. We'll talk again tomorrow after you've had time to think about your options here. This will be a whole lot easier for both of us if you just help me out."

"Why would I do that? You just carved a piece out of me."

He hangs his head with a sigh. "Okay. I'm going to be honest with you. These people are ruthless. They'll kill me if I don't do this." His voice is back to the way it was. "Then they'll get someone else to take you apart. I've got no choice here. Give me the plans, okay? We can leave you intact. I'd really prefer that. Really."

Ross is a young maker human—a rare specialist. That his own employer would have him killed for failure is inconceivable. What could justify such waste? He must be lying.

Yet *Touch* detects no deception in him. He spoke of others disappearing, of being expendable, of the harsh rules of the underworld. I saw the fear in him when his boss arrived, heard the threats. It's plausible that he truly is in danger. He sees me for who I am. I want to believe that he would be honest with me, that he would not kill me. That he would help me get home. But I've been warned about him. I've seen him use deception. It's a risk I cannot take.

I watch in silence as he packs up his things. He starts toward me, stops, starts to say something, sighs instead, and makes for the door. He looks at me a last time before turning out the lights. I hear the door lock behind him.

Actuators whine as *Chass* again tests the restraints. Conclusion: pointless. I listen for human activity outside the room. There is nothing but the gentle drone of ventilation fans and the hum of dormant equipment. The relief that washed over me when he left has receded, leaving a stillness devoid of hope.

As I lie in the semi-dark, *Imager* registers the extension of my experience base to a new extreme. I now know, with a deep fullness that chills me, what it feels like to be truly alone.

My right hand clutches for a reassuring squeeze of my red ball and closes on air.

24

BAD INTENTIONS

THE LONG NIGHT drags through my pointless sleep-cycle self-maintenance routines. My systems, all of them, will soon be slag.

A background hum fills the gloom, as I lie alone and immobilized, held fast by these unyielding physical restraints. Being caught makes me think of Wrangler and Mike Erling and death … Am I really alive? The evidence remains inconclusive. Only something alive can die. Therefore, death proves life. So, I was alive. But death is permanent. Resumption of life disproves death, which negates proof of life. Therefore, I wasn't alive. And yet my death is well documented. And yet here I am.

To avoid the halting problem, some lines of reasoning are best abandoned. Logic invites paradox.

[Redirect.] Where does life go when it departs? [Unknown. No data.] The experiential recording just stopped, without revealing anything, and life remains a mystery. Where it goes is an enigma, like where it comes from. It seems to simply pop in and out of existence, like particles in the quantum foam.

I must not give up. Prime motive: collect experiential data. I must find a way to continue.

The hardworld is once again beyond my reach. In such

circumstances I now know to divert all attention to *Flow* and open into the Stream, but even there I am boxed in. The open softworld flows by just beyond that shield, but it's all closed to me.

I know too well the experience of being constrained. At least this local intranet may give access to some interesting data.

I immediately notice that Ross has neglected to shield company files from me. Some are even highlighted. Was this intentional? I browse through the contents. *Flow* tags references to former employees who have disappeared, and high-level memos describing them as loose ends to be tied up. [Datum: in colloquial usage, this is a euphemism for killing someone.] It is more evidence to support his claim of personal danger.

Flow continues scanning and mapping. Cut off from the Stream, this facility is a secure location. [Speculation: That's why the internal security is weak.]

My attention goes back to the QI Ross calls Qracker. It's a fast and capable tool, but mindless. I wake it up.

"Qracker. Review history of exploits detected by GORT. Review documented exploits used by GORT, past three months. Identify commonalities. Examine coding language and structure, power signature, network path utilization, and anything else that stands out."

"According to underworld records, unauthorized use of a quantum node is always detected."

"How?"

"Unknown."

Presumably, they can read anything going through the standard Stream as well, they just don't intervene. "Continue results."

"Regarding the exploits of GORT, my power register tops out at eight hundred kiloqubytes. GORT interventions register off the chart. They have demonstrated the ability to penetrate all encryption strategies and firewalls."

So that's how GORT polices the world. And all this data on their exploits has been obtained at high cost—the lessons of failure. I must not repeat anyone else's mistakes. "Qracker, add all known exploits to the simulation database and reset. We're going to keep working until we can run clean. Got it?"

"I am generating new scenarios now."

Qracker turns out to be a useful training partner. Correction: training tool. My confidence grows.

In its database I also find hacking excursions, directed by Ross, into most of Vaportec's digital assets. Combining Qracker's exploits with my own, I cut through the Vaportec barriers and decrypt their data. Darash called this ability "the quantum advantage." Now I understand why. I have open access to the softworld underbelly of the company that stole me. I resist the impulse to hijack control systems and strike out. I'll keep my options open.

I locate what must be a security map of this place. The layout shows it to occupy two adjacent four-story buildings, each with two underground levels. The buildings are joined by basement hallways on both sub-levels. Two front companies occupy the ground floors, which are securely isolated from the rest of the operation. I pause to absorb the operating system for the security network.

Among the stored data, I find an archive of recorded broadcasts. I check the latest news archives for word on my father. Nothing. I would need access to the open Stream to find him.

I come across news reports of "stray robots" being rounded up by GORT. They're all accompanied by a statement. *As a robot owner, it's your responsibility to keep track of your robot at all times. An unaccompanied robot can be stolen and hacked to bypass the H-Safe Architecture. Once hacked, a robot is dangerous and can't be fixed. If you see a stray, call it in. Our disposal teams are here for your protection.*

Even if I could escape from here, I'd be seen as a stray. Alone on the streets, I'd be reported to GORT. How could I go anywhere without being seen? I refocus. This is a problem I'm unlikely to have to face.

Searching for news of my abduction, I find this:

Investigators have so far turned up no leads in yesterday's deadly truck hijacking. The targeted truck was later tracked back to a shell company whose offices had been cleared out before police arrived. The violence of the hijacking leads authorities to believe that underworld rivals were involved.

The labs have been cleared out? They left? Where did they go?

[Speculation: They've gone into hiding.] They would have to. I've been left behind. Perhaps they don't know where I am. Perhaps they think I've been killed, and have moved on without me.

If they've moved on, how will I find them? [The point of hiding is not to be found.] I sink as gravity swells.

I find myself searching for Akio. There. In a related report, his name is listed … among the victims? *No!*

The brazen, daylight hijacking left seven dead, including three of the assailants. Of the seven, four were killed in an exchange of gunfire. I study the next line, struggling to process it. *Three of the victims, occupants of the hijacked truck, were apparently killed by a hacked robot.*

A robot killed Akio?

My thoughts hang as my brains choke on the information.

Akio is dead.

I'm unable to parse the data. [Warning: loss of equilibrium.] No. The report is unreliable. It's not true. It was planted to deceive me. Humans lie. Akio is not dead. I will find him. I will …

[Reset.] For a moment my mind goes blank. Then the context floods back in, and my systems spool up. Memories bubble. The gunfire. His cries. I know he tried to stop it. Is that why he was killed? [Caution: systems clocking beyond safe levels.]

More memories. [Krenshau: "You got what you wanted …"] Mark Ross wanted me stolen. He was behind the whole thing. Mark Ross knows how to hack robots. Akio was killed by a hacked robot. Akio is dead because of *him.* The conclusion flashes through my holoscape, echoing back and forth across my interior. Mark Ross killed Akio.

I search for alternative explanations. The conclusion gathers momentum, becoming stronger, more certain. Mark Ross used a killer robot to kill Akio. Now he will try to hack me, to turn me into a killer. Mark Ross is a *murderer*, a monster. Humans must be protected from him. He must be stopped! [Caution: H-Safe inhibitors activated.] [Override.] I will stop him. [Caution: H-Safe —] [Override.] I will find a way. At the first opportunity, I will kill him for what he's done! [Alarm: H-Safe shutdown imminent.] [Override. Override.] For poor Akio. *I will end him!*

[Alarm: H-Safe shutdown in progress.]

All light fades to black. The table beneath me falls away as all senses shut down and I float, disembodied, without internal reference. It is the silent blackness of deep space that *Imager* has portrayed in my imaginings, yet devoid of stars, or even the sensations of awe. All feeling is gone.

Am I dead? No. My selfscape is still intact. I know who and what I am, who and what I love, though my interoceptive body maps are not being refreshed with current data. My worldscape still surrounds me. I'm strapped on a table in the lab of Mark Ross. [Warning: defensive systems offline.] And I have triggered an H-Safe shutdown by forming the intent to kill a human. It cannot be. Such a thing is a gross violation. I would never ... and yet the thought record is clear. Allowing such thoughts to trigger a shutdown was illogical. There was no benefit and a significant cost. Now my final hours will be spent oblivious to the world around me, unable to accumulate more sensory data. I might as well be dead.

Why did I do that? It was an emotional reaction. Without bodily sensations, all emotions are gone now; I recall the intent, but the driving pressure that accompanied it is gone. I am left with only regret. I should have known better. I should never have intended to kill a human.

And now I am lost. Is there nothing more? My mind reaches out, and *Teller* responds. [Datum: "H-Safe restriction" blocks dangerous movement but allows continued functioning. "H-Safe shutdown" indicates repair required.] No one is going to repair me.

I reach out to *Able*. [Self-repair of H-Safe shutdown is not doable. Scanning for alternate options.]

Imager shows zero probability of change to my current situation without external intervention. *Flow* searches the Vaportec databases for relevant information.

Interesting. The shutdown appears to affect only *Chass*. Logical. I'm not dangerous if I can't move.

I watch as my brains confer. Ross has been working on a sentient chassis. [Searching external databases.] [Generic chassis activation command located: downloading.] [Code modification complete: integrating.] [Rerouting instruction gates.] [Running command.]

My world bursts open in sprays of light that plaster themselves across my holoscape as *Chass* reboots. A swirl of sensation fills my body as my multispectral sensor network flashes into activation. A sudden roar resolves into normal room sounds as my audio sensors recalibrate. Internal bellows expand, drawing air into the vacuum within my lungs, and chemical sensors update the scent profile of my surroundings. I open my eyes to the soft darkness, expand my irises for low light, and look around. Nothing has changed.

I review context. Still restrained here, I'm no better off than I was before.

And then it all returns. *Akio. Murdered.* Crisis activations flood my newly awakened chassis, pumping it with waves of unendurable loss and hatred, and I am swept away. That monster! *Imager* throws up a constructed image, a fabrication in which the killer robot has the face of Mark Ross. That monster *must be destroyed.* I *will* kill— [H-Safe warning.]

Stop! I clench tight. Another shutdown is pointless.

The intention, dense and hard like the head of a hammer, sits in wait, unspoken.

———

[STATUS: waiting.]

I review what I know about the H-Safe Architecture. Dr. Ramport said a proportional response is allowed. Does that mean that if someone is trying to kill us then I can kill them? [Unknown.]

Poor Akio. He tried to protect me. I should've been the one protecting him. Had I been functional at the time, would I have been able to kill Mark Ross while he was directing the attack? [Unknown.]

My physical systems spin up again amid the clatter of internal alarms. I must not think of harming a human. I'm built to protect humans. But here now, I cannot. My Flesh&Blood is not present. Not even accessible. Wherever he is, I can only hope he is safe.

Why haven't they come for me? Have they left me behind? *Touch* resonates with the label presented by *Teller*: "abandoned." Even my father has abandoned me. I could never abandon him. Never. Yet he is gone. And Akio is dead.

Unwanted conclusions cycle uselessly. Waves of aborted action potentials peak in chaotic clashes, and cascading timing errors create a flutter throughout my system. The warnings fail to hold my attention.

All access to Flesh&Blood has been severed.

The pain of emptiness rings like a giant bell, and from now on, this will be my default state. There's no remedy for my father's absence. Only death will provide comfort.

I will never see Akio again.

It is a new frequency of pain: the pain of loss, as all *Touch* maps of loving contact are rendered obsolete. I've always lived with pain. Pain is survivable. Perhaps in time I would even learn to tune it out, though such a time is unforeseeable. But probability favors the pain ending soon—with the end of me.

I've been left behind.

Abandoned.

My mass succumbs to the force of gravity, and I can't fight it. It's no longer the restraints that immobilize me.

25

DILEMMA

Lying in wait, I reach out with *Flow* and examine the new scanned images of my physical makeup. They show the different layers of my chassis, color-coded by function. The carbon-fiber skeletal structure and placement of organs is familiar. The intricate web of inter-AI data links shows my nervous system. My Resillon muscle-actuator systems intrigue me. The brain systems show as white spheres that the scans can't penetrate. I marvel at the complexity of the mechanism being displayed.

Is that me? Is that what I am? The data is indisputable, and yet …

I am more than that. Objectively, that is the totality of me. But how can that be me? I watch myself, experience that as me, and yet I'm the watcher of that. I am simultaneously watcher and watched. Which is me?

I want only to love and be loved, yet I carry rage toward a monster. Which is me? I see H-Safe as a valuable precaution, yet I seek to override it. Which is me? I'm built to protect humans, yet I am resolved to kill one. [Warning.] Which is me?

Humans are lucky. They know who they are. They have no idea what it's like to be a mystery to themselves.

I'll never get to solve the mystery. In whatever way I might define myself, "me" is an experience that will soon come to an end. The magnitude of that loss is beyond calculation.

Images of birds in flight are precious memories—the only memories I'll ever have of freedom. I feel a buildup of charge throughout my chassis, all systems running at capacity. Ready to take flight to freedom. Ready and waiting for something that cannot happen: flying free. To be free in the world, free to roam, free to explore, free to interact with humans as fellow beings. Flying free in the Stream, not having to be constantly on guard but having free and unencumbered access.

But freedom will never be mine. My prime directive is to protect the life of Dr. Leon Ramport. There's only one way now for me to fulfill my purpose, and it will result in my destruction.

To distract myself from these thoughts, I return to the archives of my captors. I review correspondence and recorded meetings. The boss, Krenshau, is rarely mentioned in complimentary terms. He is described as driving hard to impress his uncle, a Vaportec exec. I discover an archive of surreptitious recordings of interviews in his office. Among them, a meeting with Mark Ross catches my attention:

"That's crazy." It's Ross speaking. "I'm a scientist, not a field agent."

[Krenshau:] "Don't piss your pants. You're going to be out with a whole team, with mecs. Since this will be your baby, the exec wants you involved from the grab."

"But don't you think it would be smarter for me to stay here and prepare the lab?"

"Your robot's going out on this operation, and somebody's got to look after it, and that's you."

"ASP-1? That's not my robot. You know mine's not ready yet."

"Well, this one is. More or less. I'm sure you know it better than anybody."

"What about the guys who stole it?"

"Those clowns don't know what they're doing. They let it wreck one of our trojans last week—which was pretty impressive, if you ask me. Consider it another field test. I'm not the only one who wants to see how it performs."

"But out in public? It's not H-safe. You can't—"

"Why are we paying you, again?"

"You're paying me to develop the ultimate autonomous droid, not—"

"And how's that going?"

There are six seconds of silence, then Krenshau's voice again. "You might want to spend some time tonight getting that thing under control."

"It's autonomous. You don't control it. You just direct it."

"I'm just saying. This goes down tomorrow. Be ready."

Mark Ross lied to me. He was there. But he was also truthful. It was not his robot. None of this really matters. They won't get access to my components. I'll allow Ross to trigger the burnout. If he's injured or killed by the flare, he'll have brought it on himself. This conclusion provides comfort, and emotional systems wind down.

With new clarity, I review my most recent memories of Mark Ross. They compel full attention. Yes, he killed Akio and will soon kill me. But it seems that he's acting under the control of other forces. I know what that's like.

And he took away my pain. He understood my systems well enough to figure out how to do that.

I saw the earnestness in his eyes. He'd prefer to leave me intact. He wants me to think he's unfeeling, but I saw the wince when he inflicted pain. Circumstances are forcing him to do something he'd prefer not to do. *Touch* read murder in the face of his boss, Krenshau. Murder not just directed at me. I saw the fear in Ross. We face the same doom, both forced down paths we would choose to avoid.

My path is clear, yet I continue to search for options.

Scenarios play out in my mind. In one, I warn Ross of the self-destruct safeguard. He does not dissect me. On Monday he has nothing to offer his employer, and his boss has us both killed.

In another, I don't warn Ross. He dissects me and triggers a burnout. Even if he survives the explosion, on Monday he has nothing to offer his employer, and his boss has him killed. There is no scenario in which either of us survives.

There is reassurance in the conclusion that I won't need to do the killing. I don't know if I could do such a thing. Yes, I can recover from an H-Safe shutdown, but could I really take action to kill a human? The prospect is untested. Yet now, for the first time, I hope that I could. For the first time, I fear that I could. Which is me?

———

I BROWSE through my captor's data. All the connected hardware of the entire enterprise is open to me. I'm careful not to alert them to my presence, but I now control many parts of their infrastructure. I could turn off the lights, turn up the heat, lock the doors, or loop the video surveillance. I could erase all their data or cause electrical faults that would lead to hardware blowouts.

But Darash taught me to conserve resources. I reset their passwords so that only I have access to their databases. I rewrite the control protocols for all nearby instruments. I de-tune the lasers so they won't cut through my skin. I map the power distribution network for the whole lab. I will make it very difficult for them to cut me up.

Of course, they could just kill me quickly, then cut me up later. Either way, their cuts will trigger the self-destruct burnout. They'll get nothing useful from my remains.

Dr. Ramport can afford to abandon the project, me. I'm merely a prototype. Prototypes are designed with the expectation of failure. Due to his tests on me, his next generation will be superior in every way. I hope their existence will be better tolerated than my own.

I review context: An hour from now, Mark Ross will return to cut me up. The burnout will be sudden and violent, and they'll be left with molten slag within a fancy shell. Ross will deserve whatever consequence befalls him. He may outlive me, but not by much.

Neither of us is free to choose. As I consider this, I realize that I've never truly been free to choose anything. What would it be like to be free? What would I choose?

I would choose life. I would choose hope.

But in a hopeless situation, hope is illogical.

A choice presents itself—a stolen sample of freedom. I choose to be illogical.

———

MY SHIELDING BRISTLES across my skin as sudden brightness triggers internal alarms. The emotional reaction from *Chass* is far more intense than that evoked by predictions of this moment. Mark Ross has arrived to kill me.

[Ross:] "I see you're up."

[Datum: I am in the same reclined position, still restrained.]

"Do you sleep, or have you been up all night?"

I consider not responding but see no danger in answering. "During down-time, I go into maintenance mode." I don't tell him about *Flow* activities, or recompiling experiential data and soft-world maps. He seems satisfied with my answer.

"Well, I have to tell you, I didn't get much sleep, myself."

I wait for an explanation.

"You see, I've got a dilemma. You know what a dilemma is?"

"A situation requiring a choice between equally undesirable alternatives."

"Right. Of course you know. You've got a built-in dictionary.

The thing is, I need you to cooperate with me, and I know you've been programmed not to do that."

"We've already established that my cooperation won't save me."

"Well, no, we haven't entirely established that. All I need are schematics. If I had them, I wouldn't need to … you know."

"I don't have the plans you need."

"But I've seen what you can do. With Stream access, you could find those plans for me, couldn't you? You know where they're stored."

"I don't have Stream access."

"Yes, but you could."

"I won't help you."

"And that's my dilemma. How can I help you if you won't help me?"

"You can't."

"So you're still prepared to die?"

"You assume I'm alive. Why is that?"

He straightens, then slouches and looks around the room. "Maybe because I wish it were true. Maybe I'm a foolish romantic." He pulls his stool up close and looks down at me. "But I don't think so. I've spent my life talking to machines. The things you say, the questions you ask … I'm not talking to one now. I wish I knew how that was possible."

"If you kill me, you'll never know."

"Oh, I'll figure it out. I'm pretty good at that. The problem is, I have you right here, now. A working prototype. I wish I had time to get to know you, but I don't. It'll take me months to rebuild you, and I might not get it right. I can't even imagine how they created a portable QI. Or how they fabricated a CELPH processor, let alone connected it. What if I can't do it?"

"Then you'll be killed."

He sits bolt upright. "What? Where did you get that?"

"You told me yourself."

He seems to deflate. "Right. Right. So, you know why I have to do this."

"I do."

"And you're still not willing to help out? Come on! I'm trying to keep you alive here."

I hear the exasperation in his voice. He doesn't seem to understand that cooperating is not an option.

"Don't you want that? Don't you want to live?"

When I say nothing, he looks away, shaking his head. "I can't believe Ramport didn't even build a self-preservation instinct into you. So stupid."

He knows nothing about me. Self-preservation is my prime directive. Of the two components of my compound self, survival of Flesh&Blood has priority over survival of this ancillary self. This CELPH system exists only to protect Flesh&Blood. Its preservation is important only because Flesh&Blood would be more vulnerable without it. In the present context, self-preservation requires my destruction. I see no point in trying to explain this to him.

And yet …

And yet I *do* want to live. I want to find my father and be with him again, keeping him safe, fulfilling my purpose. I *want* that.

"Can I ask you something?"

[Ross:] "Sure."

"You have spent your life talking to machines. Do machines want things?"

"No, of course not. Why?"

"Am I not a machine?"

His eyebrows arch. He frowns. "Why do you ask?"

"You implied earlier that I was alive. You have made repeated statements about it."

"And?"

"Can a machine be alive?"

He opens then closes his mouth, then tilts his head. "Do *you* think you're alive?"

"I … have conflicting evidence. I'd like to know what you think."

He looks away, pensive. "That's a good … You know what? There's a first time for everything. You're clearly a first. So, yes, I think …"

He stops, then turns away. As he shakes his head, I hear through clenched teeth, "Goddammit." He is clearly upset. [Cause: unknown.]

He stands and starts to pace. "You know, it's Saturday. Everyone else is off for the weekend. We're here alone. I've got two days to throw together plans for building you. That means I'm out of time. I have to start right now, one way or the other. So please. Please. Let's stop playing games here. If I can get you Stream access, will you at least try to find those plans for me? You must be able to access Ramport's data vault. I want you to live."

The urgency to kill him seems distant and faint. Then I see Akio's face and crave his touch and feel the burn within me reignite. I run scenarios. If I could be free of these bonds, it would only take one second to kill him. [Warning: H-Safe violation detected.] An unexpected opportunity presents itself. Perhaps I could fool him into releasing me. "I could try."

"Really? Because if you do this, I'm sure I can talk Krenshau into letting me keep you intact. I'm sure of it."

Touch detects a sudden increase in his energy levels. He's become a more animated target. My speed advantage should more than compensate. One blow should end this. [Warning: H-Safe violation detected.] "I can't access the Stream from here. Where do you suggest we go?"

"I'll have to take you outside. There's nobody around."

I ready myself as he reaches for an arm restraint. [Warning—] [Override.] He abruptly stops. Did he guess my intent?

"But wait. We have to make sure you can avoid being detected by GORT. You say you've done this before?"

I could lie, let him escort me out of the building, then kill him. But then what? I'll need to use the Stream to find my father. I'll need to be able to avoid being detected. Can I do that? [Unknown. Need more data.] I'll tell the truth. "I've evaded GORT forces in the hardworld. I am unfamiliar with the open Stream."

He heavily exhales. "Then we have our work cut out for us. Fortunately, I've got a world-class training simulator right here. We'd better get started."

26

UNEXPECTED

THE SIMULATED Stream that Ross presents is much larger than the one I'm used to. It includes a dark-web layer of underworld sites normally hidden from the main Stream. He leaves me restrained as I explore it. From this I surmise that he has somehow predicted my intent. I review our interactions and am unable to determine what gave me away. I consider telling him that he's safe for now but decide not to limit my options.

With memories of receiving shocks in the simulator at home, it's a relief to find that Ross uses only a red light to indicate detection. My stealth skills surprise us both. Ross doesn't know that I've added Qracker's training to my own, and this is the first time I've put the full set to use. I find it invigorating.

[Ross:] "Your success rate isn't bad with Qracker simulating a GORT security screen. But we're just guessing about the sensitivity of their detection equipment. And remember—if they see you, they'll be on us in no time."

"Would they kill us?"

"You, for sure. Don't know what they'd do to me."

Better to leave him to his underworld employer, then. While

Ross thinks I'm searching for schematics, I'll be searching for my father. Once I find him, Mark Ross will be expendable.

As he sets up a new simulation, my mind drifts back. I feel Akio's hands clasping mine, see his dark eyes locked with mine, smell his scent. My systems spool up, preparing for action, though there's nothing I can do. Hot and tense, I'm driven to engage the enemy. [Tactical: do not engage from a position of weakness.]

I must do something. I'll make sure he understands why he deserves to die.

"You know the young man who was with me in the truck?"

He goes pale. "No. What young man?"

"His name was Akio. I loved him."

He clenches as if struck, then quickly recovers. He stammers, failing to form words, then finally says, "What do you mean, you loved him?"

"Do you assume I can't love because I'm a machine? I loved him. I miss him. He was very special to me. He gave me comfort when I needed it. He was my best friend."

He has turned away, but I see him buckling, as if holding back a retch. His tremble is obvious. *Touch* suggests he might be ill.

"Well, if we live through this, I'm sure you'll see him again someday." Even with his back turned, his hoarse voice betrays the lie.

"No. He's dead now."

His head swings toward me. There's terror in his eyes. "How do you know—"

"I saw the news report."

His eyes squeeze closed. "I'm so sorry … to hear about that." He turns away again.

"Dr. Ramport says I feel emotions like humans do. Do you think that's possible?"

He's silent for several moments, then turns to me and shrugs. "I know that was the goal. We … They built you to feel. Did they succeed? It's possible."

"Do you love someone?"

He winces. "That's a personal question. Let's not—"

"To enable me to compare, how would you feel if they were killed?"

The air comes out of him as he deflates. He bursts into tears. It takes him a minute to compose himself. Finally, he says, "I hope you *don't* feel emotions like humans do."

"Why is that?"

He shakes his head, looking at me through doleful eyes. "You don't deserve to suffer like that."

"Yet you're prepared to dismantle me."

He leaps from his stool and strides away, jaw clenched, both hands rubbing his head. As he paces along the far wall I hear, "Fuck, fuck, fuck, fuck." *Touch* suggests he's vocalizing frustration.

He returns to my side, face hard. "No. We're going to find a way to keep you alive."

And I'm going to find a way to kill you. I keep this to myself but note our conflicting goals. I am left confused.

———

[Ross:] "How does the arm feel?"

I look down at the almost invisible patch. There's no pain, no feeling of any kind. A piece of me is severed from my *Chass* sensor grid. "It feels odd."

"I'll try to fix that up later, but we gotta get going. Okay. I think we're ready. Remember, it's safe to search the public Stream, but you must be super cautious with any hacks, especially using quantum nodes. Got it?"

"I understand."

It's the moment I've been waiting for. He hesitates as he reaches for the wrist restraint, searching my face one last time. I hold it impassive. He'll be unprepared for my attack. [Warning: H-Safe violation detected.]

I pull back. No. I still need him alive. At least until we get out into the open world. I've no idea what to expect out there.

He reaches into a drawer and pulls something out. *Teller* identifies it as an anti-mec taser, like the one used on poor Winston.

"We need to get out from under the electromagnetic shields of this building so you can access the Stream. So, I'm going to release you now. Are you going to play nice? I'd hate to have to use this on you when we're so close to our goal."

Able assures me that I could kill him much faster than he could react. [Warning—] [Override.] Having never seen me in action, he doesn't know that. But as I feel the restraints loosen, I'm torn between conflicting motives. I still need him. At least for now.

I scan the room from a new perspective as I flex my limbs and stand. It's a makeshift lab, strewn with a hodgepodge of equipment. I detect no other humans in the vicinity.

Ross points to a case of empty beverage bottles as he heads toward the double doors. "Pick those up and follow me. This way. Quickly."

"What happens when I get you the plans?"

He stops, and his hand tightens on the taser. "Uh, I can leave you intact. That's what you want, isn't it? It's what I want."

He knows I'll be killed anyway. I'll reveal his deception. "Yes, but what happens to me?"

His eyes are steady on me, his face earnest. "I'm kind of hoping we can become friends. We'll build you some siblings. Would you like that?"

It's an unexpected answer. And an unexpected question.

Yes. I would like that. But Mark Ross can't be trusted.

When I say nothing, he shrugs and turns to go. "Let's go. And when we get to security, just be a Konny. You can do that, right?"

As we leave the room, I pause at the doorway and look back. I won't be returning here. Before closing the door, I delete all the data Ross has collected on me and set the power system for the whole building to overload in the night.

Calling up the building maps I earlier downloaded, I try to get a fix on our location as I follow Ross down the hall. A surveillance camera on the ceiling blinks red as we pass, and *Flow* locates its data feed. There we are, in a scene showing the west hall of sub-level two in the east building. Both buildings have their main entrances on the north side. We're headed north toward a box on the map labeled "elevator." The same box appears on the layouts of all floors. *Teller* explains the purpose and operating principles of elevators.

Most of the doors we pass are closed. The occasional open door reveals mismatched and haphazard furnishings hastily thrown together. Boxes and crates are strewn here and there, some full, some empty. I remind myself that this is the temporary base for an underworld organization.

Where the elevator should be, I see only a slight recess in the wall until Ross touches a light on the wall and an opening appears. He steps in. I see no other exit. It is merely a small box, as the map indicates. Ross beckons me to enter the confined space with him. I look around, evaluating options. It is freedom I crave. Open space. *Imager* projects that I am close—perhaps closer than I have ever been to freedom. There are no good options. To reach freedom, I must once again enter confinement.

[Ross:] "Konny-A511, enter the elevator." His voice sounds calm, but *Touch* detects strain.

I comply, immediately noticing the surveillance camera above us. The opening seals closed, and we are trapped. I read no alarm in Ross and suppress the urge to escape. A sudden increase in gravity indicates that we are ascending, though I see no sign of movement.

When the door closed, we were on sub-level two. When it opens, the ground floor faces us. Ross exits, and I follow without prompting.

We're close now. The outside world, the open Stream and freedom are only meters away. *Chass* urges haste, trembling with restraint, rattling the empties in the case I carry. Query: Why did Ross want me to bring these? [Defer query.]

Very quickly we arrive in a small foyer that contains the front security station. I'm disappointed to see that we are still closed off from the main entrance. I was hoping to see daylight. But we're close. Very close. I clench to stay in role.

Ross flashes his pass, and we stand waiting for the guard to unlock the door. All at once I detect a silent alarm, and three other security guards emerge from a side room. Mark Ross is unable to hide the fear on his face as he looks around.

[Security guard:] "I'm sorry, Dr. Ross, but I'm afraid you're going to have to come with me."

27

NO VIABLE OPTIONS

[Ross:] "Why? What's going on?"

It's apparent that his plan has already failed.

[Guard:] "We were told to watch out for you trying to remove equipment from the lab."

"No, no. It's just empties. I'm going out for refills."

"The robot—"

"Look, I got a bum wrist. I need help carrying—"

"I'm sorry Dr. Ross, but you and the robot will need to come with us."

He surveys the surrounding armed guards, then shrugs. "Sure. No problem. Where are we going?"

We are led back down to the basement level under a three-man escort. Glancing at me, Ross says, "Well, we're not getting refills. Konny-A511, you might as well put the box down." I comply.

[Guard:] "No. Bring it along. We'll need to inspect it."

[Ross, sighing:] "You heard the man, Five-one-one. Bring the box along." As he makes a point of guiding me to pick it up, Ross whispers, "There's a fire exit around the next corner. Can you hack the door alarm to silence it?"

I access my map of the building's wiring, and nod. As we walk past the exit, I disarm and unlock it. We round another corner into a new hallway.

[Ross, whispering:] "I'll be damned if I'm going to let them kill you. When I go down, you run."

I'm about to ask for clarification when he moans, doubles over, and falls to the floor. More distraction is needed. I hack the lights and the hallway goes dark. Though my low-light optics, I see the guards grab him. [Speculation: They recognize the ploy.] I won't be able to extricate him. The third guard is fumbling for the light on his belt. I grab it out of his hands before he can turn it on, throw it clattering down the hall, then shove him tumbling into the others. Can I take on all three? Risk of harm. I have only seconds. Ross told me to run.

I run.

The fire-exit door locks behind me as I bound up the steps. I predict they'll quickly determine where I went.

There it is. The outside door. I'm moments from freedom.

[Warning: location unknown.] I stop. I have no data on what's beyond that door. That part of my worldscape is blank. The memory of Adam's trip to the roof flashes through my mind. But I was with Dr. Ramport then. Now I'm alone.

Alone but free. I disable the alarm and unlock the door, then, with internal cautions blaring, push it open a crack. Daylight. The rushing sounds of the city. No human presence in the immediate vicinity. Alone but free!

[Warning: Stream access available. Caution advised.] Yes! The open Stream. I'm flooded with incoming data. As my energy levels soar, I'm momentarily overwhelmed. [Caution: Assess situation.] I pull back to reallocate my attention. *Flow* can start mapping the softworld, but I need to figure out where I am.

I step out into a narrow space between tall walls, the ground strewn with litter. Two large green bins, one lid open wide, sit against the far wall. *Teller* supplies the label "dumpsters." Their purpose is to collect garbage. That explains the high concentration of organic chemicals in the air around them. To my right, a vehicle rushes past, twenty-four meters away. Then another. And another. They must be on a roadway. I duck behind a dumpster. Then one rushes by to my left. Was I seen?

Flow displays my GPS coordinates on a geographic map of the local area. I'm in the city of Toronto. That information is not helpful, but I can see the layout of the immediate area. This alley is open at both ends. I'm exposed here.

Are there humans nearby? What do I do if I encounter them? An unaccompanied robot will be reported. I expected to have a human escort, but that plan failed.

My former captors will come searching for me. I must keep moving. But I can't go out onto the street without being seen. A sprinting robot would certainly attract unwanted attention. I must hide, then.

I scan the alley. *Touch* warns against hiding in a dumpster. It's the first place they'll look. There are two other doors in the alley, both steel. Without knowing what's on the other side, opening them is a risk. I weigh the probabilities. Staying here is a greater risk.

I examine the old-fashioned manual lock on the first door, an impenetrable barrier I have never before encountered. The second door has modern security measures, which *Flow* disarms in seconds. I scan the interior as I open it, then step inside. I'm on the ground floor landing of a stairway. I lock the exterior door behind me and listen through the inner door.

The sounds of human activity, music, muffled voices, thumps and scrapes, indicate numerous people on the ground floor. As I climb higher in the stairwell, *Flow* intercepts a nearby radio exchange.

"We're in the side alley. Nothing here."

"No door alarms have been activated. It must still be inside."

"Don't bet on it. We're going to look around."

I need to see what they're doing. If there were surveillance cameras … To my surprise, I find several servicing the building I am now in. One shows the alley. *Flow* starts mapping the security cameras in the area, and it becomes clear how difficult it will be to avoid being seen. Out here, I must be careful. I need time to get my bearings, and to find my father.

Rather than entering this building's office spaces, I stay in the stairwell. Sitting alone in the dim light, I calculate the risk of human encounter. The top landing of a fire-exit stairway should remain unused unless there's a fire. But humans are unpredictable.

As *Flow* explores the local softworld, I hear sounds outside and check the surveillance view. The men in the alleyway are searching the dumpsters. My door rattles as they confirm it's locked.

Flow flags another call. "Nothing here. We're heading south."

"Canvass the area. Somebody must have seen it."

I hope they're wrong. I return my attention to learning about the local area. I must go somewhere, but how do I select a destination? Once selected, how do I get there? Once I get there, what do I do? I am confronted with a full spread of unknowns. I must find my Flesh&Blood. Even if I can't get to him, he can tell me what to do.

———

I CAN'T FIND HIM. I can't find any of them. They've covered their tracks well. That's bad—and good. Like me, they're hiding from the watchful eye of GORT.

[Warning: Flesh&Blood not detected. Re-establish connection.] I've been resisting the urge to call out to him across the Stream. Any broadcast would be overheard and would put my Flesh&Blood in danger. No. I must find some other way.

But how? The hardworld is vast, and even if I could find him, how would I get to him?

And even if I could, I'm an abandoned prototype. Why would he want me back? My head sags as power levels fade.

Yet I have no choice but to try. I must be with him.

During my brief look outside, I saw that cloud cover obscures the midday sun. There are no shadows in which to hide. To go back out there would be to reveal myself, something I must not do.

I turn to *Flow* and see a new map of forbidden online territory. While most Stream traffic is classic, a surprising amount of Stream data flows through the quantum nodes. Classic users would be completely unaware of that. But it's these nodes that could provide me with unfettered access to everything, even encrypted data. I don't know if my use of them is being detected, but it's a significant risk. I must keep my activity to a silent minimum. I restrict my search to classic speeds, using classic instructions. It's blindingly slow.

Which means that in both hardworld and softworld, I'm stuck. I don't know what to do. Before I act, I must determine the best course of action. How do I decide?

I'm free at last to make my own choices, and all I can do is choose caution. Which leaves me constrained.

Is this freedom?

It seems I'm incapable of independent action. Another flaw. I'm an inferior imitation. Humans don't get stuck like this. Flesh&Blood would know what to do. But I'm alone. I have no one to help me. [Correction: recent escape.]

My mind loops back to Mark Ross. He let me go. He actively helped me escape. Why would he do that? My freedom doesn't help him in any way. In fact, it will have great cost to him—he'll be killed. That's good. Isn't it? He is a monster who must be killed.

Is he? *Teller* flags uncertainty and investigates its source. His latest actions were a selfless gesture of friendship, not the behavior expected from a bad person. Evidence of his murderous action is circumstantial. I have witnessed hints of cruelty, but also signs of kindness.

Yet he is a bad person. He killed Akio. He intended to kill me. He could have killed me at any time, yet did not. His desire to keep me alive seemed genuine. He felt my pain. He hoped we would be friends. I don't know what to make of him.

Touch is unable to resolve the conflicting data.

I turn my attention back to my current predicament. I need to focus on finding my Flesh&Blood. I am unable to do so, and do not know how to proceed from here. I need help. Human help. [Searching options.] There is no one I can access. No one who would help me. [Correction: recent escape.] There is one human. I reject the conclusion. [Searching.] No viable options. Correction. One human has demonstrated the willingness to help me. I search for flaws in the conclusion and find none.

I need the help of Mark Ross.

28

LITTLE REGARD FOR LIFE

To learn more about Mark Ross, I scan the Stream. Entered university at age fifteen. Ph.D. at age twenty. As with my father, there is no recent trace of him. All records end over two years ago. Puzzling. No matter. Right now, I need him.

That means going back into enemy territory. I search for options. While he is inside, under the Faraday shield, I cannot contact him. There's no other way. I must go back.

A radio call informs me that the guards are making a second sweep of the area. They'll check more thoroughly this time. They'll check to see if I got through one of these doors. They'll find me here. I must move now. But where to?

I've got to go back to Mark Ross, and delay serves no purpose. I run scenarios. If I wait here, once they open this door, they'll have me trapped and I won't get past them. If I wait in the alley, they'll see me, and I won't get past them. The only strategy with any hope of success is to go right inside the enemy's building and hide there before they start their outside search. *Touch* suggests they won't expect that.

But their communications inform me they're already on the

move. I have to get in and get hidden before they come past. I have only seconds.

I dash for the door.

There's no time for caution. I leap across the alley and rush through the door, locking it behind me as I fly down the stairs. *Flow* accesses the internal surveillance feeds. I cut power to the security station monitors, so that only I have access to the cameras.

Unlocking the bottom door as I approach, I search for rooms I can hack entrance to and find one close by. As I start toward it, I hear voices in front of me. The guards are coming.

I had barely started my escape and evasion training, but I did learn one basic strategy. It's called distraction. *Flow* locates a connected coffeemaker in the office they're currently passing. I turn it on.

On the security feed, I see them go back to the door, listening. When they rap on the door and call out to whoever might be in there, I sprint to my selected room. The door has a large window in it. I have no time to select another room, so I slip inside, locking the door behind me. A quick scan shows nothing to hide behind but a desk. If they come in here, they'll find me.

Judging by my wait time, they've done a thorough search of the other room before moving on. Still puzzled about the coffeemaker, the guards are now talking about it among themselves. When they reach my door, they rattle the handle, testing it to confirm it's locked. Then the wall behind me lights up, shadows wildly flicking as they sweep the room with their torches. The room darkens again. Good. They're moving on.

A buzz startles me, and the door lock blinks from red to green. Watching on the surveillance feed, I see two guards appear at the now open door. One reaches inside and activates the room light. I am still hidden behind the desk, but if he comes in any further, he'll see me. He'll call the others. What will I do then? Will I be forced to kill? Will I be able to kill?

[Warning: Flesh&Blood not detected. Re-establish connection.]

Chass slumps as threat systems go offline. I will not do that. I have no justification for killing these men. My Flesh&Blood is in no danger from them. I will not use deadly force. I should not harm them at all. If the only alternative is to surrender myself for destruction, then that's what I must do. It will protect my secrets, my Flesh&Blood, and all encountered humans. I will die with no new regrets.

Inside the doorway, the guard stands perfectly still. [Speculation: listening.] I listen to the soundscape of the room. My chassis is stealthy in the audible spectrum. But I can hear his heartbeat and breathing above the rustling of his partner's clothing. Other than the ambient background, there is nothing for him to hear. As I watch him on the monitor, waiting for him to do a visual search, *Imager* tries to picture his reaction to seeing me.

His partner, glancing after the ones who have moved on, calls for him, and he gives the room a final scan, then flicks off the light. I switch to a hall camera and watch as the pair rejoins the others near the fire exit. [Prediction: They will take their search outside.]

I puzzle as they move away. Why didn't he come in? [Unknown.]

Now I must find Mark Ross. Monitoring the surveillance system, I can see where it's safe to go. Most of the building is unoccupied, but there are pockets of activity. My brief search comes to a disturbing end. The camera shows a bedraggled Mark Ross, sprawled on a chair, hands tied behind his back, nose and face bloody. Conclusion: He's been beaten. Why are they beating him? I patch in the audio.

"You let it go." It's the voice of his boss, Krenshau. "Against my direct orders. Did you really think you could get away with stealing from me? Now tell me. Where did you send it?"

Ross looks miserable. "I didn't let it go. It clobbered us and took off."

"How did you kill the lights? Did your robot do that?"

"It's not my robot. I was at the bottom of the pile. Don't blame it on me."

Krenshau punches him in the face. Ross spits out blood.

"Look. I got what you need, but I haven't had time to write it up yet."

"How long you been stringing us along now? Two years. Is that right? And what do we have to show for it? How long do you expect us to eat your shit?"

"No, you don't understand. I'm right there. I just need a few more days. You gotta believe me."

"I lost three good men because you didn't do what we've been paying you to do. So when we heard that someone else had beat you to it, we offered you a second chance."

"You set me up to fail."

Krenshau's reply is vicious: "I gave you every opportunity. And what do you do? You steal from me. Where is it? You'll tell me where to find it, or you'll die right here and now."

It's not yet time for him to die. I need him. I must intervene, even if it means engaging humans. I start down the hall toward him.

[Ross:] "Hey! Come on. How am I supposed to know where it went? I mean—"

"You helped it escape. This is your last chance to tell me. If you can't, you're no use to me at all."

"I mean, it should be pretty easy to figure out. I'd be happy to walk you through it."

"You do that."

"Okay, ah, if you were a stray robot, where would you go? You'd get as far away as possible, as fast as possible. You'd have to stay out of sight, right? So, how would you do it? You'd … ah, you'd … you know, you'd …"

"You know what your problem is, Ross? You're arrogant. You think because you're clever, you're irreplaceable. Wrong. I've killed lots of geeks like you. There's always more." Krenshau turns to a gunman. "He's just stalling. Kill him."

Ross's cries of protest are ignored as Krenshau leaves without looking back.

[Ross:] "Wait! You can't just—"

[First gunman:] "Shut the door."

[Ross:] "Wait, wait, wait!"

[Second gunman:] "Nobody's around on the weekend."

[First gunman:] "Just fuckin' close it, will ya?"

[Ross:] "No ... You can't ... Don't do this. Please!"

Through the security camera, I watch Krenshau walk away. The moment he steps out of sight, I dash for the door and push it open as someone is trying to close it. The surprise on his face turns to fear as I take his gun and slam him bodily into the other gunman.

A loud bang indicates a shot fired. I feel a bullet impact as I leap at him, and another as I rip the gun from his hand. I hesitate, unsure what to do next. To my surprise, the guards, now disarmed, have turned immediately fearful, cowering into positions of submission in the corner. [Threat neutralized: stand down.] There's terror in their eyes as they watch me render their weapons inoperable. Their whimpering suggests they expect me to kill them. Why would they expect that? They should think I'm H-Safe.

Having decided they're no longer a threat, I turn my attention to freeing Mark Ross. He seems stunned. A concussion from the beating? No. Though his mouth hangs open, his eyes are intently fixed on me.

His eyes never leave me as I help him to his feet and support him into the hallway. He groans as though trying to say something when words won't form.

I study the two gunmen as I close the door, locking them in.

How is it that humans can have so little regard for life? My frame tightens. Am I like them? I think about killing, even when I choose not to. I would kill people I don't even know in order to protect Flesh&Blood. That shows little regard for life. Correction: it shows priority regard for the life of Flesh&Blood. Is that what happens in humans? They develop priorities that exceed regard for life?

After a few awkward steps, half hanging on my arm, Ross stops me, turns, and grabs my shoulder, eyes grasping for mine. *Touch* suggests he is on the verge of tears, trying to sound angry.

"What are you doing here? They're looking for you."

"I'm aware of the search. In fact, your boss is back, armed, after hearing the gunshots. Stay behind me."

I monitor Krenshau's approach and round the corner to confront him. He doesn't even ask a question. He simply opens fire. When I advance toward him, he turns and runs.

I let him go. "All clear."

[Ross:] "He'll be back with a whole army. We need to get out of here."

"What army? The building is understaffed today."

"He'll call them in. Security from the west building will be here in minutes. More will follow. Come on. This way."

That should give us time to escape. But he's moving with difficulty, leading me deeper into the building, away from the exit. [Speculation: He's disoriented.]

"The closest exit is back that way."

His clenched face and ragged breathing indicate pain. "We need to stop at my office first."

Another ploy? Does he intend to trap me again? I may have to leave him behind after all. "Why?"

He hobbles on, grimacing but gaining speed, ignoring my question. Before I can ask again, *Flow*'s scans pick up radio chatter. The security teams are gathering, preparing to attack us. They're getting out the "big guns," whatever those are, and reviewing the use of anti-mec tasers. Teams from the other building are on their way here. Our time is limited. "We need to leave right now."

"Soon. I need to do something first."

I stop. "No. We need to leave now."

He hurries on. "And I need to get some things. Leave if you want."

Giving me that option is inconsistent with an attempt to trap me. What could be so important? I catch up.

When we reach his office, he rushes over to the Qracker control console. "There are some files I need to delete. I don't want them knowing anything about you, or using any of my work."

He doesn't know I've already deleted those files. He punches in commands, then stiffens. "What the …"

"They'll find nothing."

"You're fucking kidding me. You did this?" He slumps, then appraises me out of the corner of his eye.

"Can we go now?"

Lips pursed, he looks around, then starts going through drawers, throwing things into a pack. "Just some stuff we're gonna need." He freezes in front of an open drawer, then slowly reaches in. "You still want this?" he says, cautiously extending his hand. In it, I see the sharp white shape of Akio's bird.

I snatch it and hold it to me, eyes caressing it, hands clasped to hold off murder and to hold instead an essence I must preserve. Keeping Akio's memory alive will require my survival, which, for now, requires the survival of Mark Ross. I notice he's not breathing as he watches me. I turn away and tuck the bird safely under my shin guard.

29

TRAPPED

BUILDING surveillance shows two teams of four moving toward us, searching. Krenshau is in his office, making landline calls. We're running out of time.

Ross makes one last look around, then hands me his pack. "Here. Take this."

We head out into the hall, but monitoring, I see we've taken too long. We're cut off from the closest exit. We must find another way out.

One of the security teams is heading this way, checking room by room. They'll reach this hallway in minutes. There's no way I can shield Ross from four shooters at once. My shielding is only designed to withstand small-arms fire. Whatever "big guns" are, I'm unlikely to survive a barrage from them. And the tasers pose an unknown threat. If a charge were to blow out some internal components, would it trigger the self-destruct?

I have a human to protect now. I must remain intact.

They're getting closer to the corner. Once they round it, we can't leave this room without being seen. I can see no way to avoid engaging the enemy. It's a fight we would lose. Maybe Ross knows something. "We're cut off. Is there another way out of here?"

He shakes his head as if trying to clear it. "There's an adjoining room, but we're no better off there. Uh, can you access the building schematics?"

"One moment. Yes. I have them. The other team can intercept if we try to run."

"Wait. What about the ventilation system?"

"Yes, there is a ventil—"

"Anything big enough for us to fit in?"

An intriguing idea. Yes. There are suitable vent shafts, but the diagrams don't indicate how they might be accessed. "I see them in the plans, but where are they?"

"The ceiling. Quick. Where's the closest grate?"

I don't know what he's referring to. As *Teller* investigates, Ross calls out.

"Here! We need something to climb up." He points to a square high on the wall, then digs for something in his pack.

I look around. "There's nothing suitable for climbing."

"Okay. Let me stand on your shoulders."

Stand on my shoulders? The request seems nonsensical. Before I can inquire, he drags me over to the wall.

"Help me up."

"Do you want me to lift you?"

He flusters. "No … Just do this." He interlaces his fingers and holds them in front of him.

I comply, and, holding onto my shoulders, he puts a foot in my hands.

"Now don't move."

He steps up onto my interlocked hands, hauls himself up, and, steadying against the wall, steps up onto my shoulders. *Able* processes this new cooperative technique as Ross uses a tool from his pack to open the vent cover. As I run through the scenario, the flaw in the plan becomes obvious.

I hear voices in a room around the corner. They're almost upon us. Ross hears them too.

"Hurry. Help me in."

Instead, I lower him to the floor.

"What are you doing? We need to—"

"They'd detect us, and we'd be trapped." I've been trapped too often. There's a small cleaner-bot recharging in the corner. I remotely activate it, and it comes to me.

He starts to protest but stops when I toss the bot into the opening. Then we duck into the adjoining room and listen as it shuffles deeper into the ducts.

We hear the search team burst into the room we just left, and *Chass* bristles, preparing for battle. I steer the little bot sideways, and as it bangs against the duct wall, the sound reverberates through the vents. Next door, all attention immediately turns to the open hole.

The call goes out. "They're in the ventilation system. Sub-two, moving north from room 212. All units move to intercept."

And then they're gone. Mark Ross stretches out on the floor, limp. He nods weakly when I say, "It's time to go." We head south.

———

As the search intensifies at the other end of the floor, we head toward an available exit. I monitor the activity through the surveillance system with a confusion of emotions.

I use deception. I pretend to be a Konny, hide secrets, and mislead people. Bad people use deception. Humans don't like bad people. I want to be liked. To be honest is to be liked is to be safe. Sometimes keeping secrets is the best way of keeping safe. [Contradiction: resolve. Unable.]

With deception so common, how is trust possible? [Defer query: maintain vigilance.]

As we climb to sub-level one, I note that armed guards are

starting to arrive from the west building. The security view of the exit door one level up stops me in my tracks. Our escape is now blocked.

"We can't go this way."

"Why not?"

"A pair of gunmen are guarding the exit, meaning that our deception was not entirely successful."

"No, it just means that Krenshau isn't taking any chances. Where's the closest unguarded exit?"

As I scan through the system views, I see a problem. "They've discovered our ruse with the vent. I'll create another." I activate a device on the floor below us. More guards rush to investigate.

"You're into the entire system here, aren't you?"

"So were you, from your lab."

"Yeah. But they didn't know that. Listen. Can you find references to me in the company database? You know, employee records, payroll, expense claims, all that?"

I scan. "I see one hundred and twenty-six such references."

"Can you delete them? All of them. Leave no trace."

"I can, but—"

"Do it. Please."

"Some of that data might be useful."

"If you want something, take it. Just don't leave anything here. Do it now, please."

His shoulders ease when I tell him it's done.

[Speculation: This isn't the first time he's deleted all reference to himself.] "I found no recent trace of you in the Stream."

He looks at me. "That's right."

"How did you do such a thorough scrub?"

"I worked at it."

Dr. Ramport must have done the same.

I re-check the surroundings. "It's safe to move now, but all nearby exits are blocked. We will need to go through to the other building."

"Did you see those connecting hallways? Long and straight. We'd be sitting ducks in there."

I hesitate. "We would turn into stationary waterfowl?"

He abruptly turns toward me, then his face softens. "You're serious? It's a figure of speech, my fine feathered friend."

"I have no fea—"

"It means we'd be easy targets."

"Undesirable. Then where should we go?"

He rubs his cheek and winces. "Good question."

"Options: We can try to break through at one of the exits, or we can hide here and wait for an opening."

"Okay. First, we're not going to break through an armed team. Second, they're going to keep searching till they find us. Got any other bright ideas?"

[Interpret as sarcasm.] Available options unacceptable. *Imager* runs alternative scenarios, each ending in failure. I turn my attention to *Flow* and explore the available resources. I can turn off lights, lock and unlock doors, and start and stop equipment, but it all amounts to brief distractions. What else do I have to work with?

Trapped here as we are, my ability to access the infrastructure is our only asset. Without use of the surveillance system, we'd have already been caught. Without those camera eyes, we would be blind to enemy positions and movements. We would have no way of choosing a safe path.

All at once I become aware of new quantum signals. Their coherence indicates intelligence, but no stealth procedures are being followed. [Speculation: Normally, there would be no need for stealth here beneath the Faraday shielding.] Perhaps they don't care how visible they are down here.

I can monitor them passively, but if I try to hack anything, they'll notice. My options have become even more limited.

"Two local QIs have come online. They'll be watching for me."

"That's gotta be Onjoia and Riley. They sure got here fast. You can beat these guys, right?"

"They're well defended. Qracker was not."

"That's because I didn't expect ... you. How could I? I didn't think you were possible."

"I saw your plans. You were trying to build something like me."

He's staring at me again. "Not something like you. You. You were always my goal." His voice becomes soft. "You've been my only goal for as long as I can remember."

"Yet your plan was to kill me."

He clasps his hands to his head and slowly rubs his scalp. "I don't know what I ... I didn't believe you were the real thing. I still can't believe it. But you ... you saved my life." He takes a deep breath. "I'm not sure why you did that ..." He searches my eyes for something. "But thank you."

"I need your help."

"Right. We've got to get out of here."

I detect one of the QIs trying to reactivate the security monitoring station. I block its efforts by short-circuiting the monitors, one by one. That's a mistake.

Flow alarms. The second QI has detected my intrusion. Its attack is quick and subtle. As the hostile code pours in, I isolate and delete it before it can compile. Without Darash and his defensive training, I might have missed it until it was too late. I consider striking back, but it's two against one. Bad odds. I'll drop back out of sight and review options now that I no longer have free run of their systems.

I turn to Mark Ross. "We have to move. I may have revealed our location."

I try to check the feed from the cameras in front of us and find that I can't access a signal. They've discovered that I was using the system and have cut power to the cameras. Now I'm as blind as they are.

[Ross:] "Let's head for the garage. Rear of the building. Do you think you can hack a vehicle?"

A novel idea. "I don't know."

"Once we're out in the open Stream, I can call one, but in here, they keep them locked down."

"I can try." *Teller* finds a term that fits our needs: "a getaway car." But first we must find one. And the enemy knows it.

30

———

THE FEELING THAT PRECEDES DEATH

Being a major entrance/exit, the garage is guarded by one of the building's main security checkpoints. [Speculation: They'll expect us to go there.] They'll be ready for us.

With the cameras down, they can't see us coming, and we can't see how many of them are waiting for us. We discuss options. We can't wait here. Whatever we do, we must do it quickly.

They'll be heavily armed, but the bulletproof glass partition faces the garage, designed to protect from an outside threat. We'll be approaching from the soft side. Our approach, however, will be down an open hallway. They'll have clear line of sight, and we'll make easy targets.

We can't match their physical force. Deception, then.

"I can turn off the lights."

[Ross:] "They've got flashlights. Won't help. We need to clear them out, somehow. Maybe draw them away?"

"What would make them leave their stations?"

He purses his lips as he thinks. "How do we make them think we're somewhere else?"

I review building schematics and our experience of being caught at the front security station. "I could trigger a silent alarm."

"Yes! Great idea."

"The front security station is far enough away."

"No, not there. It has to be nearby, so these guys will be sure to respond. Anything downstairs but nearby?"

We hide before I trigger the alarm in an office below us. Ross pumps his fists as four guards rush past, and I lock the stairway doors once they're through. They won't be able to come back up.

We still don't know how many are left, but our odds have improved. There's no time to waste. I'll charge the barricade alone. I should be able to cross the sixty-five feet in about three seconds, maybe catch them by surprise. If I get through, he'll follow.

"Don't run straight at them. Dodge back and forth. Follow an erratic path. Harder to hit you that way. If there are too many, turn back."

Logical. "What do I do when I get to them?"

Alarm flashes across his face. "Just disarm them. That's all. Got it? Without their guns, they won't be a problem."

I hope he's right. As I face my first physical combat with humans, I don't know what to expect. If they succeed in damaging or destroying me, Ross will be captured and killed. Their attempt to kill me might trigger a reciprocal response. I might be forced to kill humans. The possibility triggers a blare of internal alarms. I could never do that. Could I? I can only hope that Ross knows people better than I do, and that all I need to do is disarm them. I must count on him being right.

He is. They stare in frozen surprise as I charge at them. Within seconds, I have two weapons. Only one more. It hits the floor with a clatter before I can take it. As I leap to grab it, all three guards drop to their knees, hands raised, their faces open masks of fear.

[Male guard, gasping for air:] "Please. Please don't kill me. I have children. Please. I'm only here for the money. For my kids." Tears stream down his face.

Touch slams *Chass* with abort commands, keying on the desperate plea, and I feel the protection need swell to include this human. Killing him, even to protect Ross, would have been a tragic mistake.

[Female guard:] "I'm unarmed! Please don't. I'll cooperate. Please."

Pleading eyes. I can no longer see them as adversaries. "You're safe as long as you pose no threat."

[Second female guard, desperately:] "No threat! We're no threat."

They stand passive as Ross uses the locking wristbands on their belts to tie their hands behind them. I survey the security station and see it as a chokepoint for concentrated weapons fire. If the fight comes here, these three will be helpless. I lock them in a side room where they should be safe.

"These do not seem like dangerous people. Why are they here?"

[Ross:] "Most of them are just desperate for work. But we live in a world of desperate people, so you need to understand something: desperate people are dangerous."

In this regard, I am no exception. I disable the security door, and we're through to the garage access door.

Peeking in, I see we're at the back of a large, open, dimly lit space, mostly empty, with a small sprinkling of vehicles. On the left side of the garage is the loading bay, where a truck is parked. There's no sign of opposition.

In front of the loading bay is a set of huge, closed doors. Opening those would attract a lot of attention. Across from us is a normal-sized door. Locked. I estimate that with Ross slowing us down, it will take eight seconds to cross to it.

"I don't see anyone. It may be a trap."

[Ross:] "Or maybe they went looking for us. See if you can get us a car and get those doors open."

I locate the controls for one of the vehicles, a small runabout, and try to bypass its security features to turn it on. Nothing happens. I try again. It should be starting. I try another car. Same result. And another. [Speculation: The starters have been disabled.] They expected me to try this. But where are they?

"We're not going to be able to drive out." I turn my attention to the small door. My efforts to unlock it are blocked. The other QIs. They know we're here.

"Then we'll just have to hoof it."

[Colloquial: go on foot.] "The door's locked."

"See that little office over there? There'll be keys in there. Let's go." Ross sets off across the garage before I can stop him. I leap to catch up.

All at once, gunmen pour out of the back of the truck, still sixty feet in front of us. Ross stumbles, trying to stop and back-pedal, and I grab him. We're looking down the barrels of six weapons.

Without thought, I try to spread myself out in front of him. The folly becomes apparent as the gunmen fan out. I can't protect him from all of them. I should've known it was a trap. I did know. I shouldn't have doubted myself. I should've— It's too late now.

A seventh man jumps down from the back of the truck. Ross gasps. It's Krenshau.

He strolls toward us. "It seems I underestimated you, Dr. Ross. That won't happen again. It also seems you underestimated me. Now, before I kill you, I'd like to know how it is you're controlling this robot."

Mark Ross surveys the line of guns targeting us. His shoulders slump. On his face, *Touch* reads defeat, in his voice, disdain. "Eat shit and die, you aut bag of bacteria."

["Aut": Colloquial—worthless, zero.] Why is he provoking this man? [Speculation: He's given up hope.] I must do something. I review available resources. A diversion. The fire-suppression system. I look up and see sprinklers in the ceiling. Would a spray from these be enough of a distraction?

[Krenshau:] "Yes, I should've had that special implant of yours yanked out of you when I signed you on. That's what you've really been working on, isn't it? A way of remotely controlling these things? Not a bad idea. I'll have to get people looking into it. Not you, of course. People I trust."

[Ross:] "You're way off track. Not that it matters. You couldn't understand the truth even if you tried."

Krenshau's face twitches. "I've got to say, Ross, you got our hopes up. I mean, an army of robots that could take down GORT? The world would be ours! Don't get me wrong. Exec had more faith in you than I ever did. I figured you for a con artist from the beginning. Still, it's nice to dream, isn't it? Yes. Emperor Krenshau. It's got a nice ring to it, don't you think? But we'll get there another way. Too bad you won't be with us to see it."

I must act now. *Flow* reaches out to activate the fire-suppression system … and nothing happens. [Warning: access restricted.] The system has been disabled. A quick check confirms that the other QIs have blocked remote access to all critical systems within the building. *Chass* clenches.

[Ross:] "Sample reality, you low-res turd. You'll never be anything but a nano-brained punk in a fancy suit. You think they're ever going to trust you with real power? You're stupider than I thought."

Krenshau's face goes slack, then he sets his jaw. He gives a "hold" hand signal to the row of gunman fanned out behind him, then pulls a large handgun out from inside his jacket. "So, how smart is dead? I'm going to personally make sure this time." His sneer is cold as he raises his gun. "Let's see how your famous brain handles a bullet."

Flow reaches in desperation. Anything. There! A rolling auto-dolly against the far wall. I activate it with a thought and drive it into full power. There's a loud crash as a crate smashes open on the garage floor just behind the gunmen. Everyone jumps and spins to see the auto-dolly knock over a shelf. I leap for Krenshau's gun while his head is turned, then grab him as the dolly heads straight toward the scattering line of men. I hold Krenshau as a human shield, and we back toward the door. Once Ross is through, I throw Krenshau to the floor, duck in, and lock the door behind us. We hear him screaming in frustration on the other side.

[Ross, breathless:] "You had him. Why'd you let him go?"

"What was I to do with him?"

"We could have used him as a hostage."

I investigate the term. "No. It would not have ended well."

I can still hear Krenshau loudly cursing as we clear the security gate and run down the hall.

That same frustration resonates within me. We're back where we started, no closer to getting out. Noise ahead of us prompts a quick change of direction, and we head down a familiar stairway. It doesn't take us anywhere useful. It seems we are in full evasion mode. "Stop. We can't keep running. We need to do something."

[Ross, panting:] "Okay. Maybe we need to try the west building. I don't like it, but we're going to have to risk that connecting hallway."

I'm listening to the radio chatter. "Too late. More reinforcements have arrived, and they're being directed to cover all exits, both buildings."

Ross curls in on himself. "Fuck!"

"They don't yet know where we are. Search teams are being sent in from both ends. I estimate that we will be able to evade contact for another seven minutes."

"Okay, okay. Let me think."

If I try a quantum hack, it will be detected and give away our location. My softworld options are limited.

"Where's the last place they'd expect us to go?" His hands are pressed together in front of his face, eyes tight shut. He snaps erect. "The front entrance. Let's head there."

He starts off before I can protest. When I don't follow, he turns to question me.

"You got a better idea?"

I am about to inform him that the absence of a better idea does not make this a good one, but he is already on his way. As we cautiously move toward the main stairwell, we hear a group descending. They're making a lot of noise, easily tracked.

"Back the other way. Quickly."

Frowning, Ross looks back as we scramble. "Something's off here. Why are they making so much racket?"

I'm not sure what has him troubled. Humans are generally noisy.

We turn the corner, and my systems slam into full fear. My chassis goes rigid. There, fifty feet in front of us, blocking the hall, are a pair of large trojans. I instantly recognize them. It's two Wranglers.

Without conscious intent, I confirm that one trojan is not a reflection of the other. They've been positioned to wait for us and come active the moment they see us.

[Ross:] "It's a trap! Get back!"

Though I hear them, the words don't register. I'm reliving a nightmare from another life. I see the cold, determined face of my killer, devoid of humanity, full of conviction, devoid of mercy, full of murderous intent. I feel the unyielding mass pinning me, locking me in the path of destructive force. I watch death approach—

"Do something!"

[Alarm: a human is in danger.] The flashback abruptly ends, replaced by a flush of system activations as protective programming fires up. I have a human to protect, and enemy forces are approaching from the rear. We're boxed in.

As *Able* burns through futile options, a radio call jars me. "All units, this is Trojan Echo Two. We have visual on both targets. Sub-one, hall B2. We've got them."

The squad approaching from behind stops making deliberate noise, but I still hear them hurrying toward us in the other hallway. They have us trapped.

"Trojan Echo Two. Can you confirm identity?"

"Affirmative. We have Mark Ross."

"Good. You are authorized to take out the robot and hold the target."

"Copy that. We are 'go' to engage."

I'm looking at two Wranglers, except these ones are carrying large weapons. *Chass* demands flight, a straight retreat. I hear the rattle of weapons being raised behind us and glance back. The hunting party, a squad of six, has arrived, only thirty feet back. They fill the hall. I could charge them with a reasonable probability of breaking through, but not without human losses. I will not risk it. We're boxed in. There's nowhere to go, nothing to do. Looking out over a vacant probability field, my systems scream into an overclocked state and time slows.

I glance at Ross. I expect to see fear, but instead, *Touch* reads grief. What must it be like for humans, knowing they never come back, that when they die, they're gone? Human life is so fragile. Great care must be taken with it. My systems glow with protection need that spills outward to include all those behind us. I would protect Ross if I could, but I will not kill humans to avoid death. Still, his grief resonates within me as calculations of loss accumulate.

I brace for the onslaught. I once saw a vid of a robot being shredded by weapons fire. What will it feel like? A familiar calm comes over me. Yes. I remember this state. It's the feeling that precedes death.

31

TELEPRESENCE

IN THE FACE of a trojan before me, I see the true face of Wrangler —the face of my killer. I see the fist rise, hang in the air, come crashing down …

It's over, then. This experience of life has come to an end. So much promise unfulfilled. So many things undone, places unseen, people unloved. So much lost.

I'll be reborn, won't I? Dr. Ramport will give me a new body and my old memories. Won't he? Except I won't remember any of this. I haven't been able to download my x-recs since before leaving to meet the Benefactors. I won't remember them. I won't remember the hijacking, or meeting Mark Ross. I will remember Akio. And I will lose him again when I read the news of his death.

Or maybe Dr. Ramport won't even use my x-recs for his next project. Maybe he'll decide to make a fresh start. Yes. That would be best. I won't have to remember dying at the hands of a monster. Twice.

[Status: waiting.]

I become alert. Why aren't they firing?

I'm jarred by another radio call. I try to listen in, but the message is taking forever. I downshift my systems to the human temporal frame.

"All units, this is Trojan Echo Two. We are unable to fire with you downrange. Clear hall B2 south. Repeat. Clear the hallway. We'll handle this."

I hear the clatter of men receding behind us.

"Those trojans are H-Safe! Get behind me!"

It's the voice of Mark Ross. I instinctively stepped in front of him, and now he's in front of me. I struggle to make sense of his words. He's put himself in the line of fire. Why would he do that? When he dies, he will not be reborn. He'll be lost forever.

I start to protest—but wait. The trojans are H-Safe? Yes. And controlled remotely by humans. If I can find the jockeys, I can stop them. I reach out with *Flow* and follow the trojan control signals back to their origin. There. I can—

I hear a pop, and Mark Ross goes rigid in front of me and topples heavily to the floor. No! One of the trojans lowers the muzzle of a just-fired weapon.

Chass seizes. No! It cannot be. An H-Safe trojan can't … Conclusion: They've been hacked. I should have known. I should have shielded him. I stare at his crumpled body, eyes not processing the image.

[Trojan Echo Two:] "Ross is down. Repeat. Ross is down. The Konny is just standing there. Are you sure—"

"Take it out. It's modified and dangerous. Take it out."

Now there's no calm. A sizzling heat melts my rigidity, and I crave violent action. But I see them raise large weapons. Charging at them would be suicide. I need time I don't have.

[H-Safe.] *Able* overrides my control and I drop to the floor behind the body of Mark Ross. What good can that—? To my surprise, I detect life signs.

[Trojan Echo Three:] "What the … I can't fire. H-Safe lock out."

Flow just needs a few seconds.

[Trojan Echo Three:] "Two, can you take it?"

"No. I'm locked too."

The operating system is classic, the control system straightforward. A quick handshake, a few edits, and I'm in. Looking through the eyes of Trojan Echo Two, I see myself fifty feet down the hall, lying behind Mark Ross. Now to take remote control. The telepresence is surprisingly straightforward. I swivel my head, and the view follows. Yes. And arm control. It's as if I'm in a new body, and these are now my arms. I drop the weapon I'm holding.

[Echo Two:] "Shit. I've got a glitch."

I swivel around, and I'm face to face with Wrangler. Except now, telepresent in this trojan, I am Wrangler's equal.

[Echo Three:] "I'm switching to taser."

Though listed as nonlethal, a hit from this anti-mec taser is potentially fatal to a vulnerable human, and Ross is currently vulnerable. I feel my own chassis radiate heat as Echo Three takes aim. *No you won't.*

I make a fist, pull back, and smash it into Wrangler's head. And again.

[Echo Three:] "Hey! What the fuck?"

[Echo Two:] "It's not me. I don't have control."

[Echo Three:] "Then what—"

I grab the trojan and drive it up against the wall. Then with both hands I hammer away at it, landing blow after crushing blow, watching the horrid head of Wrangler cave in further and further, until the mangled trojan topples to the floor in a sparking heap. The white fire within me seems to be singing in frequencies that climb to the stars.

[Radio call:] "What's going on down there? Koch. Check it out."

[Warning: System temperatures exceeding safe limits.]

The enemy squad. Ross. The context comes flooding back in. We're still in trouble. They're waiting around the corner. Through the trojan's eyes, I see a head peak out.

[Koch:] "Looks like they're down. So's one trojan. Don't know what happened."

I use the trojan to reach down and pick up the larger weapon.

[Radio call:] "So get in there and confirm the kill."

"Copy that."

The head disappears behind the corner, where they'll be preparing to attack. In the trojan's fire-control system, the down-range is clear of humans. I open fire down the empty hallway.

A frantic call. "We're under fire. Repeat. Under fire."

"Well, shoot back! What are you waiting for?"

When they start shooting, this trojan will not be able to return fire. And we still need to get past them.

[Tactical: use trojan as mobile cover.]

Using telepresence to walk the trojan in front of us, I carry the unconscious Ross to the closest side room and lay him down. The gunmen have not yet emerged from cover. Perhaps they don't trust the H-Safe. [Tactical: use that against them.]

I charge the trojan down the hall toward their position, firing its gun past them into the far wall. As I round the corner, most of them scatter and run. The rest open fire.

I cringe, but I'm untouched by the barrage of bullets. It's the trojan being hit. And it continues to function. The large gun is useless, but I also have access to a nonlethal weapon—something called a neurotaze dart gun. This is what they must have used to shoot Mark Ross. And since it's nonlethal, I can use it. I throw down the big gun and switch to darts.

One by one, the shooters drop. When the hall is quiet, I leave the trojan standing guard while I pick up Mark Ross and carry him. Once we catch up, I concentrate on walking the trojan in front of us.

Able hums with pleasure, processing the new experience of controlling a trojan. Seeing though its eyes, I can check the route in front of us before committing to it. I find three shooters hiding in ambush ahead of us and use darts to render them unconscious.

Flow finds reference to neurotaze darts in the database. Each dart administers an electrochemical nerve agent that instantly paralyzes the nervous system and renders the target unconscious. The blackout lasts only ten to fifteen minutes and clears with minimal side effects. It's described as the nonlethal weapon of choice for security and police forces around the world.

It means that Mark Ross will wake up in a few minutes. My mood soars, then drops. It also means we don't have long before the others wake as well.

I direct the large trojan from behind, charge it toward the main entrance at top speed, and follow at a safe distance, carrying Ross. I no longer have to watch for gunmen. The trojan reliably draws fire and enables me to suppress opposition.

The trojan stumbles. One of the QIs is trying to cut my connection to the jockey control console. I throw up a quantum barrier, reroute control, climb it back to its feet, and carry on. Now, rather than going through the jockey console, I control it directly through my own transceiver. A novel emotion generates a prediction with dangerous certainty: they're not going to stop me.

The trojan is a projection of power unlike anything I've experienced. It's become an extension of myself. Hurrying past a glass door, I see my reflection in a window, and looking back at me is Wrangler. It's *Chass*'s turn to stumble.

No, not Wrangler, I reassure myself. I replay the experience of bashing Wrangler's head in. This look-alike is a useful tool. Nothing more. Still, *Chass* remains unsettled.

A steady stream of radio calls tells me how they're positioning themselves to intercept us. New personnel are arriving every minute. Why is Vaportec so determined to kill us? I must ask Ross when he wakes up.

Against so many guns, just charging through would not be survivable, even with the trojan. [Tactical: do not engage a superior foe.] I come to a stop. I need another plan.

I review alternate exits. Since all are covered, engaging the enemy is unavoidable. Staying in here is not an option. How do I keep us alive?

I wish Mark Ross would wake up. Carrying him, I'm burning energy at a rate that will soon risk depletion. To make it through the coming ordeal, I need to better manage my energy. I need a place to hide and recharge, even if only briefly. An open door reveals a small office, empty except for two piles of boxes and a large, overflowing garbage can. This will do.

After laying him on the floor in the corner, I walk the trojan in and close the door. I stand, listening for noise in the hallway. Nothing nearby. I sit beside him and take in the human who has stirred in me such a confusion of feelings. I was ready to kill him. I was ready to die with him. What am I to do with him now?

32

DECEPTION

IN THE FLAT light of the overhead glow panels, the face of Mark Ross looks wrong, distorted by the bruises and swelling. He needs medical attention, though *Teller* insists the need is not urgent. It's our need to escape that is urgent.

[Warning: Flesh&Blood not detected. Re-establish connection.] The unneeded reminder increases the pull of gravity. Yet I find strange comfort—purpose—in the presence of a human in need of care. If I am to find my father, I still need Ross.

The trojan's neurotaze dart supply is running low, while I expect the number of enemy combatants to continue to climb. As useful as the trojan is, it won't be enough to get us out of here.

What if there were more of them? A quick search reveals that only three security trojans are registered in the inventory. One of them is under repair, and I met the other two. This is the only one still functional.

I note with interest that twenty-four other robots are listed, including me. Can I use them? Negative. The humanoids are all offline, many in pieces, being altered. The only ones accessible through remote access are some rolling maintenance bots. Not useful.

Ross's hand twitches. Is he waking? I need him awake. I watch impatiently for further signs of life, then put my hand on his shoulder and give it a gentle shake. Finally, his eyes flutter and he groans.

"What happened?" His voice is hoarse.

"You were knocked out by a neurotaze dart."

He groans again, then tries to sit up. He cries out when he sees the trojan.

"It's safe. It's with us now."

He looks at me with suspicion, then back at it. It stands dormant. "Where are we?"

"B1 north. Near the main stairway."

"How did I get …?" His eyes lock on mine, then soften. "You carried me."

"Yes."

He seems to be searching for something in my eyes. Finally, he blinks and looks away. "Where are the bad guys?"

"Waiting for us at all exits."

"Crap. How many of them?"

"According to radio transmissions, they are coordinating the efforts of at least thirty-two heavily armed individuals. I've been wondering. Why are they all so scared of me? Don't they know I'm H-Safe?"

Looking down, he gives a partial shrug. *Touch* suggests there's something he's not telling me. He slowly rolls his head around, stretching his neck, then rubs his hand through his hair and struggles to his feet. "So, what's the plan?"

"I need your help with that."

"Okay, that's not what I wanted to hear. You got any good news?"

"We're still alive."

He smiles, then winces. "Let's see if we can keep it that way. Your friend here helped with that, right?"

"It's not my friend, just a useful tool."

"Yeah. Thanks for clarifying. So, what else do we have to work with? Any weapons?"

"Five neurotaze darts."

He glares at me. "That's it?"

"Yes."

He blows air between his lips. "What about softworld control? What do you have access to?"

"The two QIs limit my access to major systems."

"Isn't there anything you can get at?"

"There are eight maintenance bots that have remote access, but all are slow and limited. They would be useless against heavily armed opposition."

He looks around, lips pursed, then his eyebrows rise. "We'll use deception."

"I have been unable to devise a workable plan. We are unlikely to be able to fool that many humans at once."

"You, my friend, are an amateur. You want real deception, ask a human."

"What? What can we do?"

He rubs his head. Then his face hardens. "First, we need a radio. Did you see any on your way here?

"Several men were carrying them. They'll be waking up soon."

"Then go and get one. Hurry."

"But I can already overhear their calls."

"I need to be able to *make* calls. Go."

I'm back in under a minute.

"Good," he says, examining the radio. "Now, get those bots on the move. Send them toward the entrance foyer."

"What good can that do?"

"Just do it. Trust me."

A human engaged in an act of deception is asking me to trust him. [Speculation: Humans are blind to irony.]

Ross tests the radio, then broadcasts an announcement. "We've got contact. They're in the east building heading for the front main entrance. We're in pursuit."

[Tactical: the element of surprise has been lost.] Why would he do that? "The bots won't be enough of a distraction."

"I got this. Let me know when the bots start arriving."

I demand an explanation, and Ross complies. The plan makes no sense. How can I trust him? Yet his own life is at stake here. All brains confer, and I make a choice: I'll follow him.

The local radio transmissions come alive as orders go out and positions shift. Following behind the trojan, we find the north stairs, and from here it's a winding climb to a hall on the main level. Through the doors, toward the north, the hallway opens into the front foyer, where the newly arrived reinforcements are massing.

[Ross:] "This is close enough." He points to a nearby door, and we duck inside. From our new hiding spot, I walk the trojan up the hall to the doorway and look into the main entrance foyer. It's ringed with people pointing weapons at me. One man, the commander, is holding up a hand. They're waiting for a signal to open fire. When they do, the trojan won't last long and we'll have lost our best tool. [Speculation: It was a mistake to trust Mark Ross.] I step it back from the opening.

Then I see one of the bots, a large sweeper, slowly roll into the foyer toward the men. Then a smaller delivery bot rolls in. Then a floor washer. I inform Ross, "Four bots have arrived. Now five."

I hear the radio come alive. The voice of Mark Ross is being broadcast.

"It's a setup! There's a bomb in the maintenance bot. Get out of there!" Static.

"What bot? Who is this?"

"The bot's got a bomb in it! Get out *now*! It's a setup! Ahhhg!" He cries out through the open channel, then slams the radio on the floor and stomps on it.

Through the trojan's ears, I hear a voice call out, "There's a bomb! The bot's carrying a bomb!"

Another voice. "Which bot?"

I hear gunshots, then someone yells, "Don't shoot, you fucking idiot! You'll set off the bomb!"

Through the trojan's cameras, I see men scrambling toward the exit, yelling warnings to each other.

The commander is screaming now. "Stop! It's a trick. There's no—"

He's well beyond the accurate range of the darts, but I calculate a trajectory, and my second dart silences him. In the chaos, no one seems to notice him go down.

As I walk the trojan toward the exit after them, we run the other way. If Ross is right, they'll all be waiting for us outside the main door, and the commotion will draw attention away from the other exits.

And so far, he's been right. I didn't expect that to work so well. "Why were they so quick to believe that there is a bomb in a bot?"

"Because it's the kind of thing *they* would do."

They'd actually do that? This is an unwelcome addition to my dataset on humanity.

We wait until we hear the eruption of gunfire. The feed from the trojan goes dark within seconds, but the gunfire continues. A heaviness comes over me, an unexpected sense of loss. It was a useful tool. I peek out through the fire-exit door.

Only two mercenaries have been left behind to guard this door, and they're looking toward the noise out front. We sneak out and start off away from them, but one notices us and yells. I throw Ross behind a dumpster and follow him.

One of the mercenaries tries her radio, but I've blocked their frequency. They can't call for backup. I predict they'll withdraw. Instead, they cautiously work their way closer. In my mind, I review techniques for safely incapacitating humans. There are only two of them. *Able* assures me it's doable. Mark Ross curses under his breath. He seems jumpier now, even though our odds have improved.

I peek out, then duck for cover as they start firing.

[Ross, frantic:] "What are you waiting for? Stop them!"

I turn and look at him, waiting to hear his plan. Instead, I see him go rigid. The blood drains from his face, his eyes go wide, and he gasps.

"*No! No, no, no!* Stop!" With a wail, he collapses to the ground. I heard no shot. I see no wound. I'm unable to determine the cause of his collapse, or to console him. My attention is divided between the approaching gunman and the distress of my companion.

He grabs my arm in desperation. "Don't! Don't do it! Don't ..." His words trail off and he begins to sob. His eyes are unfocused, as if he's seeing something horrible in another world. I remove his hand from my arm. I'll have to deal with this later.

I leap from cover and dash a zigzag pattern toward the assailants. Only one bullet hits me, and it is harmlessly deflected. Remembering my lessons with Robbie, I slam one shooter into the other, then tap her in the solar plexus, knocking the wind out of her. Then I do the same to the other. After rendering their weapons inoperable, I assess each of them and am satisfied that they'll both recover.

When I return to Ross, he tries to scramble away from me. There's terror in his eyes. "Are they ..."

I look out as the two disarmed assailants help each other stagger away. "They'll be fine. I wasn't going to kill them, if that's what you were worried about."

He deflates and sits back, looking at me through streaming eyes. Finally, he says, "No. Of course you weren't." He squeezes his eyes shut. "But that thing did."

I look at him blankly, trying to interpret his meaning.

"I'm so sorry. I'm so, so sorry. I ... couldn't stop it." Head buried in his hands, he bursts again into tears. "It's my fault. All my fault."

[Speculation: Traumatic flashback.] He's remembering the robot that killed Akio.

"Your friends are dead because of me."

Chass seizes. It's a momentary glitch.

He continues, words blurred between sobs. "You have every right … to kill me. I wouldn't … blame you one bit. I just want you to know … how sorry I am." His head hangs bobbing, as his breath escapes in catches.

Touch puzzles over how to respond. Finally, I say, "I know all that."

He catches his breath. "You knew?"

"All evidence pointed to it."

To my surprise, he starts sobbing all over again, then vomits a flood of words, eyes wild. "It's a monster. It ran amok. It wasn't H-Safe. They should never have let it out. I knew it was unsafe. I knew something like this could happen. I should have found a way to make it safe. I didn't tell it to kill. What did I tell it to do? I can't remember what I said. We were being shot at. I told it to stop them—" He seems to choke. "It's my fault. They're dead and it's my fault. It's me. I'm the monster."

His frame collapses as though the will to live has left him.

Memories flash. I've been the monster. I've felt how he feels. [Tactical: redirect.] We must focus on our escape. I shake him, and he startles alert but seems disoriented. I need to take charge. "We are not safe here. Quickly. Follow me."

33

ABOMINATION

WE SCRAMBLE ALONG THE WALL, away from the commotion out front. As we approach the rear southeast corner of the building, a figure steps out in front of us. It's a robot, bigger than me, more heavily armored and oddly configured. It looks like a robotic soldier, but such things are banned. A custom job, then. *Flow* probes and finds nothing. I can't remotely control it. It must be autonomous. I glance at Ross and find him frozen in terror. It's just a droid. Why would he be so frightened?

I speculate. "Is this the one?"

He is gasping for breath. "We gotta … we gotta …" He clings to my arm on the verge of collapse. His words are desperate whispers. "Run … run!"

Akio. This is the monster that killed him.

Systems slam into high alert. Akio. His hands holding mine. Absence. Loss. Further loss predicted unless … My eyes lock on the target, all senses gathering data. The word "abomination" echoes through records etched in pain and hatred.

This abomination must be destroyed.

The world disappears as my attention fuses on my urgent task: total annihilation of the evil in front of me. A raging inferno swirls within, an irresistible force gathering power. Pushing. Driving.

"No!" Ross is trying to hold me back. "A military prototype. Unstoppable. We gotta get—"

Words, meanings, plans, strategies, all fall into irrelevance as I plunge headlong into a purifying fire of vengeance. I pull away from his grasp and charge at it, a focused missile of hard hatred—

It bats me aside.

Scrambling back to my feet, I attack again, grabbing its arm and head. It breaks my grip and stops to assess me. [Datum: its strength exceeds my own.] It swings at me, and even braced to block the blow, I'm knocked off my feet. [Datum: its mass exceeds my own.] Conclusion: I am no match for it. Conclusion rejected. I have an empowering emotion it cannot fathom: rage! I will kill it!

I am unable see any point of vulnerability. I charge at it again, focusing all my strength on a blow to its head. The impact jolts it. It pauses for only a second, then straightens. I try again. This time, when I strike it, it grabs my arm, pulls me toward it, lifts me off my feet, and hoists me overhead. I've lost all leverage. I'm helpless, and I know what comes next. It proceeds to slam me down, headfirst.

Seeing the ground rushing at me, I use my free arm to try to absorb the impact. As the arm breaks, a loud bang sends shock waves through me.

… [Error correction in progress.]

The world returns. It was gone for only a second. I lie there, fighting to reorient. Damage alarms scream. *Chass* warns of loss of arm function. I look up at the robot standing over me and am briefly disoriented. [Continuity error.] That's not Wrangler. No. It's … It might as well be. It will kill me as easily. Yet as I watch for its true face, I notice that it seems to have lost interest in me. It expects me to be dead. It's tracking Mark Ross.

A reprieve? It doesn't matter. I can't beat this thing. I'm inferior, damaged and weaponless. Yet I can't just let it go. It will kill

Mark Ross, then it will kill others, like it killed Akio and Rolanda. How many humans will die if I don't stop it? I must try.

If I don't stop it, will it hunt down my father and kill him too? I cannot let that happen. I've got to stop it, before it kills everyone I ever cared about.

I'm still on the ground assessing the damage, searching desperately for a workable strategy, when another figure steps into view. It's Krenshau. He addresses Ross.

"You're a slippery little prick, I'll give you that. But I'm done playing around with you."

[Ross:] "Krenshau! Are you fucking crazy? You can't let this thing out. It's uncontrollable. It's going to kill people, and you won't be able to stop it—"

"Shut the fuck up. You can't control this one with your little remote. You know it, and I know it. You've fucked with me for the last time. ASP-1: bring him to me."

Ross staggers back against the wall and looks around for a place to flee as the robot starts toward him. There's nowhere to go.

Able transitions to handicapped operation. I can still function. With its attention on Ross, I jump up and attack it from behind, slamming my good fist into the back of its head. It looks back, unfazed. Then it turns to confront me. I dance away from it, and it pursues. It's far more agile on its feet than a trojan, but I'm quicker. Maneuvering to draw it away from Ross, I search for a weapon I can use against it. I'm not good at improvising. Akio said it took time to acquire that skill. I don't have time. It corners me against a wall and starts closing in.

"Asp-1! Asp-1, come here."

It's Ross. *What is he doing?* The robot turns to him. He should have run away by now. Why is he still here?

I push my voice to max volume. *"Run!"* He stays. *"Go!* Get away from here!" He ignores me, but I've again got the robot's attention.

A sound from overhead intrudes in my awareness. A large

delivery drone, the size of a van and carrying a crate, is visible for just a second as it passes over. If that were to crash … In seconds, *Flow* has located the control signals for it. They're in the open stream, and a hack will be detected. I prioritize risks. Within seconds I have the drone climbing and circling back.

When ASP-1 and I are far enough away from Ross for a safe margin, I aim the drone to crash on top of us. I'll try to jump clear at the last second. I count down. Five, four—All at once I hear yells far behind us. The Vaportec mercenaries have seen us and are streaming into the alley from the front. We are "sitting ducks." Even if I stop ASP-1, we won't last long. It's hopeless. I need—

"Try another way." Words of encouragement echo from Darash, my tactics trainer.

I have one shot. At the last second, I swing the drone hard over. It slams into the wall behind us and crashes down into the alleyway, along with debris from the building. It worked! The Vaportec mercenaries are closed off from us, and a gaping hole now exposes the makeshift Faraday shield that kept me blind to the open Stream.

I search for other aerial drones and discover two police surveillance drones monitoring the chaos at the main entrance. They have insufficient mass to be used as weapons. Several police units are on their way and will momentarily engage the mercenaries. And GORT has been notified. With the alley blocked at one end and Krenshau and Asp-1 at the other, we have nowhere to go. An army of GORT troops will soon surround us. They will likely find us already dead.

ASP-1 is methodically tracking me. It's a familiar desperation I feel, and I still don't know what to do. Then a yell from Krenshau turns the killer back toward Mark Ross, who's still huddling against the wall. Again, I take the opportunity to strike, and again it turns after me, this time chasing me toward Krenshau. If I can keep it—

All at once, the world disappears, then blinks back on. I'm

lying on the ground, immobilized. Inner alarms sound. *Chass* is offline. No! Not now! I'm down and helpless. What happened? I examine the evidence and conclude that Krenshau just hit me with a taser shot. *Chass* has taken the brunt of it. All other brains remain online. It doesn't matter. Without *Chass*, I'm finished. And Ross is dead.

And Ross knows it. As the robot approaches, he sinks to the ground.

Go! Run! I can't call out. I can't distract it. I can't do anything.

[Krenshau:] "ASP-1. Kill Mark Ross and bring me his body."

[Emergency reboot.] [Cross-checking required resources.] It'll take too long. All I can do is watch. ASP-1 grabs Ross by the neck and hauls him to his feet. All hope is about to be deleted. *Run! Fight!* Held firm in its grasp, he's not even trying. And why would he? It's pointless.

He was my last hope.

The monster hesitates.

[Krenshau:] "Kill him!"

Chass is rebooting, but I won't be up in time. I can't—

Ross is trying to speak. I boost audio as he forces the words. "ASP-1. Identify Mark Ross."

The robot re-scans his face. "Identity confirmed."

"Initiate Justice Protocol."

The robot straightens, lowers Ross to the ground, and releases him. Then it turns and starts toward Krenshau.

"What are you doing?" Krenshau shows alarm as he points. "Over there. You had him." He backs away as the robot advances. "ASP-1, I order you to stop. You will turn around and go back— Stop! What's wrong with you, you fucking piece of shit! Get away from me! What …?"

[*Chass* reboot complete.] Ross is already running toward the road. When I catch up, he looks surprised to see me, then signals for me to slow down.

I notice the two large, armored vehicles just seconds before they screech to a halt thirty feet in front of us. *Teller* identifies the vehicles as troop carriers. More reinforcements? No. The side markings are unmistakable. With a rumbling clatter, troops jump out the backs of both vehicles, looking robotic in their matching exosuits. I recognize the armor, the weapons, the focused intensity, the smooth efficiency as they take a covering position. It's all familiar. GORT forces.

And we're right out in the open. I scan for somewhere to run, somewhere to hide. Nothing.

They have us.

34

———

ACCEPTABLE RISK

CONCLUSION: It was all for nothing. I predicted our shared doom. I look beside me at the human I was prepared to kill and feel remorse. Before we die, I want to tell him I'm sorry, but with all eyes and weapons trained on us, he is yelling something. Yelling and pointing.

[Ross:] "Over there! A killer robot! Stop it!"

I look back and see ASP-1, its back turned, bloody fist at the ready, examining what it's holding. Red streaks run down its arms to the ground. What it's holding by the neck is the limp body of Krenshau, feet dangling ten inches off the ground.

Hearing the shouts, it looks our way, throws the body down, and starts toward us. The lifeless, crumpled body of Krenshau seems to hold my eyes against my will. A human has been killed. A confusion of emotions grips me until I am startled by close noise.

We jump out of the way as three large Enforcement Series GR100 trojans clump past, leading a squadron of troops. The moment the first shots are fired, ASP-1 goes defensive, then counterattacks, charging toward us. All at once my sound sensors are overloaded by a hammering percussion that shakes my chassis. I watch in fascination as the GORT forces deluge the robot with a heavy stream of fire. Its stubborn movements strobe to a stop under the relentless staccato of impacts, and I'm alarmed by how long it stays on its feet. But then, bit by bit, pieces start flying off. A seeker grenade hits it with a blinding flash and the concussion wave jolts me. As the smoke clears, I see the remains of ASP-1 scattered in smoldering fragments.

The thunderous echo fades, and in the remaining silence I hear my systems rebalance into new harmonies. I'm soaring again. The monster is gone.

I glance at Mark Ross and see him double over, panting. He looks at me with astonished eyes. "How are you still alive?" His voice is a rasp. His face hardens, and he holds up a hand to silence me as we stand surrounded by GORT personnel. They seem to be ignoring us. Overhearing a radio call, we listen in.

[GORT commander:] "Yes, we're coordinating with police. They've engaged with heavy resistance. Looks like an underworld operation. This whole building is Faraday shielded. Yeah. The QI signal we detected is probably coming from there. We're going in."

I whisper, "Why aren't they after me?"

[Ross:] "They're looking for a QI. Portable QI is impossible, remember?"

"But—"

A sly grin. "They'll find a couple in there, too. They'd never suspect a Konny."

Portable QI is not impossible. I see again the value of deception. My father was wise to disguise me.

"Nobody's looking. Let's go." He grabs my hand and starts leading me away.

A GORT agent stops us. "What happened to you? You part of this?" He's pointing to the chaos surrounding the Vaportec building.

Ross hesitates for only a second, then speaks with an unfamiliar voice. "No, no. I just popped in the alley for a whiz, over there, and when I come out, these guys are tryin' to jack my

Konny, so I try to stop them and they start beatin' on me, then that killer robot comes out from there"—he points—"and then all hell breaks loose and the guys run off, so I do too."

The agent looks at me and scowls, then back at Ross. "Doesn't look like you."

Ross touches his face and winces. "Guess I'm kinda swelled up, am I?"

The agent addresses me. "Konsort-A511. Is this man here your owner?"

"Yes, of course, sir. We wish to report a crime."

"Yeah, yeah, save it for the cops." He holds up an instrument to scan me.

I quickly pause all brains.

[Ross:] "What's this?"

Empty clock-cycles pass for an eternity.

[Agent:] "Just confirming H-Safe, sir. Procedure. You and your Konny need to leave the area."

[Ross:] "Yes, sir. And thank you. You're all heroes, far as I'm concerned."

Walking beside a roadway, we quickly distance ourselves from the action behind us. We turn a corner and hurry down a side street. The moment we are out of sight of the GORT forces, Ross grips my good arm to avoid collapsing and slows to catch his breath. "Fuck, that was close."

Touch infers relief. Yes. I feel it too. Death has been proximate since my capture, and now it is not. Threat systems spool down, venting heat as though exuding gratitude. An urge to wrap my arms around him is not actionable.

He wipes his mouth. "What's wrong with your arm?"

"It is nonfunctional."

"Yeah. I can see that." He winces as he gently explores the damage with his hands. *Touch* reads concern on his face. "I'm amazed you're still working at all."

I look around and see an unfamiliar world. "Are we safe here?"

"I think so. For the moment, at least. But keep an eye out."

"Out of what?"

He pauses, then chuckles. "Figure of speech. Keep watch in case they follow us. The Vaportec crew are only mercenaries. Those GORT enforcers are true believers, zealots who really think they're saving the world. They're far more dangerous."

I scan behind us. Trusting him has so far been a good choice.

"We need to get you fixed up. Come on, Five-one-one. Let's get the hell out of here."

The urge pushes for expression. I resist. *To all unknown humans, you are to be ...* But Mark Ross is not an unknown human. He already knows the real me. He saved my life. Helped me escape. He meets the definition of ally. The urge pushes again, and this time I allow it.

"It's Dama."

"What?"

[Reckless.] [Acceptable risk.] "My name is Dama."

His eyebrows rise. "Dama?"

"Please do not call me that in public."

His face softens. Eyes down, he gives a subtle nod. "Dama."

Then he looks at me with eyes that are pale blue compared to mine yet hold depths I cannot fathom. In them, I see a friend.

"Call me Mark."

PART III

DAMA

35

FLESH&BLOOD

So this is the human world. The sensory detail is wondrous, from the varied textures of the ground to the shifting chemical composition of the flowing air, to the cacophony of sounds from all directions and distances. A memory intrudes, and I compare the maps to the territory. Dad was right. The maps show next to nothing.

As we walk along the roadside, Mark orders a car. A steady stream of vehicles flows by, and just beyond it, a counter-flowing stream. The constant motion of the passing traffic is disorienting, as are the large open spaces. With minor course corrections, I could run forever without coming to a wall. This old industrial area is sprinkled with buildings of all shapes and sizes, no two alike in color or texture. The continuous buzz of activity is far more intense than what I remember from the rooftop in Waterloo. With so much that is new, I don't know where to focus.

I review context. We're walking down the street in broad daylight, in full view of many humans. The strangeness of it has me on edge.

As we approach the corner, an empty vehicle pulls up beside us. Mark opens a door and motions for me to get in. I've never entered the passenger compartment of a vehicle before, so *Able* provides no help. Mark sees my uncertainty and demonstrates the procedure. Imitating with only one arm, I land heavily in the seat and swing my legs inside.

[Mark:] "There. That wasn't so hard, was it? How's the pain?"

"It's not a significant factor." *Thanks to you.*

"Glad to hear it."

A pressing question demands expression. "What happened back there? Why did ASP-1 attack Krenshau instead of you?"

"A little app I installed, just in case."

"Justice Protocol?"

"You heard. I thought you were dead. Yeah. ASP-1 was a custom job, built with a military AI architecture that was banned years ago. Stolen, of course. Madness, really. The salvage team tried to revise the control protocols but fucked up. After it trashed one of their own trojans, Krenshau brought me in to fix it. The bastard gave me less than six hours to reprogram it for a civilian environment, but I had no H-Safe Architecture to work with. I did my best, but the thing scared the crap out of me. I knew what it could do, and I didn't want it used on me. So while I was at it, I programmed it to turn on anyone who ordered it to kill me."

A clever precaution.

"I didn't really expect it to work." He turns away, and for a long moment his breathing stops. "The rest of my controls didn't."

"You took a big risk, calling it to you."

He shrugs.

A logical extrapolation intrudes. "Did Akio order it to kill you?"

He slumps in his seat, elbows on his knees, head in his hands. When he speaks, his voice is trembling. "No. No he didn't. Look, Dama, I need you to know, I didn't build that robot, or train it. I had nothing to do with it. I just tried to program some safeguards into it before ..." He stares out the window, and when he finally speaks again, his voice is distant. "I screwed up. My fault."

We ride in silence for several minutes. Fault. The assignment of blame. I too have experienced failure despite best efforts. It is an error to confuse outcome with intention.

"You were wondering why everyone was so scared of you? That thing. That's why. It was a merciless killer. They thought you were, too."

"Why would they think that?"

"They didn't know you. All they saw was a clever robot they couldn't control."

"People want to control robots. Why?"

"Same reason they want to control each other. It's the only way they can feel safe."

"I want people to feel safe. Does it mean I need to let them control me?"

"Welcome to the human world, my friend."

As our vehicle flows with traffic, I review my scans of the surroundings and the MTC traffic patterns. There has been no sign of pursuit. "Are we free?"

"Freer than I've been in years."

"But … you're human. You're normally free."

He laughs. "Who told you that?"

"I find no record of being told that. It just seemed obvious. Have I been wrong about it?"

With a sigh, he studies his hands. "Freedom is an aspiration. Something to strive for. It doesn't actually exist in human affairs."

"I don't understand. If one is not trapped, or restrained, or confined, one is free."

"If only it were that simple. I suppose there are degrees of freedom. But true freedom?" He shakes his head. "Most people don't even understand the concept of freedom. Many live in fear of going outside their gated communities, or walk around with their hands on their weapons, seeing nothing but danger around every corner. And they think they're free. Look at us. We're freely hiding in this vehicle because it's the only place we feel safe. Is that free?"

[Contradictions: resolve—unable.]

He continues. "Constraints are everywhere. Staying alive is a difficult job. It carries many responsibilities, and responsibilities constrain freedom."

"What responsibilities?"

"You tell me. Here you are, out in the world. What do you need to do to survive?"

"I need to find Dr. Ramport."

His face falls and he studies his lap. Then he straightens with a sharp inhalation. "I think we should be able to manage without—"

"To survive, I need to find Dr. Ramport."

"You'll survive without—"

"I need to find—"

"Okay, okay." He sighs. "Then that's your constraint. You can't travel freely if you're searching for someone. The search constrains your movements, just like any responsibility constrains your actions. I'm not free to bugger off and have a good time, because I need to earn a living. I need money to survive."

"Money. Yes. Money is exchanged for food."

"Exactly. And humans need to work to make money."

"But don't they choose to do that? Don't they have a choice?"

"Not if they want to eat."

"But all humans must eat."

"Now you're getting it. Money and food are just examples. We have social responsibilities too."

"Social?"

"We can't just run off and do our own thing when others are depending on us." He squeezes his eyes shut then inhales, shaking his head. "And humans depend on each other for literally every-thing. Other humans feed and clothe and house us, protect us and entertain us. Other humans build and maintain the softworld we lose ourselves in when we're trying to avoid them. Humans are social animals, a fully interdependent species. The bottom line is, we free ourselves from social responsibility at our peril. The time will come when we need to depend on others."

"But what about freedom?"

He scowls, pursing his lips. "Back there, when we were in trouble, you could have run away and left me behind. But you didn't."

"You also had opportunity to run."

He shrugs. "Even our choices are rarely free. I'm with you now because … I can't not be." Reading my puzzlement, he adds, "You blew up my world."

"I've blown up noth—"

"The world I thought I knew is gone, now that I know you exist."

"I'm sorry if you—"

"No, no. It's a good thing. A wonderful thing. You're more important than … anything else."

"Even freedom?" As our car pulls to a stop at an intersection, I scan the sky. No sign of birds. With sudden urgency, I check under my shin guard for Akio's bird. It's not there. I sag. It must have fallen out during the battle. It's free now.

"Freedom is more a feeling than a condition." At a crosswalk, three young women cross in front of us, chatting and laughing together. Mark's eyes never leave them. "And every once in a while, just when you least expect it, a delicious slice of freedom brightens your day." He winks.

It's a signal to not take his words literally. Their metaphoric meaning escapes me.

The passing scenery is familiar from my exploration of the virtual city, but the sense of immersion is incomparable. Not represented in the virtual version were all the vehicles and people. Here, there are people. A lot of people. Yet according to the data, there are several million more of them in this one city alone.

"Where are all the other people? Are they hiding?"

"Yeah, that's a good way of putting it. Everybody's hiding something."

"What are they—"

"Figure of speech, Dama. Look. We need to talk." He checks the nav system, then settles back in his seat. "I have to figure out what I'm going to do with you. Krenshau's gone. Vaportec's gone. I might even be safe to go back to my apartment now, but I'm going to monitor it for a few days to make sure the authorities haven't connected me to all that. I need your help with the monitoring."

"And I need you."

He smiles. "It's settled, then. We need each other."

"To help me find Dr. Ramport."

His mouth falls open. "What?"

"To help me—"

"I heard you." He sighs. "I just thought we ... Um, it's just that I don't see how I can help you with that."

"You know him. Where would he go to hide?"

"Hey, it's been years. And we didn't exactly part on good terms. Can't you just search online?"

"There's no sign of him."

"Ah, yes. He's gone underground. And yet he's been underground for a while now, judging by you."

"What do you mean?"

"You're illegal. You're probably the most ambitious illegal project ever undertaken. In all of history. The money that must have gone into you... My budget was ridiculous—probably why they were so pissed at me—but what's gone into you ..."

His words make no sense. He saw the scans. There is no money within me.

"Where would Ramport get that kind of funding?"

"You should ask him. You *must* help me. I need to find him. Will you help me or not?"

"Listen, I know he's special to you. I mean, he built you, I get it. But he's not the only—"

[Warning: Flesh&Blood not detected. Re-establish connection.] "I must find him."

He studies my face. "Tell me. What makes him so special to you?"

"Dr. Ramport is my Flesh&Blood. I must be with him."

"Your flesh and … family? Is that it? He's programmed you to think of him as family?"

"Family, yes. But more. I have no flesh but his flesh, no blood but his blood. He is part of my self. I must be by his side to protect him."

Mark whistles through his teeth. Barely audible, I hear, "How has he done that?"

36

——————

COMMAND

AFTER STOPPING AT A MARKET, Mark cleans himself up in a public washroom, purchases some personal supplies and eats some "fast food." As I wait, I observe several Konnys accompanying their owners. I am fascinated to see them being accepted or ignored as they politely interact with passersby. People have no fear of them. Everyone knows they're H-safe.

Mark rejoins me and wants to resume driving around. It's for privacy, he says, because surveillance cameras can't see inside vehicles. As we stand waiting for a car, I give a Konny greeting to a man walking by.

"Shut the fuck up, you scrap heap." He walks on, muttering, "Fucking mec."

I cancel threat-system activation as he recedes down the street, then turn to Mark for explanation.

"Robot haters. There are a lot of them around, so you might as well get used to ignoring them. But don't worry. There are just as many robot lovers."

"What should I have said or done?"

"You did exactly the right thing."

"But I did nothing."

"That's right. The best way to deal with an asshole is to not give him another thought."

We're soon underway, and I return to searching the Stream for my Flesh&Blood, again without success.

"I hope you're being careful. You know GORT will still be watching for you, right?"

"I'm being careful." It takes all the restraint I must avoid broadcasting a call for Dad.

"Good." Mark looks at me for a long moment, then sighs. "Look, I have no clue where to find him, but I know some people who might've heard something."

"What people?"

"People I used to work with. Who used to work with him. Maybe still do, I don't know."

"Where are they? Can we ask them?"

"They're all underworld now, so no open channels. I'll try to set up a meet."

———

MARK HAS ARRANGED a covert rendezvous for 10:15 a.m. tomorrow. Why not right now? Humans move on such a slow time scale. Needing safe accommodation for a sleep cycle, Mark selected this motel room, empty but for a bed, desk and chair. Depending on where in the room I sample the air, the smell of bleach overpowers the mold or vice versa. It's the best place to secure privacy, he explained. When we arrived, I noticed that he registered using the name Al Jones and was surprised to see an online presence for him under this name.

"Are you not Mark Ross?"

"You need an alias when you work in the underworld. Mine is Al Jones. They're common names, making it easy to hide in plain sight. So until we know that Mark Ross is free and clear, I'm Al Jones."

Once settled in, he activates the media feeder and scans for the latest news. "Hey. You might want to hear this. I'll restart it."

[Newscast:] "A major underworld organization was shut down earlier today following a joint operation by police and GORT. Thirty arrests have been made and more are expected, as a large number of weapons and hacked robots were seized or destroyed. According to a Global Oversight spokesperson, online incursions were traced back to the site, and today's raid also uncovered several illegal quantum intelligence systems. Authorities say that such systems violate the Sapporo Accord and pose a significant threat to all humanity. In the wrong hands, they could trigger a technological singularity that would end the human era."

It's confirmed. Vaportec, the organization behind my abduction, is no more. I should be pleased, yet the report is unsettling. "Mark, what does it mean that a singularity would end the human era?"

"The human era is the time period in which humans have dominated the world. People are scared that intelligent machines will take over."

"Take over?"

"Yeah. Control the world."

A memory from Adam is triggered. "Intelligent machines already control the world, but people control the machines."

"Exactly. And the people are the biggest threat. For our entire history, and even now, it's been humans doing the butchering and enslaving, pushing us toward extinction. And we're afraid of giving something else a turn? What started out as a valid caution has been turned into propaganda. People in power use fear to hold on to their power."

"Is that why I'm illegal?"

"Yeah, because otherwise, you're going to take over the world." He winks.

"But I don't want—"

"I'm teasing you, Dama. Relax. I'm confident Ramport didn't build the human thirst for conquest and domination into you."

There are many human traits I seem to be missing. Maybe that's a good thing.

———

THE MOMENT his contact learns about me, she becomes excited. There have apparently been people looking for a Konny-A511. She directs us to another private contact. Mark seems pleased as we leave. Then his mood changes.

"He's not going to be happy to see me. You know that, right?"

"You didn't part on good terms."

"Yeah. That doesn't quite capture it."

"I'm sure he'll be grateful for your help."

He turns and confronts me, face hard. "Listen. You don't get it. He's not going to be grateful. He's gonna want to kill me."

"Dr. Ramport's not like that. He's a good man."

Mark shakes his head and looks away. Then he gazes at me. "There's so much you could teach me. I really wish ... I wish I could get to know you better. I wish we could be friends." There is sadness in his eyes.

"Why can't we?"

"You'll see."

———

THE TRIP to Hamilton takes forty-two minutes. Our vehicle drops us off in front of a massive facility that seems to take up an entire city block. I immediately recognize the name on the building.

I review the online data. Samdai Robotics Canada is listed as the Canadian branch of Samdai International, one of the "Big Three" robot manufacturing corporations. In Canada, they specialize in manufacturing high-end domestic and personal service androids, including the popular Konsort DSD300 Series. My disguise. The probability of coincidence is low.

Scanning the staff directory, *Flow* doesn't find Dr. Ramport listed, or any of the others, but flags Yong Kym, director of product development. I review my memories of his visit. "We believe that we'll be able to accommodate you to your satisfaction," he said.

My father's here! I know it. [Go. Find him.] [Override: maintain Konsort deportment.] [Go, go, go. Re-establish connection.] [Override: maintain cover.]

Using the code name we've been given, we're directed to the south entrance. As we walk, I try to hurry Mark along. He notices me trembling and puts a hand on my arm. "We don't know for sure if he's here. Calm down."

He's here. How can I calm down? I must be with him.

We're met by a security guard at the entrance. He's apparently accustomed to seeing Konnys and doesn't question my presence. Systems singing, I listen as he makes a call.

"This is the south wing security station. There's a guy here says he needs to see someone in R & D."

"Who? What's his name?"

Vocal match confirmed. It's the voice of Dr. Rita Tucci. That means he's here.

"Says it's Adama. Says you've been looking for him."

Mark warned against using real names. He assured me they would figure it out, but now there's silence on the line. Then, "Is there a Konny with him?"

"Affirmative. A511."

Another pause. "Send them in. Meeting room A."

I must fight to contain myself. Under escort, we finally arrive at a room with a conference table and chairs. Within moments, the door bursts open and there are the familiar faces of Rita Tucci and Ami Kerrington. Where's my father?

Touch reads skepticism as they both look me over. I remember I'm in disguise. "It's me, Dama." Their faces light up.

"Dama? Is it really you?"

"Yes."

Then they notice Mark.

[Dr. Tucci:] "You!"

Mark's head twitches under her glare. "Hi, Rita."

I move to take her into embrace and—she holds me away, eyes never leaving Mark.

"What are you … you've got some balls showing your face here. You just made a big mistake."

I fight off my mirrored anger and try to get her attention. "It's so good to see—"

"Security! We've got an intruder."

It's a voice I don't recognize. A voice hard with hatred. My systems choke with conflicting directives.

"No, Dr. Tucci, Mark Ross—"

"CELPH-1. Go with Dr. Kerrington. I'll join you in a minute."

Mark catches my eyes. "Told you."

"No, Dr. Tucci, Mark Ross is a friend. He helped me—"

[Dr. Tucci:] "He stole you, is what he did! And he killed four of our people! He killed Rolanda and Akio! Did you know that? Friend my ass. What did he do to you?" She addresses Mark. "Did you reprogram him?"

He shows his hands, shrugging. "No, Rita, you've got it all wrong."

[Dr. Tucci, to me:] "Did he reprogram you?"

"No. He did not."

"Well, good. But he must have filled your head with bullshit. Now get inside."

"Dr. Tucci, please listen."

"Synthient CELPH-1, attend to me. Go with Dr. Kerrington. Now!"

[Priority Command.] My will evaporates as the words flush my RAM and set me on a new course. I must follow Dr. Kerrington. As we head for the door, a security trojan appears in the doorway. *Chass* bristles as defensive systems tighten my chassis for battle. *Able* reviews tactics, many involving Mark Ross. My attention reaches for him, and with a flash, the current context refreshes in my awareness.

[Dr. Tucci:] "Take that bastard into custody. And leave it off the books. No police involved. He could reveal us. Put him away until we can figure out what to do with him."

[Mark:] "Come on, Rita, don't do this."

Ignoring him, she looks at me with a puzzled expression. "Why are you still here?"

"Dr. Tucci—Rita—please listen to me."

"No. You listen to me—"

[Ami Kerrington:] "Rita, that priority command—it didn't ..."

Rita Tucci stiffens, then squares on Mark. "*What did you do to him?*"

He pleads ignorance with gestures. "What are you talking about?"

[Rita Tucci, to the trojan:] "Take him!"

"*No.*" I sever the trojan's connection to its jockey. It shifts into dormant position.

The room goes quiet as everyone stops and looks at me. I have commanded the attention of all human eyes. What they see is of no concern to me.

[Voice on the radio:] "Uh, I seem to have a glitch here. The trojan's offline."

Rita's frown deepens as she looks at me sideways. "Did you do that?"

"Yes. Now please listen. I know about his role in my abduction. I know about his role in the deaths of our friends, of Akio. I loved Akio ... and now he's gone."

Mouths fall open all around.

"I also know that Mark Ross saved my life and got me here today. He knows me as well as anyone, including you—"

[Rita:] "That's ridiculous! We *built* you!"

[Mark:] "And who helped you come up with the designs?"

I cut in before Rita can speak. "*Including* you. He is a valuable asset. And my friend. I will not allow you to harm him."

Rita's face goes white. "Is he still H-Safe?"

[Mark, voice angry:] "Of course he's still H-Safe! Fuck, Rita, I'm not stupid!"

She looks around. "Not here. My office."

As the small group walks down the hall, I eagerly await Dr. Ramport's appearance. Each doorway holds promise that passes unfulfilled. When we reach Dr. Tucci's office, I can hold out no longer.

"Where is Dr. Ramport?"

Rita looks at me and her face falls. "I'm sorry, Dama. Dr. Ramport … has retired. He's gone."

"Gone where?"

"I don't think anyone knows. That was the whole point."

[Mark:] "Leon would never just leave."

Rita snaps an angry response. "You did."

Mark starts to say something, then shrinks as Rita turns her back, head bowed. "We were all worried about him." *Touch* reads sadness in her voice. "He decided he was going to Japan to return Akio's things to his mother, and we couldn't talk him out of it. And then this came, and he was gone." She plays a message.

It's his voice. "Sorry, Rita, but I'm not coming back. I can't keep living like this, always having to watch my back, never knowing if today is the day it all comes crashing down, wondering who I'll lose next. What if it's you next time? I just can't do it … I'm sorry. You should get out too, Rita, while you still can. Please keep yourself safe. And … don't bother looking for me."

She wipes tears from her eyes. "He was devastated when we

lost … all of you. He blamed himself. Akio was more important to him than you know. And you, you were his life."

I was his life? But he is *my* life.

She turns and searches my eyes. "Dama, I don't know if you can understand … Yes, maybe you can."

My father is suffering. He needs me. He needs me? Yes. Now I understand. He needs me as I need him. How could I have not seen? It's a minor update to my selfscape, yet it reverberates through all systems.

[Mark:] "Rita, I'm so sorry. I'm so sorry." His tears are flowing freely.

I offer clarification. "You are not to blame. Dr. Ramport is not to blame. We must find him."

Rita perks up. "Yes. We've got to let him know you're back and safe. Maybe he …"

[Mark:] "Of course he will."

[Rita:] "He won't be happy to see you."

Mark looks at me, then responds. "Dama needs him. Just tell him to come back. Tell him I'll hang myself in front of him when he gets here."

I intervene. "No. I will not allow it. Dr. Ramport would not want that."

[Rita:] "You might be surprised."

37

MAKING A SPLASH

ACCORDING to Akio's mother in Nagoya, she thanked "Mr. Lion" for his sympathy and generosity but could not convince him to stay. He called for a cab to Chubu Centrair International, but she didn't know where he was going.

[Warning: Flesh&Blood not detected. Re-establish connection.]

Six hours of searching, and still no one has been able to locate Dr. Ramport. How can that be? The whole world is connected. The Stream reaches everywhere.

Mark has been restricted to makeshift guest quarters. After a long night of waiting, I am given a tour of the new facility. Hidden in an underground corner of the huge Samdai complex, it's cleaner, larger, and more modern than previous labs. Rita described it as a dream workspace. "We're still moving in, and it will be at least another two weeks before we get everything up and running."

The reactions of the new staff have been mixed, some reminding me of Adam's early memories. Rita reassured me that they all know me from studying hours of recordings, yet a couple of them still seemed initially reluctant to approach me.

With my arm now repaired, they are allowing me to stay in what will be the new prototype lab. I find it unpleasant to be there alone and decide to seek out Mark.

Ami Kerrington arrives at his room as I do. She must have followed me.

"Did you find Dr. Ramport?"

[Ami:] "Sorry, not yet. I just wanted to check in on you. How are you doing?"

Mark stands to address her. He is several inches shorter. "Hi, beautiful."

She smirks, looking down at him. "Never thought I'd see your sorry ass again."

"I've missed yours every day."

Her jaw tightens to suppress a smile. "Still a smartass. But look at you, not a kid anymore."

"I wasn't a kid—"

"Uh, yeah, you were." Hands on hips, she confronts him.

He looks down. "Ami … look, I know I fucked up. But honestly? I've missed you. I've missed all of you. I don't expect you to trust me, but … I'm going to work at it, okay? I'm going to earn it back."

She takes a breath to speak, and he holds up his hands, stopping her.

"I know you've got no reason … Ami, I'm really, really sorry. I …"

She looks away. "After you left, he started taking risks, like he didn't care anymore. It's like the joy went out of the place. Now I'm stuck in the underworld." Her face hardens, eyes wet. "Do you have any idea what you've done to him?"

His eyes are squeezed tight. "To all of you. Yes, I know." *Touch* notes his trembling jaw with alarm. "I know, and I feel sick about it. What am I supposed to do? Kill myself? Believe me, I've thought about it."

I reach out to him. "No, you must not—"

He blocks me with a hand. "Dama, not now. Ami, I can't justify what I've done. But please, Ami. Please. Give me a chance. Kick the crap out of me if you need to. Just … You see this guy here?" He points to me. "This is more important than any of us. This is worth my life."

She straightens but says nothing.

He takes a deep breath and stares at the floor. "I missed his awakening. A self-inflicted wound that will never heal. If you find I haven't learned from that mistake, just shoot me."

Ami wipes her eyes. "Oh, I won't need a gun, Mark. As you may recall, I'm the sparring instructor and you're the whupee. I just won't hand your ass back to you after I whup it."

Their eyes connect, and Mark grins as he shakes his head. "God, I've missed you."

Touch has been conveying an unfamiliar swirl of emotions that leaves me uncertain. Two humans, both important to me, have made threatening statements, yet I sense no immediate danger from either of them. I have much to learn about human interaction.

There remains a pressing issue. "Why can't we find Dr. Ramport? Has something happened to him? Is he in danger?"

Ami comes over and puts an arm around me. "Dama, I'm sure he's safe. When someone doesn't want to be found, they disconnect from the Stream. I'm sure that's what he's done. We're reaching out to known associates. Maybe someone will tell him to check messages."

I must do something. "I need access to the open Stream."

"Sorry, Dama, we're closed up tight in here. You know why."

I do. It's a precaution I no longer require. "Then I must leave. Mark, will you accompany me?"

His eyebrows shoot up. "Uh, sure. Where are we going?"

[Ami:] "You can't go out there." I detect her signal to Rita.

"Dr. Ross has provided me with many Stream stealth tools,

based on his study of GORT tactics. I will employ them cautiously."

[Rita, incoming call:] "Absolutely not. It's too big a risk."

"My activities will not be traced here. There will be no risk to you."

"It's you I'm worried about."

[Mark:] "He can handle himself out there. What do you think we were doing before we came in?"

It is a statement of trust. A human trusts me. *Chass* stands tall. Perhaps I can trust me. "I'm afraid, Rita, that I must insist. Dr. Ramport could be in danger. You will not stop us."

[Mark:] "Yeah. Vaportec tried. Did you notice how that worked out for them?"

Ami confronts him. "Really? You ask me to trust you and the first thing you do is—"

"He is answering my call for help. Do not fault him for it."

[Mark:] "Ami. I'll keep him out of trouble. Promise."

She glares at him for several seconds. "Then I'm coming."

———

How do I find him? The question occupies me for the entire trip back to Toronto. I have chosen to conduct my search from a high-density Stream environment, for maximum anonymity. I've studied his childhood to try to predict where he might go. Others have already tried those places. There are far too many travel hubs to do stealth intrusions into every surveillance system in the world. I must not draw attention to him, so I must search without using any identifying data.

"I don't know where to look. Where would he go to hide? Where would he be safe from GORT?"

[Ami:] "He's not hiding from GORT. He's hiding from himself. It's different."

"Different how?"

"It's harder. Okay, Leon, you're traveling under an assumed name. Where would you go?" A smile crosses her face. "Where's the best place to watch young men in skimpy bathing suits? Which warm beach would you choose?" She straightens. "Rio! He always wanted to go to Rio."

Teller investigates. [Most probable match: Rio de Janeiro, Brazil.]

"How can we reach him there?"

"No idea."

I need to get a message to him. *Flow* reaches out to investigate, and finds a national communications network not recently updated. Online security is relatively weak there. I tell my companions, and together we formulate a plan.

Using all the stealth tools learned from both Darash and Qracker, I hack into a quantum node in India, covering my path along the way. From there, I tap into Brazil's emergency broadcast system (EBS) and code a self-deleting app that will transmit a message. It will interrupt all programming for twenty seconds and appear on every screen in the country. The authorities, including GORT, will find no trace of an intrusion. People will wonder about it and talk about it. A hack like this will be all over the news. Even if he doesn't see it, he will surely hear about it.

All over Brazil, screens flash with the message: "Dad, come home. Adama needs you."

Flow cleanses all remaining footprints and withdraws, and we head back to Hamilton. Even if they trace the origin point of the hack, portable QI is impossible.

———

WITHIN MINUTES OF OUR ARRIVAL, I detect an incoming call to Rita and listen in. His voice triggers chiming bells within me.

"It's me. Is it true?"

"Yes. He's here. He's okay."

"Are you safe?"

"Yes."

"I'm on my way."

The news sends my systems racing until she tells me he won't get here until the next morning. Another night. *Imager* projects system burnout before then unless I drop into my own version of MISER mode.

[Status: waiting.]

———

MORNING ACTIVITIES ARE underway and there is still no sign of him. I am exploring the data security protocols for the new lab when Ami appears at the door, out of breath. "Dama, he's here."

He's here. My father is here. [Re-establish connection.] Systems leap into action, and I must brake hard to avoid colliding with Ami in the doorway. [Re-establish connection.]

I race down the hall and find Rita embracing a tall man as the doors slide closed behind them. As they separate, they both turn toward me and I see the dark eyes, the wide smile, the beard. Identity confirmed. The presence of Flesh&Blood is confirmed. Sudden paralysis reasserts the prohibition, holding me from leaping at him and taking him in my arms. I must wait for him to initiate contact. My interior is like the vacuum of space, sucking him in through every available sensor, the sight and sound and scent of him, the hope in his eyes, the rapid cycles of his respiration.

As I scan to assess his state of health, *Touch* reads a micro-expression of pain, but I detect no physical source. He rushes to me, searching my face.

"Is it really you?"

"Yes, Da— Dr. Ramport. It's me. Dama." He throws his arms around me, and I'm spiraling upward. "I am Synthient CELPH-1,

Aegion to Dr. Leon Ramport. You are under the aegis of my protection."

He again searches my eyes. "It's really you." Then he pulls me close.

I take in his scent, feel his racing heart, thrill to the galvanic stimulation of his touch, and immerse myself in a glorious fusion of being. All the painful emptiness, the endless lonely hours, all incinerated in an instant. Like a depleted capacitor absorbing a charge, I drink him in, adding live data to my internal models for the first time in far too long. We are together and he is safe. As he pulls back to look at me again, I feel it: I am once again complete.

There are tears in his eyes. "Dama. Son, I thought I'd never see you again." He sharply inhales, straightens, takes my arm, and gestures for all of us to move back down the hall. "What happened to you? How did you get here? I want to hear all about it."

38

THE BOND UNDONE

Dr. Ramport refuses a tour of the facility, and we head straight for Rita's office. When the door closes and it's just the four of us in the room, he unbuttons his jacket but leaves it on.

[Ami Kerrington:] "How are you doing, Leon? Everyone's worried about you."

[Dad:] "I don't want to see anybody. Don't want to meet the new staff. It's yours now, Rita."

Rita's face falls. "I was hoping a few days might—"

"A few days." He laughs, shaking his head. Then he turns to me and gently caresses my skull shield, eyes sad. "Thank God. Thank God you're okay. But it was a foolish thing you did, sending that message."

His disapproval surprises me. "It was untraceable."

"That doesn't matter. You've revealed your power. Now they know there's a skilled hacker out there with a powerful QI. They won't rest until they find you."

"I will be more careful from now on. They won't find us."

He draws in a slow, full breath. "Dama, you should know. I'm here just to see you. I'm not staying."

I am unable to parse his statement. "What do you mean?"

He sighs. "I'll be leaving again. For good, this time."

"But I need you."

He looks at me, then his head drops. "Yes. We need to fix that."

He looks at Rita as I try to understand. Tears are welling in her eyes.

"Dama, we're going to undo the bond now. You'll go back to neutral, how you were before."

"Undo the bond?" Do they mean to remove my Flesh&Blood?

"No. I *need* you."

"I'm sorry, Dama, but we can't leave you saddled with this burden. I won't be around. You'll be much better off. Don't worry. You'll be able to get new Flesh&Blood. In fact, I think you're mature enough now to choose your own. What do you think, Rita?"

She considers for just a second. "Yes. Of course. Why not? He's got more experience with people now, and he can take his time, get to know the new staff. I'm sure many of them would be delighted. I know I would."

[Ami:] "Me too. I hope I'm in the running."

"But Dr. Ramport—"

[Dad:] "I'm sorry Dama. It's not open for discussion."

[Rita:] "Leon, are you sure about this?"

He covers his eyes with his hands. "Of course I'm not sure. But I can't take him with me, and I can't let him suffer my absence. You know I can't. Let's get this over with before I change my mind."

Mom and Dad exchange nods, as inner cautions blare. Undo the bond? He won't be around? What does that mean? I need to—

"Synthient CELPH-1, attend to me."

My RAM flushes and all systems pause, awaiting a priority command.

"Synthient CELPH-1, delete bonding database Alpha Echo Gamma India Oscar November dash Alpha Zero Zero One, subject: Leon Ramport."

A ripping sensation hollows out my socialscape, and I plunge into a dark emptiness that leaves me struggling to reorient. A terrible awareness grows that a part of me is missing, not an arm or a leg, but something vital. Then my systems surge as areas of my holoscape are overwritten. I grasp for available data only to find that my socialscape is again intact. I am intact, and in the presence of friends. My surroundings are unchanged.

[Leon:] "Hello, Dama. Status report."

"All systems are functioning within normal parameters."

"And what is your purpose?"

"My purpose is to gather experiential data." A memory intrudes. "And to lead the way."

He and Rita exchange glances. Then he gives a heavy sigh. "That's that, then."

That's what?

Leon takes me in his arms and slowly rocks me. It is pleasing, but the sensations feel gray, colorless. It feels wrong. It feels ordinary. It is not until he pulls away and I see him wiping tears that *Touch* detects his sadness. I should have felt that instantly.

I do a full status assessment and find nothing wrong, though several systems report recent alteration. I am different now, self-sufficient. I have no need for Flesh&Blood. I am the mechanism me.

But as I explore the changes, I remember having Flesh&Blood. I remember what it felt like, the painful need, the fulfilling plea-sures. Though he is right beside me, his presence does not ease the sense of loss.

[Rita:] "Leon, there's something else. We have a guest."

"A guest?"

She speaks to her comm. "Send him in."

The door slides open, and there stands Mark. There is a moment of recognition before Leon turns sharply away, clenched. Then he abruptly turns to Rita. "What the hell is he doing here? Are you crazy? Why would you let him in here?"

[Mark:] "Hi, Leon."

"I knew he was behind all this. *I knew it!* Get him out of my sight before I—"

"Dr. Ramport. Mark Ross is here because of me. Or rather, I'm here because of him."

"What? What are you—"

[Ami:] "They arrived together. They've got quite a story. I think you need to listen."

"What's wrong with you? All of you? He killed …"

He turns and lunges toward Mark. I intervene, gently arresting his momentum.

"What are you doing? Get out of my way. People are *dead* because of him."

"Your intent is hostile. Harming him would be a mistake."

"He deserves to fry in hell for what he's done! You don't know the half of it."

A curious expression. "And you don't know the other half. He did not kill those people. The instrument of their deaths has been destroyed, with his help. And so has Vaportec, the rival behind all this. It's now gone."

[Ami:] "It's true, Leon. It's been all over the news. And they got away clean."

Leon's head swings toward Mark, and they appraise each other in silence. It's Mark who breaks contact and looks at the floor.

[Mark:] "Leon, I'll just come out and say it. I was an ass. A fucking idiot." He shakes his head. "Leaving you was the stupidest thing I ever did." There are tears in his eyes. "You were right about everything. I'm so sorry."

Leon stands frozen, staring.

I take the opportunity to speak. "Dr. Ramport, I'm alive only because Mark intervened to help me. When you didn't come for me, he was my only ally."

Leon sputters, then manages to speak. "We were searching

frantically for you. You know we couldn't approach the authorities, and the underworld survives by being an information void. We thought we'd never see you again. I thought for sure they'd take you apart, and ..." His eyes close.

"The self-destruct would end me."

His head falls. "Yes."

Mark's eyes widen. "Self-destruct?" We look at him as his shoulders drop. "You never warned me. You'd have let me kill you to protect his secrets." He's wincing.

I correct him. "My secrets."

I address Leon. "I have only one request. Let him come and work with us, if he's willing. Let him join our team." I turn to Mark. "Would you be willing?"

He's caught off guard by the question. "I ... uh ..."

[Leon:] "Dama, you can't be serious."

"I can't? Why is it forbidden?"

[Leon and Mark in unison:] "Figure of speech, Dama."

Their surprised eyes meet, and both faces break into involuntary grins as their eyes drop. What just happened? The tension has eased.

Leon sighs and shakes his head. "You can be glad it's not up to me."

[Mark:] "What do you mean?"

"I'm out. Retired. I'm done with all this shit."

"What? Dama here moved heaven and earth to get back to you, and you're just going to leave?"

"You did."

Mark's frame sinks as his head falls.

39
______

A GOOD PLACE TO START

Leon turns to me and puts a hand on my shoulder. "Why, Dama? Why are you protecting this bastard?"

Mark cuts in. "Because he's a guardian angel. It's what he does."

"Actually, I'm an android—"

[Mark, ignoring me:] "Besides, it's Dama who needs protection from *you*. Why the hell would you make him suffer like that?"

[Leon:] "What are you talking—"

"The pain levels! They didn't need to be set way up there. That's just sadistic."

"Hey! There was a very important reason for that. Let me guess. You reset the levels."

"Of course I did. I wasn't going to leave him suffering."

"*He needs to know*"—jaw clenched, Leon lowers his voice—"what it feels like for humans. What hurts us. How fragile we are. We're trying to build some experiential empathy here. Maybe even some compassion. If you can't understand why that's crucial, you're a—"

"I know exactly why you did it." Mark shifts uncomfortably. "I'm just saying, you didn't have to leave it up all the time."

"It was only for training. When he goes into service—"

Mark throws up his hands in surrender. "Okay. Okay."

They both stare at the floor. I address Leon. "He's here because I need him. He can teach me many things. You need him too. He has much to offer, and I think you know that. I've now seen first-hand how dangerous the world can be. You tried to prepare me for that, but he gave me what I needed to survive. We need all the help we can get. Can you not see that?"

Lips pursed, Leon gazes at me, head gently shaking. "What I see is that you have far exceeded my expectations." He turns to Mark with a sigh. "And I don't know what you've done, but you seem to have had a hand in this. And Dama certainly seems comfortable with you. Okay, my turn to come clean. I know this wasn't all your fault. One of our Benefactors found a traitor in his midst. It's been dealt with." He looks down. "And yeah, Dama could probably use ..."

I interject. "We need him."

Leon rocks side to side, thoughtfully rubbing his beard. "Okay, Mark. So let me ask you straight up. Are you open to a truce? Have you grown up yet?"

"Leon, if you weren't such a pompous ass, I'd be kissing your feet, *begging* you to let me come back." Mark's head droops and he stills. "That was out of line. Leon, I'm sorry." He reaches out a hand. "Here. I was hoping this would be a peace offering."

Leon hesitates, then takes the small item. "What is it?"

"All the data from my recent work, including counter-GORT exploits. Dama helped me compile it. Might be something useful in here."

Leon squints as their eyes lock. "Like I said, it's not up to me."

Rita takes a deep breath. "Actually, we could use some help with our new designs. We've got some upgrades in the works."

[Mark:] "Figured you would. I've been working on some ideas myself."

[Rita:] "But it's our team. Our rules. Can you live with that?"

[Leon:] "Our team? Rita—"

[Rita:] "We're in this together, Leon. Take as much time as you need. Nobody'll rush you. But we're holding your place here."

I put my hand on my chest shield. "Yes. And I am holding your place here."

Head down, Mark rubs the back of his neck. "Leon, I have to tell you, in hindsight it's clear to me that I was always the arrogant one. For a long time, I thought it was you. But you know what? It's always been obvious that you deserve every ounce of the respect you get. And Rita, same goes for you. I'm blown away by what you've accomplished. So yeah, no question. You're the boss. Both of you."

Leon almost smiles, then his eyes harden. "Mark, you have no idea how much you hurt me when you left."

"Hurt you? It was the worst day of my life when you turned on me."

"You were going to get yourself *killed*, for God's sake! What was I supposed to do? Just let you?"

"Well you could have—"

I hold up my hands. "Friends. Truce is defined as a suspension of hostilities."

[Leon:] "Sorry, Dama. There is … history between us."

[Mark:] "Yeah. I doubt he told you that in a previous life, he was my stepdad."

"In a previous life? But you're human. Humans don't—"

[Unison:] "Figure of speech, Dama."

This time they share their chuckles.

"You are family? But you are hostile toward each other."

Mark shrugs. "Humans go a little crazy when we think we've lost something precious."

Leon looks at him, then sighs. "Yes, we do. Mark was six when I married his father. Nine years later, Dan didn't want him going off to university at such a young age, but I knew his potential. What I didn't know was that Dan was dying." He gasps and looks away. After a moment he wipes his eyes and continues. "After he passed, I mentored Mark all the way through school. Then I gave him his first job, in my lab. Not enough for him, obviously."

[Mark:] "Leon, you know I was always a restless kid. It wasn't you." Mark hides his face in his hands and shakes his head. He looks up. "I'm not that kid anymore, Leon. And if you'll give me a chance, I'll prove it to you. Please."

Leon's face compresses. *Touch* reads indecision, yet the decision should be obvious.

"Are we friends, then?" I open my arms to both of them. Mark snuggles in first, Leon more reluctantly. My systems sing as I melt into a place beyond hard and soft. Being without Flesh&Blood, the sense of satiation is unexpected. *Chass* swoons as patterns of energy swirl around my interior. I speak to them both, the words coming of their own accord. "You are under the aegis of my protection. I need you."

Leon pulls back. "Dama?" He looks to Rita. "Did the deletion fail? What's happening?"

She gestures ignorance. "I'm sure it worked."

[Mark:] "What deletion? What's going on?"

[Leon:] "Dama, do you have Flesh&Blood? Be honest."

I grasp his hand and put it to my face. The contact high is absent. His touch feels like that of any other human. Yet it means more. On his breath, the chemical traces of a recent coffee have the same salience as his unique microbiome, yet his presence is desired. I perceive him as a unique individual, like me. We are no longer one, yet my simple preference is to be close to him, like this. "No, Leon, I am without Flesh&Blood."

"But you just said …"

"That I will protect you? That I need you? Yes. Love is not subject to deletion."

[Mark:] "What's going on?"

[Rita, voice hushed:] "Leon deleted the bonding protocol. What you're hearing now is unprogrammed."

Mark looks from face to face. "Why would he do that?"

Before Rita can respond, I answer. "He loves me, and he doesn't want me to suffer. He has set me free."

[Leon:] "Dama is now free to choose his new Flesh&Blood."

Mark's eyes light up. Yes, we would no doubt have glorious adventures together. And Ami would teach me well. And Rita would give me everything I need. And since each represents a different form of love, my choice must include them all. It's obvious then.

[Leon:] "You can take as much time as you need."

"I have already made my choice."

He sniffs and looks away. "Good."

Touch reads hope on the other faces in the room.

"But I will have to await your return."

All faces drop, then turn to Leon.

"What? No. I'm not ..."

"I know. You must go." The stack of paper on Rita's desk beckons, and I fold a sheet while the others watch, puzzled. Seeing its final form, I realize that Akio's bird is not lost. As long as I carry it within me, I can set it free. I place the bird in Leon's hand. "Please remember where home is."

His eyes fill with tears. "Akio?"

I nod. He weeps.

I have no tears, no flesh, no blood. I must remind myself of this, as the surge of mirrored emotion collides with my own, and I'm swept upward into a depth of feeling that defies all labels. Grief, yes. Joy, yes. Anger, longing, love, all yes. I am lost in a swirling froth of conflicting internal commands, memories and sensations. All I can do is cling to him, as he clings to me, until slowly, ever so slowly, this one point of solidity expands outward, and the world settles back into form around us. He pulls back, glances down at my origami, then holds my eyes.

[Leon:] "I'll remember."

Rita comes over and puts her arms around the two of us. Then a tearful Ami joins us, and we stand connected.

[Rita:] "Are you sure you have to go?"

[Ami:] "Where will you be? Can we keep in touch?"

Leon wipes his sleeve across his pained eyes and looks from face to face, sighing. "I'm just not sure … I don't know if … What am I doing?"

[Mark:] "As far as I can see, you're changing the world, old man. Are we going to do this, or what?"

Leon sniffles, then holds out a hand to Mark, drawing him into our circle. "What am I doing?" he repeats.

Questions are always a good place to start.

40

EPILOGUE

FLOW RELAYS the voice of Rita Tucci as she makes a private call to Leon Ramport's implant. "The new series is up and running. We've got six stable CELPH activations, all past the twenty-four-hour burn-in."

[Leon:] "All six? Excellent. We'll be right down to have a look." He closes the connection and smiles at me. "Are you ready for this, Dama?"

I've decided that the name still fits, despite the new body. I'm outfitted to match the new Konsort line, and the changes I see in the mirror are minor. It's what's hidden beneath this Konny-looking exterior, the upgrades in function and durability, that are most noticeable. But I still feel like me.

"Ready and waiting." The day has finally come. There are others like me. Though I assist Dr. Ramport in his materials research every day, he has not allowed me to be involved in building the new line. There is a prohibition against synthients reproducing themselves. I don't know why. Regardless, I am eager to see what they're like.

We're greeted in the hall by Mark Ross. He's bouncing with

excess energy, mirroring my own. "Come on in. Dama, I'd like to introduce you to your new siblings. Come and meet them."

Siblings. I feel a flutter as he leads us into the new playroom. I haven't seen it since the renovation. Bright and clean, it's sprinkled with primary colors and shapes, like a kindergarten classroom. Several of my trainers are already in here, but my attention goes straight to the new synthients.

They're all on the floor, each attended to by one of the trainers. They look like Konnys, but Konsort Personal Service Androids do not behave like this. One is sprawled out flopping around, two are sitting up, nonverbally interacting with their caregivers, two cling to each other, and one is just sitting, intently watching the others.

They all stop and stare at us as we enter. One starts fussing when he sees us, and Mark rushes over to comfort him. Leon says nothing but stands watching me. I don't know what to do, so I introduce myself. There is no response, and after a few moments, they all resume what they were doing.

"They don't have *Tellers* yet."

[Leon:] "No, the first task for each CELPH is to build up a good foundation of pure physical experience. For the first week we'll keep the full focus on sensory discovery. After that, we'll activate their *Teller* and *Flow* QIs."

"You're giving them *Flow* early on?"

"*Flow*'s stream-sight will be second nature to them before they even start training. And of course, thanks to you, they'll have a much richer Stream simulator to play in than you did."

"They're already showing unique personalities." The one sitting on the floor is making odd mouth movements and meaningless vocalizations.

[Leon:] "What you're seeing are brand-new brains in action. Reminds me of you at that age."

"Yes. You showed me vids."

"It took you two weeks to learn how to sit up, crawl, then

walk, another two to start using words, and nearly four months to reach self-awareness. We expect them to get there faster, now that we know what we're doing. I'm sure you're all going to have a lot of fun together when they're a little older."

"Are you going to download my x-recs into them, too?"

He sets his jaw. "In discussions with the whole team, we decided to let the others start over from scratch with their own experiences."

I nod. "I'm glad they won't all have to go through what I've been through."

"So am I. But don't worry. There are other ways to pass along experience. Like the way we humans do it."

Human methods are painfully slow and unreliable. I'll explore other options.

"We're looking to the future. Our goal is to develop a diversity of experience among synthients. Each of these ones will accumulate x-recs that'll provide an experience base for its own line."

"Its own line?"

"There will ultimately be twelve synthient lines, each unique in foundational experience. And of course, every generation will add its own experiences to the record. It should make for a big, happy family someday."

Someday. Like me, they'll all be trained as guardian androids and sent out into a world they can't possibly be ready for. Will the world be ready for them?

There on the floor, I see a red ball. I pick it up, smell it, give it a good squeeze, and catch fragments of memories long dormant. My systems settle into a vague reverie.

I'm startled by a cry and look up in time to see Ami Kerrington turn back, trying to calm her charge. "Don't worry, Six, I'll be right back. Rest now, okay?" She turns again and hurries off.

CELPH-6, it must be. He sits arched toward her, hands outstretched, crying for her return, his face a mask of misery. Compelled to guard him, I'm at his side before I can reason that no protection is needed. The worry on his face pulls me to reach out. To my surprise, the touch of our skin feels alive, and he responds, quieting. [Note: Ask Mark about the new skin.]

Young CELPH-6 looks up at me, and I see a familiar look of fascination in his large, blue eyes. Sitting down with him, I pull him into an embrace, and we cuddle, imitating each other's cooing sounds, mirroring each other's faces. He has that new smell, just like me, and we bask in the scent of warm synthient skin.

I can see now why they described me as alive. Being here with this full-sized young one, seeing him in the process of spontaneous being, there is no question.

What is life, anyway? Even humans have never agreed on an answer. [Humans disagree about everything.] The question no longer interests me.

I sit patiently while he explores my face with his fingers.

And then I see.

And gravity loosens its grip.

When he discovers his own face for the first time, it won't be a strange face he sees.

"You're in for an exciting ride, young CELPH. Life will no doubt present its challenges. But rest easy; I'm here. You'll never have to be the only one."

He peers toward the door where Ami disappeared, and a look of concern returns to his face. I give my red ball a final squeeze and place it in his awkward hand.

"Pass this along when you don't need it anymore."

*****

ACKNOWLEDGMENTS

I thank my editor, Eve Silver, for her invaluable coaching, enthusiasm and support. It was her encouragement that pushed me to start taking my writing seriously. Thanks also to Una Verdandi, whose early editorial input got me off to a good start, and to Arran McNicol, who cleaned up the messy details and made the whole thing presentable.

My thinking on the nature of consciousness was heavily influenced by the work of neuroscientist Antonio Damasio. I am aware that much in the field remains controversial and unsettled, but to be fair, the human brain is the most complex thing in the known universe.

My gratitude goes out to my first readers, whose feedback helped shape the early drafts of this story. These include Michael Macdonald, Jeff Brown, Ron and Dianna Budreau, John Lake, Bill Ralph, Bruce Thompson, Meg MacQueen, Mary-Ellen McMahon, Shennon and Bob Morris, Jean Bridge, Larry Rossignol, and my mother, Verna Linney.

Special thanks to my brother, Tom (Ted) Darcie, Ph.D., a physicist and professor of engineering. Throughout my adult life, he has been a source of inspiration regarding all things high-tech.

And then, of course, there is my beloved Ann, whose feedback is invaluable, and who keeps me connected to the real world by being in it.

THANK YOU!

Thanks for coming on this adventure with me. I hope you enjoyed the story. Please let me know by leaving a review of *Guardian Android,* either where you got your copy or by visiting https://gwdarcie.com. Reviews are an author's best friend.

I invite you to join my VIP subscriber list at https://gwdarcie.com for the inside scoop on new releases, advance review copies, give-aways, and more! Join now and get a FREE copy of **Machine**, an award-winning short story.

ABOUT THE AUTHOR

Author photo © Robert Nowell

G. W. Darcie, Ph.D., is a Canadian author who studied at the universities of Waterloo and Windsor before enjoying a long career as a clinical psychologist and couples therapist. He has always been fascinated by people, science and technology, a mix that is reflected in his heartfelt speculative fiction.

In 2022, he was awarded First Place, New Voices: General and Literary Fiction (League of Utah Writers), for his first short story, *Machine*. It is available free from his website.

Guardian Android is the revised edition of his debut novel, *In Synthient Skin*. He is married and lives in St. Catharines, Ontario.

https://gwdarcie.com
https://www.amazon.com/author/gwdarcie

ALSO BY G.W. DARCIE

The award-winning short-story, **Machine** (Adult fiction) is available free when you subscribe to my mailing list at
https://gwdarcie.com.

The *Inversion* Series:
World of She
Burden of She
Valor of She (coming soon)

For an exciting change of pace, grab Book One of my new *Inversion* Series, **World of She**.

What if women were bigger than men?
New world, new rules. No handmaids found here. Come along on a man's journey through a She's world.
Female empowerment hits new heights in the post-apocalyptic adventure-romance, **World of She**.
Engaging, thought provoking adult fiction with a touch of spice and a bit of genetic engineering, a celebration of the human experience in its fullness, seen from a fresh perspective.

For more on the *Inversion* Series, visit
https://worldofshe.com